"You don't tr

No matter how many tir innocence Mallory wasn't going to believe him. You haven't even asked me if I killed those two marshals."

"Let me and Ben go, Nash. You don't need hostages. We'll only slow you down."

"Right on both counts."

"Why, then? Do you really think you're going to raise your son on the run, always looking over your shoulder? And what about me? You think I'm just going to go along for the ride? We have a good life."

"That life's over," he said, feeling the need to put an end to false hope.

Uncertainty filled her eyes. If she hadn't been afraid before, he could see she was now. "What are you not telling me, Nash?"

He pushed to his feet and stopped alongside the couch beside her. "I'm sorry if you can't trust me, Mal, but you've got no one else you can trust."

He continued walking and then stopped. "And for the record, I didn't kill those two marshals. No matter what anyone else says.

Dear Reader,

Have you ever felt like chucking your old life for a new one? While this has always been a favorite fantasy of mine, the reality is I'm far too attached to my life for that kind of change. But what if you'd lost everything and had nothing more to lose?

Such is the case for Kenneth Nash. Wrongfully convicted of his wife's murder, the navy SEAL accepts a deal from the Feds that allows him to go deep undercover in search of the real killer. Seven years later, his cover is blown and he must choose between the integrity of his original mission or saving the son he's never known along with the sister-in-law who testified against him.

There are somewhere between 9,000 and 10,000 families in the Witness Protection Program, also called Witness Security Program (WITSEC). According to the U.S. Marshals Service, no witness who's followed the rules has ever been killed.

Some interesting facts about the program:

Witnesses can choose their new names, but are advised to keep current initials or the same first name.

Name changes are done by the court system just like any other name change, but the records are sealed.

Witnesses must not contact former associates or unprotected family members. Or return to the town from which they were relocated.

If the witness has a criminal history, local authorities are made aware of the situation. Only a small percentage of criminal witnesses return to a life of crime.

Can't wait to find out what you think. You can contact me through my website, www.rogennabrewer.com, my Twitter account (@rogenna) or on Facebook: /rogenna.

Happy reading!

Rogenna Brewer

ROGENNA BREWER

—

The SEAL's Special Mission

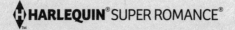

HARLEQUIN® SUPER ROMANCE®

Recycling programs
for this product may
not exist in your area.

ISBN-13: 978-0-373-60845-4

THE SEAL'S SPECIAL MISSION

Copyright © 2014 by Rogenna Brewer

Printed in U.S.A.

HARLEQUIN®
www.Harlequin.com

ABOUT THE AUTHOR

When an aptitude test labeled her suited for librarian or clergy, Rogenna Brewer joined the United States Navy. Ever the rebel, she landed in the chaplain's office where duties included operating the base library. She's served Coast Guard, Navy and Marine Corps personnel in such exotic locales as Midway Island and the Pentagon. She is not now, nor has she ever been, in the Witness Protection Program. But her grandfather did cross paths with Al Capone once and lived to tell about it. There may or may not have been bootleggers in her family history.

Books by Rogenna Brewer

HARLEQUIN SUPERROMANCE

Other titles by this author available in ebook format.

To those who keep me grounded in reality:

My husband and sons. My mother.

My best friends and fellow writers
Tina Russo Radcliffe and Debra Salonen.

My lifeboat Linda Barrett, Jean Brashear,
Dee Davis, Ginger Chambers, Annie Jones,
Julie Kenner, Day LeClaire, Barbara McMahon,
Lisa Mondello and Karen Sandler.

And to my editor Karen Reid who had to put up with
a little too much Rogenna Reality TV for this book.

PROLOGUE

Coronado, California

"Freeze!" Her voice shook almost as badly as the SIG Sauer in her hand. After twenty weeks of G-man U in Quantico, Virginia, twenty-three-year-old rookie FBI Agent Mallory Ward never imagined facing down her first perp in her sister's kitchen. "Freeze, Nash. I mean it, damn it!"

Her false bravado lost all conviction as she tried to comprehend the bizarre scene playing out in front of her. Her brother-in-law, covered in her sister's blood, cradled a blue bundle in the palms of his hands.

"Dear Lord, Nash, what have you done?"

Mallory shook her head to clear it. She'd stepped outside for just a moment.

One minute Nash was giving her sister mouth-to-mouth. The next he was ordering Mallory to grab his cell phone from the pack he said he'd left outside the back door. When she couldn't find his phone, she'd taken those precious extra seconds to grab hers from her rental car parked out front at the curb.

Mallory kicked past an overturned chair and stepped over the cordless phone unit that had been ripped from the wall. Her sister's still-warm body lay lifeless on the cold tile floor where her brother-in-law had been performing CPR.

Mallory couldn't remember if she'd punched 911 before dropping her cell phone to reach for her gun. Though only seconds, it seemed like a lifetime ago. She'd initially been willing to give Nash the benefit of the doubt when she stumbled upon him at the center of an obvious crime scene....

Until she watched the Navy SEAL slice the swell of her sister's belly.

"She's gone, Mal." His voice never wavered.

"You have the right to remain silent..."

"There was nothing more I could do for her, except save our son." Nash dropped his KA-BAR in the puddle of blood.

Sidestepping the slick pool, Mallory still managed to leave the imprint of her sole behind. Biting back the copper tang of panic, she continued to read him his Miranda rights—Article 31 in the military. "Anything you say or do can and will be used against you in a court of law...."

Nash ignored her, concentrated on the little bundle in his arms. He covered the teeny nose and mouth with his own mouth. The tiny concave chest expanded and then contracted with each puff.

"Do you understand these rights as I have read them to you…?"

She couldn't afford to make another rookie mistake.

Sirens blared in the distance—emergency responders, too late to save her sister. Mallory's world spun out of control.

The tile floor rushed up to meet her.

CHAPTER ONE

Denver, Colorado
Seven months later

"Muh, muh...muh," Benjamin babbled from his crib.

"Up already?" Mallory carried her coffee into the baby's room. Strong. Black. A reason to get out of bed at zero dark thirty and make it through another day.

Of course, Benji was the real reason she bothered to set the timer on Mr. Coffee. He pulled himself up to gnaw on the guardrail while bouncing on his tiny toes. He couldn't walk yet, but he sure gave those chubby baby legs a workout.

"Stop before you knock out a tooth."

Her words startled him into stopping. He reached for her and fell back on his diaper-padded bottom. "Mama!" he cried with his arms outstretched.

"Say, what—"

"Mama, mama," he continued to blubber.

"Oh, Benji." Mallory set her happy face mug on

the dresser and lifted her nephew out of his crib. He rewarded her with big tears and baby drool all over her new black suit jacket. "I wish your mama was here, too."

"Mama," he insisted, latching on to her nose. How much plainer could it get? Benji wasn't asking for his mother—Mallory was the only mother he'd ever known.

He didn't understand that the woman who'd carried him for thirty-six weeks was dead. Benji's only world was the one Mallory created for him. That's why she needed to push past her grief and do more than just go through the motions…for both their sakes.

Hugging her nephew tight, Mallory repeated, "Mama, mama."

Until she almost believed it.

She kept a firm hold on her little wiggly worm while she changed his diaper and then carried him out of her old room. It wasn't much of a nursery. It wasn't much of a room, either. She'd pushed her twin bed against one wall and then hauled the old crib down from the attic.

The baby crib was a beautiful piece of heirloom furniture in a rich cherrywood. It was so well crafted that it still met safety standards decades later—she'd checked. Someday she'd bring down the rest of the ensemble and turn the room into a real nursery. Hopefully before Benji grew out of the nursery altogether.

At first, she'd slept in her old room with him.

Now more often than not she fell asleep in front of the TV on the leather sofa in what had once been her dad's study. She kept her clothes in one huge pile on her parents' bed, with the intention of eventually moving into their bedroom located across the hall with its en suite bathroom. Though she already showered in the en suite and dressed in the bedroom, she still couldn't bring herself to clear out the closets.

To her it was still her parents' room, her parents' house—the home where she and Cara had grown up. Just passing Cara's old room next door to hers made Mallory want to cry.

She'd opened the door once.

Everything remained as Cara had left it before going off to college—with the addition of her wedding dress, which had been hanging in a storage bag on the back of the closet door since Cara and Nash's wedding. It's where their dad had stashed Cara's personal effects brought back from San Diego. And where a short while later Mallory had found her mom crumpled in a heap on the bed— an empty pill bottle in her hands—among boxes of Cara's childhood, college and wedding mementos.

There were more memories in that room than Mallory could handle.

The whole house was haunted by a not-too-distant past. At some point, though, she'd have to find the strength to deal with it and make it her own or put her childhood home up for sale. She simply wasn't ready to do either.

Mallory carried Benji downstairs to the kitchen, where she settled him into his high chair for breakfast. While making him a bowl of rice cereal with applesauce, she grabbed a carton of yogurt for herself. Shoving aside the stacks of bills and legal papers, she made room at the table so she could sit down to feed him.

One of her father's colleagues was helping her sort out her family's financial and legal mess pro bono. Her parents had considerable assets and the foresight to have both wills and living wills. But even they were not prepared for the tragic turn of events that would require shifting power of attorney and property to their younger daughter so soon after their older daughter's death.

Cara hadn't owned anything of real value that didn't also belong to Nash, except for a small burial policy the insurance company refused to pay out because Nash was the sole beneficiary.

And even though Mallory was Benji's court-appointed guardian, she had a big battle ahead of her in order to gain full custody. Kenneth Nash was still the baby's father and Benjamin Nash was legally a ward of the state of California until a judge said otherwise.

She couldn't discount Nash's family.

His mother, his aunt and uncle, numerous cousins, including a married cousin in New York, had all expressed interest in adopting Benji. And that was just on his mother's side. But it seemed wrong somehow—disloyal to Cara's memory—to allow her murderer's family to raise her son.

Mallory might not yet have her act together at twenty-three, yet she was determined to pull it together fast—she had to, for her nephew's sake.

Life had been anything but easy these past few months, between the trial, and the responsibilities of a preemie nephew *and* aging parents—make that aging parent, since her mother had died after collapsing in Cara's room. And without her mother's help, she'd had no choice but to put her father in an assisted-living facility. And, to add to everything else, Dad wasn't adjusting very well to the loss of Mom or his new home.

The telephone rang as Mallory shoveled another spoonful of rice cereal into Benji's eager mouth. She glanced over her shoulder at the shrill disruption. The call appeared to be coming from a blocked number.

With an eye on the clock, she got up from her seat and picked up the wireless receiver. Mallory had only been back to work a couple of months and couldn't afford to be late again. *Please do not let it be the assisted-living facility.* "'lo?"

"Ms. Ward, it's Tess Galena." The NCIS special agent worked out of the San Diego field office and had been assigned as the special agent in charge of Cara's case. The woman was somewhat of a legend in her field. Mallory had once dreamed of that kind of professional recognition and respect, until circumstances beyond her control landed her behind a desk.

Galena's investigation into Cara's murder had led to Nash's conviction.

"Ms. Ward, are you there?" Galena asked.

"What?" Mallory wiped Benji's face with a clean cloth. Offering a reassuring smile as she exchanged his bowl of mush for a few Cheerios he could manage on his own. "Sorry. Yes, I'm here."

"I need you in San Diego today. My assistant has booked you a flight."

"I'd have to check with work—"

"Your superiors are aware of the situation. Plan to be here for a few days."

The woman must have some serious pull.

"What's this about?" The yogurt in Mallory's stomach soured as the possibilities, none of them good, ran through her mind. "I don't have anyone to watch Benji."

NCIS Special Agent Tess Galena never hesitated. "Actually, Ms. Ward, we need both of you. We'll brief you when you get here."

"Is it Nash?"

"I can't say anything more over the phone. Someone will meet you at the airport, Ms. Ward."

Naval Brig Miramar
San Diego, California

As soon as they landed at San Diego International Airport, Mallory and Benji were taken to the brig at Miramar. Once a naval air station, made famous by the movie *Top Gun,* the base now belonged to the Marine Corps. The brig itself, run by the Department of the Navy, consolidated Level I and Level II military prisoners.

Nash, as a convicted murderer, was housed at Fort Leavenworth, a Level III disciplinary barracks in Leavenworth, Kansas, and the sole maximum-security penal facility for the U.S. military. Mallory couldn't have been more confused, but neither of her special agent escorts had deemed it necessary to fill her in on the details during the drive over.

Shifting Benji on her hip, she adjusted the diaper bag and purse on her opposite shoulder as they breezed through security with a show of agency badges. They were buzzed through several more gates and then led to an interrogation room by a uniformed guard.

The otherwise nondescript room consisted of military-issued furniture, a gunmetal-gray table and four chairs. Her escorts took up positions outside the steel security door, which locked with a quiet click behind her.

She recognized Commander Mike McCaffrey—Mac—Nash's former commanding officer, leaning against the wall next to a large mirror, which was likely a two-way. Nash had served under McCaffrey as executive officer of SEAL Team Eleven. The commander straightened to his full height as she entered the room.

Tess Galena sat at the table. The NCIS special agent wore a pin-striped suit, obviously tailor-made for her curvy figure—there was no mistaking that the woman in designer duds was the woman in charge. Mallory's own slobber-stained, off-the-rack ensemble made her feel dowdy in comparison.

"Ms. Ward," the woman said, uncrossing her long legs and rising to her feet. "Please have a seat." She indicated the chair across the table from hers. "I apologize for such short notice." Galena's sharp glance toward the commander had Mallory wondering who exactly had called this meeting.

Mallory sat and then adjusted Benji on her

lap. Tugging at the sleeves of his little jacket, she dropped it into the diaper bag at her feet.

He was a quiet baby, prematurely taken from his mother's womb in a grizzly scene Mallory wouldn't soon—if ever—forget. She hoped they wouldn't be here long enough for Benji to get tired or hungry during this major disruption to his routine.

"Are you going to tell me what this is all about?" Mallory forced herself to make eye contact, first with Galena and then the commander. "Nash," she whispered, reading it on their faces with a sinking sensation in the pit of her gut. "He's escaped."

She didn't know why escape was the first thought that popped into her head. But as a Navy SEAL trained in escape and evasion, Nash certainly had the skills. If anyone could break out of a military prison, he could.

"Not yet." The commander sauntered over to the table. "But he will. With your help."

The absurdity of his statement took a moment to sink in.

"Like hell I will." Only a cold-blooded killer could do what Nash had done to his pregnant wife. "Not in this or any other lifetime will I be helping that man escape—"

Galena leaned across the table. "Mallory… May I call you Mallory?" She continued without waiting for the consent, which Mallory would have given gladly. "Kenneth Nash can serve a higher purpose than any death sentence handed down to him."

Mallory wasn't so sure about that. She didn't necessarily believe in capital punishment. But if anyone deserved to pay the ultimate price, Nash did.

"To put it bluntly," the commander interrupted, "we're proposing a mission few men are even qualified to undertake. You're aware, of course, that Nash is half Syrian—on his mother's side. He has the looks and the know-how for a deep-cover op to infiltrate al-Ayman." She knew al-Ayman to be a terrorist organization with ties to al Qaeda.

"What are you suggesting?" She looked from one to the other.

Galena cleared her throat. "The president has reviewed the case and is prepared to offer Kenneth Nash a full pardon for the murder of his wife, your sister, in exchange for certain, shall we say— services. What you need to understand, Mallory, is that he'd be a free man. And we need you to be comfortable with that."

Mallory smoothed a hand over her nephew's dark head. "You've got to be kidding." A presidential pardon? So much for the president getting her vote of confidence. "There must be other men, loyal Americans of Middle Eastern descent—"

"None with Lieutenant Commander Nash's

background and training who are already serving a prison sentence." The commander had a grim certainty about him Mallory found disconcerting. "We're proposing a move to Gitmo under an assumed name. He'd be so deep undercover not even the marines guarding him would know his true identity."

"His main objective would be to gather intel from the detainees held at the military detention center in Guantanamo Bay, Cuba," Galena clarified. "Specifically the youngest son of Mullah Kahn. Mullah, also known as the Cobra, is the head of the al-Ayman terrorist network. His son, Bari Kahn, was captured last year, right here in California. Additionally, Nash would be tasked with finding security leaks within our own system."

Mallory shifted uncomfortably in her seat. "And if he's caught—"

"If he's caught by *either* side," the commander said with emphasis, "he'd be a marked man."

That shouldn't bother her as much as it did.

She shouldn't care.

She didn't care.

Galena directed a sharp glance at the commander. "Or he may come out of all this unscathed." The NCIS agent drummed a pen on a pad, a sign of restlessness Mallory wouldn't have associated with the woman. Perhaps she had her own reservations and was just as uncomfortable with the situation as Mallory. "Detainees in Cuba won't be held forever. There's plenty of public outcry as U.S. involvement in the war comes to a close, and when the last prisoners are released or transferred to other countries, as many have been already, Nash will be among them."

"You'd let him go? Just like that?"

"Gitmo is no cakewalk." The commander crossed his arms. "Even if he were to go free, you're not in any danger, Ms. Ward," he said with the unwavering confidence of his rank. "I strongly believe in Lieutenant Commander Nash's innocence."

He might believe it. She might even want to believe it. But she'd seen what she'd seen. And Mallory's testimony had convicted the man, for crying out loud—what was to stop him from coming after her?

Or Benji?

There was no doubt in her mind Nash would come after his son.

She felt it with bone-chilling certainty.

Mallory stared out of focus at the two-way mirror. As if looking at it through a haze of raw emotions would allow her to see more clearly. That's when she felt it, the eerie sensation of being watched.

Of course, there was someone behind the glass,

watching them. She took a deep, shuddering breath and held Benji tighter. "Are you saying this assignment somehow hinges on my approval?"

She fixed her gaze on the commander this time. He shifted his to Galena as if this condition was a point of contention between them. "No," he said, returning his attention to her.

"Then why am I here, sir?" Benji shoved a pudgy fist into his mouth. "Why are *we* here?"

Galena stepped in and answered for him. "We can't just waltz a high-profile prisoner like Lieutenant Commander Kenneth Nash out the front gate of a federal prison."

Mallory sensed the commander's growing impatience with this conversation.

He hunkered down eye level to her nephew and allowed Benji to grab his thumb as he cupped the baby's chubby cheek. Benji immediately became intent on bringing that masculine digit to his mouth like a new teething toy. She knew the commander was a new father himself and wondered what he really thought of this whole mess.

"We're taking Nash out of here in a body bag," he said. "Stone-cold dead. Kenneth Nash will no longer exist."

He'd said it with such finality as he lifted his gaze toward hers that Mallory shivered and turned away from the glimpse of resignation behind the man's eyes. Was that supposed to make her feel guilty?

"We're going to fake his suicide." Galena straightened in her seat. "We didn't want you caught off guard. There will likely be renewed interest in your sister's case as well as press coverage. We need you to keep a low profile for the next few days."

"Out of sight, out of mind." Mallory shook her head in disbelief.

The commander gently disengaged himself from the baby's grasp and pushed to his feet with his mask securely in place. "We weighed in heavily against telling you anything, Ms Ward."

"So why did you?" She glanced at the two-way mirror again.

"Frankly, Nash's odds of survival are better on death row," the commander said. "He may be a free man, but he won't be free. *And* he won't be Kenneth Nash." His firm mouth held a grim line. "There's no reason for you to be afraid. Should he survive this operation, Lieutenant Commander Nash has agreed to no contact with you or his son. *Ever.*"

He might want to believe there was no real danger to her or the baby, but the pounding in her chest told Mallory otherwise. She choked back a laugh as she looked the commander in the eye. "A lot of good a restraining order did my sister."

He didn't balk at her accusation. The facts were irrefutable.

At the time, Mallory had tried to talk her sister out of filing the protection order. The marriage had never been volatile. But Cara had kicked Nash out of their off-base housing for reasons that were still unclear to everyone, except perhaps Nash, and he wasn't talking. He'd left without incident but had later returned drunk and dismal. Mallory had to drive him back to the bachelor pad where he was staying with friends.

Even then, she'd been on his side.

But the next morning Cara had insisted on filing a restraining order to keep him away. Mallory thought the whole separation ridiculous. Yet Cara was dead before Nash had even been served the papers—which proved, only too late, Cara had reason to fear him.

"Nash *has* made one stipulation," the commander said.

"Just one?" She might have known.

"He wanted to see you and the baby one last time."

"Seriously?" She jerked her head toward the mirror. "He's behind that glass, isn't he? That's why you really brought us here?"

"He's not asking—"

"What does he want?" She pushed to her feet

with her nephew in her arms and faced off with her own reflection. "Forgiveness? Forget it!"

"To say goodbye, Ms. Ward. The man just wants to say goodbye to his son."

Protected by that pane of glass, she put on her bravest facade and continued to stand there as tears pricked behind her eyes. She would not cry.

How had the boy her sister had dated since high school become the man who'd murdered her? No tears. Not for him.

She'd cried them all for Cara. Her best friend and big sister.

Gone forever.

"Fine. I want to see him, too," she demanded. "I want him to look me in the eye as he begs for his get-out-of-jail-free card," she hissed at the mirror.

"That's not what's happening here."

"Even I know he has a better than average chance of survival, Commander—freedom. Anyway, why tell me any of this? What's to stop me from going to the press?" Mallory knowingly put more than just her career on the line with that threat.

The commander's demeanor changed in an instant. "That would be ill advised, Ms. Ward. I don't think I need to remind you that this conversation is highly sensitive."

Sensitive, meaning *classified!*

Every government agency out there—no matter what its initials—needed a deep-cover operative of Middle Eastern descent, more than they needed another homogenized desk jockey with unruly red hair and freckles like her.

Mallory scoffed at his words. "I'm not very good at keeping secrets."

A muscle twitched in the commander's jaw. Mallory clamped down on her back teeth to keep from saying something she shouldn't. Tension filled the room as they squared off against each other.

"If you promise to keep quiet, Mallory, then Kenneth will sign over custody of his son to you—right here, right now, today. Plus, he trusts you." Galena's words broke through strained nerves and forced Mallory to look in her direction. "Otherwise you wouldn't be here at all."

Her ex-brother-in-law had no reason to trust her. He had to hate her as much as she hated him. But maybe this highly irregular request for her presence and then Benji's was finally starting to make sense.

She wouldn't be surprised to find the proposed undercover op was Nash's idea. Something he and the commander had concocted and then taken up the chain of command, maybe even directly to the secretary of the navy, who'd taken it all the way up the chain to the President of the United States.

The president who'd pardoned her sister's murderer.

She might just have to change her whole party affiliation.

"I want to see him now," she demanded a second time as Benji began to fuss.

The commander nodded to whomever watched them from behind that plated glass. Mallory bounced Benji on her hip to keep her trembling body under control. A few pulse pounding heartbeats later the door opened.

A marine guard ushered Nash into the room with his hands and legs shackled.

Mallory forced herself to look at him—at the stranger he'd become. He'd lost weight since she'd last seen him at his court-martial. The prison uniform hung on his lanky frame and washed out his olive complexion.

The dark stubble on his head and clean-shaven face brought out the high cheekbones and the prominent nose descended from the nomadic princes of the Lost Tribes of Israel. But he'd always be that boy from Brooklyn, New York, to her. Just as he'd been the day he moved into their Denver neighborhood.

That distinctive New York boroughs accent had set him apart more than his mixed heritage. She remembered him as being street tough and smart—an irresistible combination for most teenage girls. She'd been younger than Cara by almost four years and halfway in love with "Kenny" Nash herself by the time she was twelve.

Her unrequited crush had evolved into something much less painful over the years and they'd become fast friends, family.

He'd lost that accent somewhere along the way. But not that edge.

Though she hated to admit it, even he would have a hard time pulling off a mission of this magnitude. Yet somehow she knew he would.

Fluent in half a dozen Semitic languages, including Hebrew, Arabic, Aramaic and Tigrinya, Nash had carried a double major in political science and theology while at Harvard. He'd graduated from the prestigious university with honors, and a B.S.D.—Bull Shit Degree, as he liked to call it—before joining the navy.

The navy had seemed like such an odd career choice for him at the time. And her sister had been less than thrilled to have her fiancé and future husband join the military.

Mal distinctly remembered their father saying the military was a good choice for a young man with political aspirations, although Mal just couldn't see Nash as a politician. She thought his enlistment had more to do with the fact that his father had been a marine—either that or a restless desire to see the world. Nash had an insatiable curiosity with world religions and religious artifacts. He even went on to earn his master's in education while in the service.

For a long time she'd held on to the romantic notion that he was more Indiana Jones than Navy SEAL.

Part scholar, part mystery. Passionate in his thinking.

She also knew better than most not to argue politics or religion with him.

Christian, Muslim, Jew. As far as she was concerned, a person's religious beliefs and practices were his own business. But in some parts of the world, the distinction could get a person killed. This was why his mother's family had fled Syria for Israel, and then later America, when his mother was a young girl.

Nash's dark brown eyes remained sharp and focused on her. The chains rattled one last time as he settled against the wall.

Benji swiveled toward the sound. Resting his small head against her shoulder, he shoved a sloppy fist into his mouth as he stared without recognition at the man who'd brought him into the world.

Nash stood with his head high and met Mallory's hate-filled glare before shifting his attention toward the son he'd delivered by cutting open his wife's womb. Cara had died before help arrived. But was she dead before he'd slaughtered her?

That question haunted Mallory to this day.

The autopsy had been inconclusive at best. Medical experts testified to both scenarios, depending on their allegiance to the prosecution or the defense.

There were those who'd called Nash's extreme measures heroic. He was a Navy SEAL, trained to assess and react in critical situations without hesitation. Then there was the fact that his actions were criminal.

He might have been EMT trained, but he was not a surgeon.

Hero or killer? He'd saved his son's life either way.

A traumatized fetus couldn't survive more than four minutes without oxygen from its mother. So if Nash's story was to be believed, less than four minutes separated him from the real murderer. But his account of those two hundred and forty seconds was as muddy as his defense.

Regardless of how Cara wound up on the floor fighting for her life, Mal believed Nash sealed her sister's fate with his knife.

Why didn't he just continue CPR? Especially after she arrived and could have helped. Only Nash knew his real motive for sending her outside for a phone he knew she wouldn't be able to find because he'd had it on him all along.

Records indicated he'd actually dialed 911 before she did. So there was no reason to even send her outside, except...

To save his son's life? Or to cover up his even more heinous crime?

Or both.

The pinch near the corner of his mouth might have gone unnoticed if Mallory hadn't been searching for a reaction from him.

"Take a good look," she spat. "Because it's your last."

Until that moment, there'd been some niggling doubt that maybe she was wrong. Maybe he was innocent. She wanted to believe with her whole heart he'd fought off a one-armed man like Dr. Richard Kimble in *The Fugitive*. Because for as long as she could remember, Nash had been her real-life action hero.

But maybe there was no one-armed man. What there was, though, were telltale scratches on Nash's face, his skin cells under Cara's nails, and his partial prints on the phone cord that had been ripped out of the wall and then wrapped around Cara's neck.

No forced entry, nothing missing.

Cara had trusted her killer.

Mallory wouldn't trust Nash again if her life

depended on it. If there was still such a thing as a firing squad, she'd volunteer to be the one and only shooter. She'd riddle his body with bullets just to watch him bleed. She wanted revenge, vengeance. *Not* freedom for her sister's murderer.

The Uniform Code of Military Justice provided the death penalty as possible punishment for fifteen offenses, most of which had to occur during wartime. All nine men at present on death row had been convicted of premeditated murder or felony murder. The president had the power to commute a death sentence to life, and no service member could be executed without the personally signed order from the Commander in Chief.

Eisenhower was the last president under whom a military execution had been upheld. In fifty years, only George W. Bush had signed a single death writ, and that order was still under appeal.

Nash had plenty of time to plead his case.

The man she'd known wouldn't have gone down without throwing at least one punch. If he was innocent, he would have—should have—fought harder to prove it.

He wouldn't do the unthinkable.

Mallory took an involuntary step backward and plopped into her chair as Nash moved to sit across the table from her. Galena set some papers in front of him and then handed him a pen. His hand shook as he signed at the flagged lines without reading.

When he finished, he set the pen aside and pushed the papers across the table toward Mallory.

Her lower lip threatened to tremble. The man didn't deserve her pity. Strengthening her resolve, she raised her chin to look into Nash's eyes.

"You just sold your son for your freedom."

CHAPTER TWO

"COFFEE?" A PAPER cup appeared within easy reach of his cuffed wrists, chained to the table. Nash ignored the cup while the man who'd offered it scooted around the table to sit across from him. It was Good Cop's turn to have a crack at him while Bad Cop scowled from the corner. Actually they were both Feds. But he wouldn't hold that against them. "Sayyid," Good Cop said as if confiding in his new best friend. "We know you're his number-two...."

They didn't know shit about him, but he wouldn't hold *that* against them, either.

The man flipped through a file full of misleading information. Sayyid Naveed, born in Syria, educated in the U.S. as a devout Muslim. Detained at Gitmo for suspected ties to terrorism. Escaped from Gitmo—which was true. Though the actual account was classified and well above this guy's pay grade, he probably had some version of that truth in front of him. As well as Nash's mug shot on an FBIs Most Wanted bulletin. He was somewhere in the top one hundred, not high enough to attract any real attention, but high enough that anyone coming into contact with him would know they had someone important on their hands.

His file also read that he'd spent six years working his way up to a position of trust within the al-Ayman terrorist network—that was true, too. Helping Bari Kahn, the youngest son of Mullah Kahn, escape from Gitmo had all been part of his plan—the part he hadn't disclosed to the authorities that had sanctioned his assignment. Nash had known going in that if he got the chance to escape—with or without Kahn's son—he was going to take it.

He'd left it to Mac to smooth things over with the top brass.

The years of intel Nash had been feeding U.S. intelligence agencies since hadn't hurt his case, either, but he'd always known he was in this alone. Which was why he'd hedged his bets with the Israelis. He might be working more than one angle, but he wasn't a traitor to his country or his beliefs. The Allies wanted to put an end to the al-Ayman faction of a global terrorist network, and so did he.

Only his reasons were more personal.

"Just tell us what we need to know and we'll go easy on you."

His new BFF had made all sorts of promises over the past eight hours.

Nash stared past the man's shoulder to his own reflection in the two-way mirror and remained silent. Most days even he didn't recognize the man he'd become. His shoulder-length hair was long enough now that the natural curl had taken over and the scruff on his face was more beard than not.

He hadn't asked for a phone call. A drink of water. Or to use the bathroom.

All of which were within his legal rights.

"Well, why don't I tell you what we know?" Good Cop said. "We've shut down the entire al-Ayman operation today."

Big Dog was barking up the wrong tree. Nash had supplied intel for the fifty-city sweep across the Americas and Europe from the inside.

Hitting al-Ayman hard at the sex trafficking level was one way to mess with their cash flow. Unfortunately they had other means.

Drugs. Prostitution. Money laundering.

You name it. If it was illegal, al-Ayman was into it.

It would take years for Nash to wash away the stench of his own participation in such activities.

No, today was about one thing—catching the

man at the top in the wrong place at the right time. Seven long years he'd waited for justice, and now he was going to get it through the federal court system in the state of New York.

In the good old U.S. of A.

Kahn wasn't the kind of terrorist that could be taken out with a drone.

He was a well-connected international businessman. With enough money and clout to make certain countries look the other way.

He'd have to be taken down by the legal system on a bigger, more public stage.

"Guys like you don't last long in prison. Tough on the outside. All jelly doughnut on the inside." Good Cop took a big bite out of a jelly doughnut for emphasis. Goop oozed from between his thick, smacking lips and a glob landed on his tie. He picked up a napkin and made an even bigger mess.

Hunger gnawed at Nash's insides, a hunger for justice. Besides the scene in front of him was enough to curb his appetite for food. The box of doughnuts had been sitting there all day— They were probably stale by now anyway.

"A pretty boy like you—" Bad Cop shrugged from the corner "—you'll be someone's bitch inside a week."

"How long do you think before one of your cohorts rolls over on you, Sayyid?" Good Cop asked. "We're questioning them right now. Why not do yourself a favor? I can get you a nice cozy cell in isolation, away from the general population."

The man pushed a pen and pad of paper toward Nash for his confession.

Seriously? The pen was a mistake. He could kill both of the agents and be free of his handcuffs before whoever was watching the box could enter the room.

Not that Nash would.

He'd done enough bad shit in the past seven years.

Honed his skills. Acquired new ones.

But it was all sanctioned shit.

Killing a Fed for no justifiable reason? Well, even Mac wouldn't be able to get him out of that one.

Nash wished his ride would hurry up and get here.

As amusing as these guys were, he was getting kind of bored hearing the same fairy tale over and over again. Just to prove wishes really do come true, the door opened. Nash caught a glimpse of Mac and two U.S. Marshals reflected in the mirror. Another man, important and harried looking, wearing dress pants and a white dress shirt with rolled-up sleeves, entered the room behind them. "This one belongs to the Marshal Service now."

The captain, or whoever he was—whatever police precinct had assisted the FBI with the raid—

walked over and unlocked the chains that tethered Nash to the table. The look on the faces of Good cop/Bad Cop was worth the wait.

Without a word, Nash stood and followed the lead U.S. Marshal out the door while the other marshal and Mac walked behind. He was still shackled and for good reason—his very life depended on him never blowing his cover.

As they exited the room, Mullah Kahn was being hauled out of another room in shackles. Flanked by two federal agents and trailed by a couple of designer suits with leather briefcases, Kahn was on his way to Booking. The al-Ayman leader might have a couple of high-priced attorneys on the payroll, but he wasn't making bail this time.

The snake turned to stare at Nash in passing. Saw Mac's uniform and the Windbreakers identifying the marshals. "Where are they taking you?" the al-Ayman leader demanded.

"Gitmo," Nash said with the expected contrition of an underling.

"Shut up and keep moving." McCaffrey shoved him from behind.

Kahn shouted in Arabic as the FBI led him away.

"What the hell was all that about?" Mac asked once they were outside and beyond earshot of anyone else that might be listening.

"He still thinks he's in charge." Kahn had called

him son and promised to keep him out of prison. "Nice touch with the shove, by the way."

"Just doing my part. How are you holding up?"

"About as good as I look."

"Well, you look like crap," McCaffrey said. "So I guess that answers my question."

"What's the word on Bari?" Bari Kahn, the little weasel, had slipped out before the raid on the warehouse down by the docks.

Mac shook his head.

"Lieutenant Commander Nash." The redheaded marshal opened the back of an unmarked white van used for prisoner transport. "Sorry, sir. Protocol. I've been instructed to leave the cuffs on. You'll be riding in back."

Nash had been through this once or twice before. He'd be taken to a secure location for debriefing before they'd let him out of his cuffs. Only this time he wouldn't be given a new assignment.

Federal prosecutors would be present to take his statement and then he'd be moved to a safe house. Because this time he was testifying.

Safe house somewhere in the Catskill Mountains

"NASH, YOU IN OR OUT?" Irish tipped the kitchen chair back on two legs to poke his head around the corner.

"Go ahead and deal me in." It's not as if he had

other plans. They'd been cooped up in this house close to fourteen weeks now. Only two more weeks to go until the trial. Nash eased the ache in his neck and then flipped from the Weather Channel to Thursday Night Football before setting the remote aside.

He'd been daydreaming through the forecast for the Western states again.

The snowstorm closing in on the Rockies in time for Halloween had him thinking of things other than the extended forecast. Things he shouldn't be thinking about.

He hadn't been this close to—or felt this far from—home in years.

He was born within a hundred-mile radius of where he stood right now and had spent several summers as a boy in the Hudson River Valley.

If he wasn't for all intents and purposes a ghost, he could call on his mother for a visit.

As for Colorado…well, that was some sixteen hundred miles away and another lifetime ago. Yet he felt the pull. But this caretaker's cabin in the Catskills was as much a prison as Leavenworth or Gitmo. And he wasn't free to move about.

U.S. Marshal Reid "Irish" Thompson finished dealing as Nash and U.S. Marshal Salvatore Torri joined the freckle faced kid for a little three-handed Texas Hold'em. Thompson claimed marshals invented the game out of sheer boredom, though little was known of the actual origins of Hold'em poker, except that it first appeared in the early 1900s. The Texas Legislature laid claim before the game migrated to Las Vegas, Nevada, in the 1960s and became synonymous with the word *poker.*

All Nash knew was they'd played a lot of poker these past four months.

And he'd bet those marshals of old didn't sit around playing cards in their body armor. Long johns, maybe. But not Kevlar.

His guards were cautious and he appreciated it.

"You're not still thinking about what the federal prosecutor said this afternoon?" Irish asked once he finished passing out the chips.

Nash picked up his stack of red chips and let them fall through his fingers in a rhythmic motion. After this was all over and he'd given his testimony, he intended to let his chips fall where they may so to speak. Checking his hand against the flop, he plunked two chips off the top and then tossed them into the pot. "There's no reason for Sari to testify."

Sal raised his bet. "Can't blame her for wanting to."

Needing to was what Nash was afraid of.

Irish took his time rearranging his cards and then comparing them to what was on the table. The kid was into them for some twenty grand now.

It wasn't as if Nash planned to collect; they kept the running tab purely for bragging rights and weren't even playing for real money, but maybe he should let Thompson win a few hands before he left.

"I think it's messed up that her brother could get away with something like that," Thompson said. "And if her father ordered it, then he's just a sick bastard."

Sal passed around the pizza box from the Torri family's pizzeria in nearby Albany—if forty miles could be considered nearby. Nash took several slices and a cold Near Beer.

His marshals didn't drink on duty.

And Nash didn't drink, period.

As far as he was concerned, Sari's father and brothers deserved worse than prison for the mental and physical abuse they'd subjected her to. But Sari's story was so personal there'd be no hiding her identity.

That would be bad news for her. And for him.

He'd like nothing better than to testify in open court himself. But that wasn't going to happen when transmitting a pixilated image and altered audio from another room could protect his identity.

And for one very good reason....

Suddenly Nash's thoughts went some sixteen hundred miles away again.

He could go days, weeks, without even worrying about Ben. Knowing he'd left his son in capable hands. But then there were days—like today—when he'd realized the reality of his choices meant more than just missing out on the first seven years of his son's life.

And it always hit him hard.

Of course, he'd known the sacrifices he was making in going after Cara's killer and then not killing the man. He could have had his revenge a long time ago and no one would have been the wiser—and maybe he should have.

But he wanted to clear his name for Ben's sake.

Even if Nash was no longer his last name. Or Ben's.

Sal Torri was telling a story about his own son, and Nash forced a laugh. Swapping sea stories over Near Beer, pizza and poker with the guys was almost like being part of the Team again.

Only back then the beer had been genuine.

And so had he.

Sal did the majority of their cooking and grocery shopping. Once a week he drove into Albany for supplies and—Nash suspected—a quick visit with his large Italian family, which included a pregnant wife and a young son.

While they played cards, Sal also did most of the talking. The man's familiar street-tough accent lulled Nash into slipping back into his own every now and again.

As far as safe houses went, this one was rather low tech.

Security cameras. Perimeter alarms.

A panic room.

Once a popular vacation spot for New Yorkers, the row of vacation homes had burned to the ground in the late '70s. For whatever reason, the owner had been unable to rebuild and his heirs further neglected the taxes.

Eventually the government seized the property along with the only building left standing. The caretaker's residence had been a safe house for close to thirty years without a single breach. In fact, no witness in the history of the U.S. Marshal Service had ever died while under protection—with the caveat—while following the rules of the program.

The rules were simple—but maybe harder for some than others to follow.

You could never return to the town from which you were relocated. You could never connect with known associates, or friends and family not in the program.

Never was a long time.

And this wasn't a reflection on his babysitters, but he'd already decided against going into the Witness Protection Program once the trial was over. He wasn't stupid, though. He knew he'd have to don another identity and then move on regardless of whether he entered the program.

But this time he wanted to be truly anonymous.

Outside government control and way beyond government contact.

Nash could make a good living in the private sector or he could retire to a quiet life. He had enough money to do whatever he wanted. Either way, he was willing to disappear so that Ben wouldn't have to.

As far as the al-Ayman network knew, Kenneth Nash was already dead. And the identity of the undercover agent testifying against them, the man they knew as Sayyid Naveed, would remain anonymous.

Suddenly the perimeter alarm wailed and lights flooded the exterior.

As a precaution the house went into auto lockdown.

All three men abandoned the card table. At first glance, the monitors above the duty station built into the kitchen revealed nothing going on.

One camera focused on the only road in or out, barricaded with a warning that a nonexistent bridge had been washed out. The others focused along a footpath and the outer and inner perimeters.

The cameras were motion-sensitive and this wasn't the first time they'd gone off. Any movement, a deer, a skunk, or the rustle of the wind through the trees, and it appeared on the screen.

Torri did a quick computer scan. "I've got nothing. Irish, get the asset to the basement while I check this out." He drew his weapon and picked up a transmitter and then tossed one to Irish.

Translated: they were locking him in the panic room as a precaution.

Witnesses weren't allowed to carry. Though Nash was the exception—being more agent than criminal—this was their show, not his.

He knew better than to argue. He was no good to anyone dead.

Thompson put a hand on Nash's back. But before either of them could take a single step in the right direction, the front and back doors exploded. Followed by two pops. Torri slammed backward with his brains all over the kitchen floor. Two men dressed in black leather from head to toe and wearing motorcycle helmets entered through the back and then another one from the front.

Irish put himself between Nash and the first shooter. He got off a couple of rounds in each direction before dropping to his knees from a bullet to the leg. He took another bullet to the arm before he could get off another round.

Nash made a move for the kid's gun and instantly had two beads on him.

He raised his arms and straightened slowly.

Irish raised his arms, but couldn't rise above his knees.

The first shooter through the door, the one who'd shot Torri, sauntered over to within feet of where Nash stood in the middle of the small living room. He lifted his dark visor on his grotesquely scarred face. "Sayyid, my brother," he said with a big grin on his face.

And then Bari Kahn shot Irish twice more, once to the neck and once to the face without so much as a passing glance at the young marshal who would die thinking Nash was a traitor.

Nash winced on the inside. On the outside, he played it cool.

Bari kicked Irish's firearm under the couch as he eyeballed Nash through his drooping lids. "Or should I say Lieutenant Commander Kenneth Nash?"

So much for playing it cool.

"Remove the Kevlar." Bari motioned with his gun. "You won't need it where you're going," he said as his two henchmen ripped the protective vest off Nash at the Velcro tabs.

They also relieved him of the weapon he'd hoped to keep hidden. And then forced him to his knees, facing the window so that his back was to their leader.

"I'd be happy to take you to hell *with* me, Bari," Nash said over his shoulder.

Bari stepped farther into the room and over Irish's limp body, circling around to level the barrel of his gun at Nash's chest. "Tell me where my sister is."

"Even if I knew, you know I wouldn't tell you."

"Sadly, I do know." Bari continued his circle until he was at Nash's back again.

The TV went from being background noise to being the *only* noise as Nash caught Bari's reflection in the window. The man raised his gun to the back of Nash's head and then lowered it.

Nash blinked. Surprised to find he was still alive.

"Father wants you alive. So he can have the pleasure of torturing you himself, I'm sure." Bari's reflection shrugged as if it made no difference to him. "Lucky for you he ordered me not to kill you."

"Since when have you ever listened to your father?"

"Exactly."

Nash caught Bari's reflected nod toward his man.

In that same instant, Nash grabbed Bari by the arm and wrestled for possession of his gun. Bullets went flying through the cramped space. Nash angled the weapon at Bari's men. One man went down. Nash shoved Bari into the other and then launched the downed man helmet first through the window.

Diving after him through the shower of glass and bullets, Nash landed in a heap outside the window. He reached for the downed man's Glock mere inches from his own torn and bloody hand and then rolled onto his back, firing through the empty window.

Scrambling to unsteady feet, he angled toward the heavily wooded area with Bari and his man not far behind him. Nash ran full tilt, dodging stray bullets and low branches for several heart-pounding miles until he was sure he'd outrun them.

Even then, he only slowed enough to access the damage.

ATVs rumbled in the distance. Bari and his man?

That would give them a light source and the ability to cover more ground, but it also meant Nash would hear them coming.

More than likely, Bari had changed up his plan. From here on out it would be a race against the clock to try and stay one step ahead of the terrorist.

How in the hell had Bari found him in the first place?

Nash had been in this business long enough to know that when enough money exchanged hands, almost anyone or anything could be found. Had

Bari bribed someone in the federal prosecutor's office? Used his father's fancy lawyers to get to someone on the inside? Blackmail, maybe?

Could they have been followed back from the federal prosecutor's office in New York City that morning? All this speculation was just that, speculation. The one thing he did know was that his cover was blown.

Trust no one.

Right now his priority was to stay alive.

More important, he had to keep those he loved alive.

His mother, his son.

Nash didn't even want to think about what might happen if Bari reached Ben before he did. Running headlong into a trap was the least of his worries. Nash removed some of the larger, more uncomfortable shards of glass from his palms and did his best to stanch the flow of blood from the apparent bullet wound at his side.

He'd been struck from the front at close range with no exit wound—more than likely in his struggle with Bari. Only he'd been too pumped full of adrenaline to feel anything until now.

No telling how much blood he'd lost.

Fatigue had already started to set in. He could feel it in the weight of his limbs.

By the time he reached the nearest town, the last of his strength was fading. He barely remembered stealing a car and driving into the city. Once he got there, he ditched the stolen vehicle and grabbed what he needed from a locker he kept for emergencies.

Then he hopped on a subway to sanctuary.

Nash hunched his shoulders and kept his head down. Shoving his hands deeper into the pocket of his dark hoodie where he cradled the Glock, he entered a long-forgotten alley on the west side. He used what little strength he had left to knock on the door. It took several minutes for someone to answer.

When the door opened, an elderly man stood on the other side.

"Rabbi Yaakov?"

"Yes?" The old man studied him from behind wire-framed glasses.

"I'm with the Institute." Nash kept his voice low, using the literal English translation for Mossad.

The Institute was responsible for covert operations and counterterrorism, as well as bringing Jews to Israel from countries where official immigration agencies were forbidden and protecting Jewish communities.

The rabbi looked up and down the alley before pulling Nash inside. "You can't be here," he hissed.

"I need your help." Nash unzipped the hoodie to reveal his blood-soaked T-shirt. "I can pay in cash." He dropped his backpack to the floor at the rabbi's feet.

"Oy," the old man said. Nash's knees threatened to buckle as the rabbi ducked under his arm to support his weight and led him to an industrial-size stainless steel kitchen. "If you're going to pass out, do it up here."

WHEN NASH CAME to, he was stretched out on one of the stainless steel workstations, watching the rabbi drop the last of his instruments into a stainless steel bedpan. The rattle must have been what had woken him. Nash glanced at the pan full of instruments. He eyed the bullet and bloody gauze with distaste, wondering if he'd just traded that bullet for a lifetime of hep C.

"You want I should call a doctor?" Rabbi Yaakov said when he caught the frown on Nash's face. The old man snapped off the latex gloves with equal disgust. "The Institute sees to it that I'm well equipped. I use only sterile instruments."

Nash did not dare question the man's medical practice further.

Mossad took care of its own.

Besides which, beggars couldn't be choosers. Any emergency room staff would have to report him to the authorities.

"I need a plane." Nash pushed to sit up and then dropped back to his elbows. He turned and then threw up into the bedpan. "Preferably one with a pilot," he said, wiping the back of his hand across his mouth. "To Denver."

CHAPTER THREE

Less than twelve hours later

IDLING IN A black Ford Explorer on the crimson and gold tree-lined drive, he could pass for any other parent waiting for his son or daughter after school.

Except the snowcapped mountain license plates had belonged to an abandoned junker in an overgrown backyard. And the tamper-resistant expiration stickers had been lifted off a newer vehicle.

Grit scratched his sleep-deprived eyes like sandpaper. He removed his Ray-Ban Predators and wiped at his weary lids. If he closed them now he wasn't sure he'd ever open them again. Replacing his sunglasses, he pulled his ball cap lower.

The three o'clock bell signaled an end to the school day *and* the school week since it was Friday. Boys and girls poured out of the building, clamoring to be heard above the final peal. Mallory had put him in a private school, which made the boy harder to find. But not hard enough for anyone looking.

Not that he believed she'd hidden him out of

fear or as a precaution. If that were the case, she and the boy wouldn't be living in the same house she and her sister had grown up in.

He was sketchy on the details of the past seven years, but he knew her mother had passed away some time ago and that her father now resided in a nearby nursing home.

Nash glanced at the dated surveillance photo on the seat beside him. Hell of a thing not to know your own son. But he would have recognized the boy anywhere, right down to the Transformers T-shirt—it could have been his own second grade photo staring back at him.

Nash spotted Benjamin among a group of boys in uniform skipping down stairs despite being weighted down by backpacks bigger than they were. Quickly folding the photo along worn creases, he tucked it back into his pocket. As he watched, a man in a black turban approached the group of small boys. Nash reached for the door handle but pulled back at the last minute as a dark-skinned boy broke off from the crowd and ran up to embrace the lucky bastard.

Nash relaxed his grip on the Glock in his lap hidden beneath a newspaper.

He should have known better. His enemies wouldn't be that obvious. *If* they even looked like his Middle Eastern brethren.

The group of second grade boys thinned out

as they reached the sidewalk, with two of them breaking off in one direction and Benjamin in another.

"Damn it!" Nash checked his mirrors and then shoved the Explorer into gear. She didn't seriously allow the boy to walk those six blocks to the house alone, did she?

After everything he'd seen and done these past seven years, he wouldn't let a kid wander next door to his own house, let alone down the block in his own neighborhood. Urban jungles were some of the most dangerous.

As he pulled away from the curb, a teenage girl with two-toned, blond-on-black hair, rushed up to Benjamin. He heard her simultaneously scold him for not staying put and apologize for being late. The apparent babysitter and the boy continued down the block toward a rusted-out red Volvo.

The combination of an old car and a young driver didn't make Nash feel any better about his son's safety. But he drove on without so much as a glance in passing. Turning left at the third stop sign, he avoided the unmarked car parked across the street from his former in-laws' home, which now belonged to Mal—not just his former sister-in-law, but also his son's aunt and guardian.

If not for that familial connection, he would have braked at his first opportunity and snatched the boy right then and there. He checked the rearview mirror as the Volvo stopped at the same intersection before continuing toward the house.

Nash turned right at the alley and slowed the Explorer.

Modern pop tops punctuated the row of American Craftsman homes that made up the old Washington Park neighborhood that lay within spitting distance of downtown Denver. He'd scouted the area earlier. The stakeout appeared to be limited to the two Feds sitting in a black sedan out front.

At least a dozen federal agents should have been swarming the place by now. Unless, of course, they thought he was dead like the two federal marshals assigned to protect him.

In which case, they should have taken even more precautions.

He winced as a spasm in his side reminded him of his narrow escape and just how much blood he'd lost at the scene. Shoving back the brim of his ball cap, he swiped the beads of sweat forming on his brow.

Focus, Nash.

He tugged the ball cap back down and then took a familiar left turn out of the alley. He knew these lanes well—he'd grown up here.

After he'd entered the service, his mother had moved back East to be with family. As far as Sabine Nash knew, her only child—a convicted murderer—had died a coward in prison. He'd had to rely on Rabbi Yaakov to see that his mother paid a visit to their relatives in Israel for the time being. He didn't have the time to get both her *and* his son to safety. Nash beat back a twinge of guilt.

Thank God his father hadn't lived to see this day.

Though it was unlikely anyone from the old neighborhood would recognize him, including his own mother, Nash continued straight instead of taking another right. He didn't want to drive past the old house where he'd grown up just in case their elderly neighbor, Mrs. Rosenberg, had lived to see her eightieth birthday.

MALLORY PUSHED HER father's wheelchair, enjoying the relatively warm autumn weather as they strolled the parklike grounds between the assisted-living facility and his nursing home. The late afternoon sun reflected off the pond as they followed the winding path toward a chorus of honking geese who were making a pit stop on their way south for the winter.

"Slow down, Margaret! You're driving too fast."

"It's me, Daddy, Mallory. Mom—" There was no point in bringing it up again. He'd just relive the pain of losing his wife of thirty-five years. Or worse, would only feel frustrated because he couldn't remember her at all. "Mom couldn't make it today."

"Mallory?" He cranked his neck but couldn't turn his head far enough back to look at her, so he shifted his frail body to face her. "I have a daughter named Mallory."

"I know." Mallory sat on a bench and then angled his chair toward her, hoping for some sign of recognition from him today. At least this seemed to be a good day.

"Going to make a damn fine lawyer someday." The pride in his voice turned the remembrance bittersweet.

Her father had just made deputy district attorney when she'd told him she wasn't going on to law school after receiving her undergraduate degree. Instead she'd applied for, and had been accepted into, the FBI Academy.

She'd told him that she still intended to put her pre-law studies to good use, but in law enforcement. Mallory had explained that she had a hard time seeing herself stuck behind a desk for the next thirty years.

She'd always been a serious tomboy, with no time for boys, at least not in the boyfriend and girlfriend way—she'd been too busy competing with them both academically and physically. Despite that, she'd always had more male friends than female friends in high school and college. She just found it easier to relate to men. More often than not, her male friends considered her one of the guys, and she'd come to accept that that made her a better friend than girlfriend.

These days she had very few friends of either sex, though she still preferred the company of men—to a point. Because by both male and female agents she'd forever be known as that rookie whose brother-in-law murdered her sister. The one who pulled her gun and then fainted.

She'd spent most of the past seven years behind a desk, constantly passed over for promotions. But it turned out to be in the best interest of the two most important men in her life, and she couldn't regret that. Putting herself in the line of fire and leaving her father alone and Ben an orphan was not an option.

Being a single parent came with its own set of rules and responsibilities.

More recently, however, she'd made her own opportunities and finally felt as if she'd put the past behind her. She'd become part of an evidence recovery and processing team.

It might not be the job of her dreams, but at least she found her work interesting and maintained special agent status. This also meant she did a lot more fieldwork these days and carried a badge and a firearm again, which Ben thought was kind of cool and she found comforting.

Goose bumps raised the hairs on her arms, and she shivered.

"Are you cold, Daddy?" She tucked the lap blanket around him.

"Cold, no. I'm not cold." He took a moment to assess his surroundings. "Maybe a little." He amended his answer.

Mal lost track of time as the afternoon sun faded into evening and the temperature dropped. A slight breeze blew through the umber and gold trees with their scattered leaves. The afternoon sun had warmed their earthy fragrance and she breathed in the crisp, clean scent as it clung to the evening air.

Halloween was just around the corner. Exactly one week from today.

She must remember to stop by the grocery store on her way home for the pumpkin she'd promised Ben.

Taking the remnants of stale bread from the bag inside her purse, she handed a slice to her father. They took turns tossing bits and pieces into the water. Whenever the honks died down, one or the other of them would toss out another bit of bread for the geese to clamor over.

Her dad used to take her and Cara to Wash Park—Washington Park—to feed the geese on days just like this.

If he had to be lost in his memories, she figured that would be a nice one to get lost in.

While it often felt as if she and her dad were

having two different conversations, every once in a while they connected over something as simple as the weather and a flock of geese.

Brushing the crumbs from her lap, Mallory reached out to her father and just sat holding his fragile hand in hers. She listened to the familiar nuances in his voice while he talked as if she were away, studying pre-law at Colorado University in Boulder and her mother and sister were still with them.

Cara married to Nash and living in San Diego.

Their mother having no greater care than tending her rosebushes and vegetable gardens.

After Cara's death, Margaret Ward had simply given up on life. Even a grandbaby couldn't bring her back from the brink of despair. She'd needed pills to get up in the morning and then pills to fall asleep at night. She'd died of an overdose shortly after Nash's conviction.

An accidental overdose. At least that's what Mallory chose to tell herself…when she wasn't blaming Nash for her mother's suicide.

Mallory's father was made of sterner stuff. Older than his wife by a decade, he'd been diagnosed with Alzheimer's nine years ago. Charles Ward had stubbornly controlled the onset of dementia with medication and had succeeded in having several lucid years after his diagnosis. Not so much lately, though.

Consigning him to an assisted-living facility, and then later the nursing home, had taken all the fight out of him. But it had been the right thing to do.

Mallory hadn't been able to care for both her nephew and her father with his deteriorating mental and physical condition. Exhausted from trying, she came to a time when she had no choice.

She couldn't take an afternoon nap or lie down at night without worrying her father might take the baby out for a walk and leave him somewhere, or give him a bath and then become distracted. Or worse, become confused and frustrated when he heard the baby crying.

Even as a twenty-three-year-old, she'd realized the baby's safety had to come first.

Otherwise the consequences could have been tragic.

To her surprise, Nash's mother never contested Mallory's appointment as Ben's guardian. Nor her subsequent adoption. Mallory supposed there wasn't much the woman could do since her son had signed over Ben's custody to Mallory on that day at Miramar. She tried never to think about that day or the days that followed.

The way Nash attempted to control the tremor in his hand as he signed papers relinquishing his rights as a father and making way for her to adopt his and Cara's son...

The next day news broke in grizzly detail of Nash hanging himself with bedsheets, following a family visit—a custody hearing in San Diego being the excuse for Nash's temporary transfer to the Level II facility.

Even though none of it was real, she still found it disturbing, watching the events unfold while she sat holed up in her hotel room. Even though she'd attempted to stay below the radar, the reporters had been relentless in tracking her down, wanting to know what she might have said or done to provoke his actions.

She'd known it was coming. Yet she hadn't been prepared for the onslaught of questions. "What were Kenneth Nash's last words to you, Ms. Ward? Did he confess? Did he leave a note? Your mother also committed suicide. Tragic coincidence? Suspicious circumstance? What's the connection?"

She couldn't leave the hotel room without microphones being shoved in her face. "How do you feel about the role you played in the arrest and conviction of your own brother-in-law and a decorated war hero? Are you aware your brother-in-law is being buried without ceremony in the Fort Leavenworth Military Prison Cemetery? Will you be attending the funeral, Ms. Ward?"

She'd been as unprepared for those questions as she had been for the profound feeling of loss that accompanied them. Another part of her had died that day. She'd lost her sister, her mother and to some extent her father.

What more did she have to lose?

Nash had taken everything that was youthful and innocent about her and destroyed it, irrevocably changing her and the direction of her life at twenty-two.

And yet she'd still mourned the brother-in-law she'd once known.

For a long time afterward, she felt as empty as the wooden crate lowered to the ground with nothing more substantial than sandbags to weight it down—assuming they'd weighted down his casket with sand. They could have interred an unidentified body for all she knew.

Cremation might have been easier but would have gone against the traditions of his faith.

Of course, most faiths had at least a moral objection to suicide and she was sure that included faking death. In any case, she did not attend the mockery of a funeral. The commander and several of Nash's Navy SEAL buddies were there for the show...or perhaps some other reason.

His mother had also attended the service. To this day, Mallory could barely look the woman in the eye, knowing what she knew about Nash. At the time, she didn't know how they'd kept her from claiming the body when she had every right to do so.

Prisoners did not have to be buried inside prison walls.

Later Mal discovered they'd simply handed his grieving mother a letter stating it was his preference—since he couldn't be buried beside his wife or near his father.

If he had even tried to use the family plot next to Cara, Mallory would have had something to say about it. She didn't understand canon law governing Jewish burial, but suspected not being able to be buried next to his father had something to do with suicide, which used to be the case with the Catholic Church until the pope declared it otherwise.

What did it matter? He didn't commit suicide.

And though she might wish otherwise, he wasn't dead.

As far as she knew anyway.

It had been years since that fateful phone call.

The man was a ghost. Not just the kind that haunted her past, but the living, breathing, deep-cover-operative kind. That thought alone was enough to raise the goose bumps on her flesh. Ghosts had a way of popping up when you least expected them.

God, she hadn't thought about any of this in so long.

A hand curled around hers with surprising strength and she jumped. "Will you come back to see me, Meg?"

Mallory didn't bother to correct her father even though the emptiness of it all squeezed at her chest. Meg was his pet name for her mother. "Of course I will."

NASH WAITED INSIDE the house. In a working-class neighborhood, it was just as easy to break in during the day as at night under cover of darkness. He kept quiet upstairs while the young sitter and the boy moved around downstairs. The creaky, century-old house would have given him away if he was any less cautious and if the kids were more alert.

In the hall bathroom, he tended his torn sutures as best he could without running tap water. He could hear the babysitter moving around in the kitchen. The boy had settled into the front room with a video game. Something age-appropriate, he assumed, from the lack of bloodcurdling screams.

And because he was fairly certain Mal would curb the kid's activities away from violence.

He didn't know why he thought that. Maybe he was confusing what Cara would have done, and what he and Cara would have wanted, with how Mal was actually raising his son.

Truth be told, he didn't have a clue how Ben

was being raised. He wanted to believe the boy was growing up in a healthy and happy environment. One that wasn't haunted by his mother's murder and his father's failures.

The smell of popcorn wafted up to him. Nash hadn't eaten anything more substantial than a protein bar all day, and his stomach churned out a reminder. While he didn't have much of an appetite, he did need to keep up his strength. Tugging his bloodstained T-shirt back in place, he zipped the equally dark hoodie over it as he left the bathroom.

On his way into the boy's room, he knocked a photo frame off the dresser.

It hit the carpet with a soft thud.

Nash winced and waited for any indication the kids had been alerted to his presence. After several seconds, he uncoiled his tense muscles.

It wasn't like him to be so careless.

Endless energy drinks were making him jittery.

For good reason.

Mallory should have been home from work by now. Even a quick stop at the grocery store or for a carry-out dinner shouldn't have taken her this long.

He picked up the frame and found Cara smiling back at him from what was probably the last photograph he'd taken of her at Mission Beach. The digital photo frame changed from one picture to the next, flooding him with memories of happier times. It had been a lifetime since he'd seen the exact shade of his wife's strawberry blond hair and green eyes. Images of her beauty had faded to soft-focus memory.

A look. A laugh.

The punch line of a joke she could never get right.

Not a day went by that he didn't think about how much he'd loved her. How much he still loved her. How he'd failed to protect her as a husband.

And as a Navy SEAL.

The first rule to starting a new life was that you couldn't take the old one with you even though the personal baggage always came along for the ride. This would be his second incarnation. Kenneth Nash was dead and buried along with his wife—if not literally, then figuratively. The man standing in their son's bedroom was nothing more than a cold, empty shell.

Here to tie up loose ends. That's all.

Having a picture of Cara wouldn't bring her back.

Still he hesitated before setting her photo back on the dresser. There were others, none of them framed, tucked into holders and around the dresser mirror.

There were photos of Benjamin with each of his grandparents. The one with Margaret was taken when the boy was still a newborn. The one with Charles in a wheelchair looked recent, as did the one with Nash's mother, which appeared to have been taken in New York City outside F.A.O. Schwarz around Thanksgiving. Last year if he had to guess. Had they visited the city for Macy's Thanksgiving Day Parade? Done some Christmas shopping?

Spent Hanukkah with his mother?

Had the boy experienced both Hanukkah and Christmas last year for the first time? Or had he done so every year?

He and Cara had worked through those fundamental differences before marriage—or at least that's what he'd thought.

Until Cara got pregnant and they found out differently.

He needed to believe they would have worked things out eventually.

They weren't the first couple of different faiths to marry and have children. They would have found their Jewish/Catholic compromise, and their kids would have been just fine being raised with the diversity of two faiths. That's what he believed.

But he hadn't expected his wife's side of the family to have anything to do with his side after his conviction. He'd asked his mother not to interfere with his unorthodox decision to allow his sister-in-law—his non-Jewish sister-in-law at that—to raise his son.

On a practical note, Mal was young. His mother was not.

He had other family, but he'd never even considered them when it came to raising Ben.

Mal would be on a constant lookout and was physically and mentally better equipped to handle trouble, which made her the best choice as Ben's guardian.

But it had been more of an emotional decision. Mal was the closest thing he could give the boy to a mother, and she'd see to it that Ben grew up knowing Cara—even if that meant he would also grow up hating his father.

It was good to see Mal had kept in touch with his mother, but that relationship added another wrinkle to the current situation. He'd been operating under the assumption that Mal and Ben had no close ties to his family.

Yet oddly enough, there was even a picture of him in uniform in the photomontage, which included several more pictures of Ben with friends, his babysitter, his aunt Mal.

How old had she been the last time he saw her, twenty-three, twenty-four? Staring daggers at him from across that table in the interrogation room.

The clever and carefree girl from their youth—with flame-red corkscrew curls hanging down her back—was long gone. From the moment she'd stuck a gun in his face, lawyers had seen to it that they never got the chance to talk again before the trial. She wouldn't even make eye contact with him while on the witness stand and wasn't allowed to sit through the proceedings until after her testimony and the closing arguments.

But at one time they'd been more than family—they'd been friends.

Even after all these years, sadness still etched her smile and he bore the brunt of responsibility for putting it there. Beyond that sad smile, there were other changes to her physical appearance. For one, she'd straightened her hair, and she apparently wore dark designer suits these days, looking every bit the professional government agent.

A real G-man, government man. Or G-woman—person—as the case may be.

Kidnapping the kid would be difficult enough without dragging an armed and angry aunt along for the ride.

But he owed her that much at least.

No one else should have to die because of him. Humbled by the sacrifice Torri and Thompson had made, he knew he had to make his escape count. He had to save his family. And he had to honor the two marshals, and Cara, and countless others, by staying alive to testify.

He grabbed the boy's backpack from the bed

where Benjamin had dumped it after school. Nash stuffed a change of clothes inside, and then moved on to Mallory's room, where he found her gym bag and then shoved some of her clothes into it.

It dawned on him that the gym bag's presence was not a good sign. If it wasn't a workout keeping her late, what was it?

He checked his watch again. It'd be fully dark soon. If she wasn't here within the next twelve minutes, he'd have some tough choices to make.

Stepping into the adjoining bathroom, he grabbed her toothpaste and toothbrush. It struck him as odd that there was no sign of a man in her life. Not so much as an extra toothbrush to indicate a sleepover. But he didn't have time to dwell on whether or not there was the complication of a boyfriend. Other than how unfortunate it would be for any guy who walked in the door with her tonight.

While he couldn't account for every variable, he had to hope she didn't spend Friday nights away from home—or at least not this Friday night.

Nash scowled at his reflection. While there was no love lost between him and his former sister-in-law, leaving Mal behind was not an option. If she wasn't here by nineteen hundred hours, he'd find out from the boy where she was and they'd go get her.

Worst-case scenario, Bari or one of his hench-men had already gotten to her.

Just the thought was enough to send chills down his spine.

Ben's safety had to come first. Not Mal, not his mother—not even Sari—came before Ben, and those were just the cold, hard facts.

But he'd have a hard time living with himself if anything happened to Mallory—or with any of the women on the periphery of his life—because of him. His conscience would demand that he go after her. His conscience was why he was here now instead of already on the road.

Back in the bedroom, he checked both night-stands looking for Mallory's handgun.

Assuming she had more than one firearm, where would she keep them? Some place out of the kid's reach. He scanned the room and then settled on the closet, where he found a fireproof lockbox on the shelf underneath some sweaters.

He felt along the dusty ridge of the doorframe inside the closet until he came across the key. The most logical place to look was usually the place to find what you were looking for. The lockbox contained her SIG Sauer and a box of 9 mm bul-lets among life's important papers—birth certifi-cates, death certificates, adoption papers.

Dead presidents.

Not the amount of cash needed to start a new

life, but enough for a household emergency or a quick getaway. He didn't think twice before shoving the money into his pants pocket.

Checking her unloaded gun, he grabbed the box of bullets. The 9 mm shells would fit both their weapons.

Tucking her SIG into his waistband at his back alongside his Glock, he wondered why she'd kept the weapon. There was no doubt in his mind the SIG Sauer was the same one he'd given her as a graduation present from Quantico. The one she'd pointed at him while reading him his rights.

A car door slammed. Nash drew the bedroom curtain aside to check it out. Mallory had just gotten out of her white Prius with a bag of groceries in hand and a pumpkin tucked under her arm.

The two agents parked across from the house approached her with a flash of agency badges. Nash couldn't make out what they were saying, but Mal dropped the pumpkin and everything else she carried with a splat as she ran toward the house.

CHAPTER FOUR

MALLORY RAN UP the front steps. Fumbling for the right key, she unlocked the door and in her haste tripped over the threshold. "Ben, Benjamin!"

"Yeah?" He looked up from his video game on the big screen. "Whatever it is, I didn't do it."

Her heartbeat slowed to normal at the sight of him playing his favorite video game. "Is there something I should know that you're not telling me, Ben?"

"No." He returned to *Skylander Spyro's Adventures*.

Mallory turned to the two agents who'd followed her as far as the door. "Looks like we're fine." She kept her voice low so Ben wouldn't overhear.

"We'll be right outside." FBI Special Agent Stanley Morgan set the groceries inside the door and handed over her pumpkin-gut-splattered Kate Spade handbag. The one she'd saved for six months to buy and then ruined in six seconds with the first words out of his mouth a couple minutes ago.

"When was the last time you had contact with Kenneth Nash, Ms. Ward?"

No contact. *Ever.*

He'd promised—a convicted felon was as good as his word, after all.

"Would you mind telling me what's going on?" She took a step outside, backing the agents up onto her front porch. She left the door cracked behind her and kept a watchful eye on Ben through the picture window to the front room.

Stan, with his basset hound eyes and long overdue for retirement, exchanged a look with his young bulldog of a partner, an ex-marine named Christopher Tyler. Though not well acquainted with either of them, Mallory knew both men from the downtown office. Tyler even hung out on the fringe of her social group and had asked her out once or twice. But she gave dating him or anyone from the office a wide berth.

At the very least these two men owed her the professional courtesy of a response. "Guys?"

"Nash was in the custody of two U.S. marshals found dead early this morning," Tyler said. "He's a person of interest."

"Meaning what, exactly?" She crossed her arms. "Are you saying he killed two federal marshals?"

Stan shifted uncomfortably. "I'm sure that's what the Marshal Service would like to find out."

"There's enough ballistics and blood evidence to suggest he was wounded at the scene," Tyler said. "They really want to find the guy."

"Where was this?"

"Back East, somewhere."

"That doesn't tell me anything, Stan. New York? D.C., Virginia…? Where back East?"

"Mallory," Stan said, sounding rather paternal as he ignored her question—he reminded her of her father and everything about him that she would miss once he was gone. "Kenneth Nash is considered armed and dangerous. He's been a deep-cover operative for a while now. It's not unheard of for these guys to turn rogue. If you come up against him, do not try to take him down alone this time. He's not the same man you knew seven years ago."

"The man I knew seven years ago killed my sister. I wouldn't put anything past him." She brushed back a loose strand of hair before tucking her hand back in her crossed arms. "Why was he in custody?"

"They didn't tell us much," Stan admitted. "Until we got the call a few hours ago, we were under the impression the guy was dead."

"Suicide or something, wasn't it?" Tyler's watchful eyes became piercing. "Of course you must have known different?"

"I don't know anything." She ignored his subtle

probing accusations and held his gaze as she offered up that half-truth. Deep down she'd known this day would come and had prepared for it. "Good night, gentlemen."

She turned to step back inside the house.

"Mallory." Stan stopped her from closing the door. "We can't protect you and the kid if you don't tell us what you know. Where is he?"

"What I know?" she said. "What I know is that you can't protect us from him. But if he was here, you'd already be dead."

She closed the door and then leaned against it with a resigned sigh.

"Ben, turn off the video game." She forced a calm she was far from feeling into her voice. "I dropped the pumpkin. We need to run to the grocery store for another one or we won't be able to carve it tonight. If we go now we can stop by the party store and pick up that Iron Man costume you wanted. Hurry up, okay?"

"'Kay." His response lacked enthusiasm and she knew from experience it would be several minutes before he turned off the game. She needed those minutes to compose herself anyway. If Nash was coming from the East Coast, it would take him at least a day to get here, unless he hopped a plane. Assuming he'd avoid major airports, train and bus depots, he was mostly likely traveling by car. *Assuming* being the operative word.

She had no idea what Nash would or wouldn't risk to get to them.

Only that he would get to them. Unless she managed to stay one step ahead of him.

She scooped up her purse and the bag of groceries by the door. She found Jess, Ben's babysitter, in the kitchen, eating popcorn—iPod so loud she could hear the faint strains of music without the benefit of earbuds herself. It was no wonder the girl hadn't heard Mallory calling for Ben.

Jess removed an earbud. "He got bored with my project." She let the handful of orange-colored popcorn fall into the bowl.

"Thanks for staying late this evening, Jess." Mallory dug out her checkbook, scribbled out the amount for the week with a sizable bonus and then tried not to appear as if she were rushing the girl out the door.

Stay calm, Ward. This is no time to panic.

"No problem." Jess stuffed the check into the pocket of her strategically ripped jeans without so much as a glance at the amount, and then grabbed her hoodie off the wall rack on her way out the back door. "See you next week."

Next week was too far into the future to think about when the next few minutes were all that counted. Mallory followed the girl to her car parked in the drive at the side of the house. Jess could just as easily have crossed the alley to her own yard, but try telling that to a seventeen-year-old in her first year of unrestricted driving. With one eye on the back door and the other on the car, Mal watched headlights fade as Jess backed around the Prius and then out onto the street.

It might very well be the last time they saw the girl.

For peace of mind, Mal had to make sure she left safely.

Darting a quick glance toward the unmarked car parked across the street, Mal hurried back inside and grabbed the keys to her father's vintage Mustang off the same rack where they hung their jackets. She seldom drove the car except to keep the battery charged for the occasional Sunday drive with her dad. It was parked in the detached garage off the alley, which meant they could get to it before anyone stationed out front even knew they were gone.

A well-tuned muscle car had the added advantage of being fast.

"Ben!" she called out as she stepped back into the kitchen. Unpacking the groceries by rote, she paused to check her cell phone to see if she had any new messages. She'd taken the afternoon off to run her father to his doctor's appointment, but she'd had her phone with her the entire time. No calls.

Nothing from Special Agent Galena. Or Commander McCaffrey.

If something was up, wouldn't one of them have contacted her? She dropped the phone back into her purse.

For years now Nash hadn't even been a blip on her radar screen. About a year after he'd been transferred to Guantanamo Bay, under an assumed name known only to a select handful of important people, three prisoners escaped. A fourth was shot in the attempt. Mal knew upon hearing the reports that Nash was among the escapees.

It was all hush-hush. As far as the public was concerned, no detainee had ever escaped from Gitmo.

Shortly after that, he appeared with wild hair and a full beard on the FBI's Most Wanted list under the alias Sayyid Naveed. If it wasn't for his eyes, she never would have known it was Nash. He was unrecognizable to the point she would have passed him on the street. The very thought gave her chills.

Shortly afterward she learned that asking questions invited trouble.

The commander himself came to debrief her. He even threatened to have her security clearance downgraded.

That's when she realized she might need an escape hatch someday and began systematically socking away resources in storage lockers around the state. But Nash had never appeared on her radar again, until tonight.

"Ben, now," she said in her best mom voice. That should get him moving.

"Coming." His answering whine meant he'd heard the seriousness in her tone and would wind down the game. These next few hours, days— maybe even weeks and months—were not going to be easy for him to understand, so she'd allowed him this small rebellion. It wouldn't be easy leaving everything behind.

If she'd known today was going to be the last time she'd see her father, what might she have done differently?

Don't even go there, Ward.

It was going to be hard enough walking out the door and never looking back.

She'd spent that first year after Nash's "suicide" looking over her shoulder, preparing for this moment. Panic set in now that her day of reckoning had come and she realized just how unprepared she really was. She *should* run up the back stairs and grab the stash of cash she kept in the lockbox.

But the hairs on the back of her neck kept her rooted to the first floor where she could see both the front and back door from the kitchen, while remaining within an arm's reach of Ben.

No. There was no time to waste. She was already

wearing her service revolver. And she had her badge and handcuffs, too.

Best to leave with as little as possible. They'd still need cash, but a single withdrawal from an ATM close to home would get them to their next destination. She'd planned this carefully enough so that no matter what direction she was forced to take, she and Ben would be able to start a new life.

Shoving the carton of broken eggs to the back of the fridge, she closed the door and then jumped. Nash stood on the opposite side of the refrigerator, looking scruffy in his ball cap with his overlong hair and five o'clock shadow.

"Hello, Mal."

"There are two FBI agents out front." She put the center island between them and picked up the butcher knife from the block of knives next to the cutting board. Reaching for the celery, which hadn't made it into the crisper, she began chopping the bunch without washing or removing the rubber band. "I'll give you a ten-minute head start before I scream."

"I don't need ten minutes. And you're not going to scream."

She didn't scream as he moved right up behind her and stilled the knife in her hand with his hand. She let go and the butcher knife dropped to the cutting board. He picked it up and tossed it out of reach to the sink.

It would be futile to resist. She wasn't about to challenge him in hand-to-hand combat—until she had to.

"They think you killed two marshals."

He didn't move from behind her. "What do you think?"

That he was capable of doing just that.

She ignored his loaded question as he reached inside her jacket for her gun. Her breath caught on the intake as his arm brushed the underside of her breasts and pinned her against his chest as he checked the safety on her firearm before tucking it into his own jacket pocket. "What are you doing here, Nash?"

"Smart move not going for the gun."

He began patting her down underneath her jacket.

His impersonal check felt far too personal and she slid around to face him. With her back to the island, she groped for a steak knife and managed to get a good grip on one. He blocked the jab, took the knife and the whole block of knives and dumped them in the sink out of her immediate reach.

"Enough games, Mal. You and the boy are coming with me."

He latched on to her elbow and she shook off his grip. "We're not going anywhere with you."

"We don't have time for theatrics. Call him

again." He picked up what she recognized as her gym bag and tucked her gun from his jacket into a side pocket, and then picked up Ben's backpack and tossed it over his shoulder as he nodded toward the back door.

"Ben." She modulated her tone so there was little to no urgency in it, hoping he'd be too engrossed in his game to break away. Heart pounding, Mallory moved toward the living room as if to hurry him along. She flicked the kitchen light switch in passing.

Nash was no dummy. He hauled ass toward her with menace in his stride.

She stood there with her hands on her hips and made sure she had plenty of room to maneuver before picking a fight with him.

She was a trained professional. All she had to do was stand between Nash and Ben until two armed agents burst through the doors. If Nash dared to make a move in Ben's direction, she would lay a world of hurt on him. Not even a Navy SEAL could easily get past a mama bear intent on protecting her cub.

"Can we get a big pumpkin this year?" Ben asked as he entered the kitchen. "I mean really big." He held his arms out wide and then stopped just inside the doorway, frozen in his big pumpkin stance staring at Nash.

"Do you know who I am?" the man asked.

The boy nodded. "You're him. You're my dad."

From one heartbeat to the next, Nash swooped up Ben along with their bags, and then ran for the back door as Tyler burst through the front door, splintering it off its hinges. Mallory barely had time to react before Special Agent Tyler shoved her out of his way. She went down hard, hitting her head against the granite countertop.

"You all right?" He glanced back without stopping.

Dazed, she waved him off. "Go, go! He's got Ben!"

But Special Agent Tyler was already gone and so far ahead he probably didn't even hear her.

NASH CROUCHED NEXT to the boy as they took shelter in the overgrowth, waiting for Mal to come out of the house. They'd hopped the chain-link fence across the alley just ahead of the first agent out the back gate. The narrow space beside the detached garage, bordered by the six-foot wooden privacy fence on the other side, hadn't seen a lawn mower in years.

Since both houses were third from the end, Nash had counted on the agents to assume that he'd run the short distance out the alley. But instead of trying to chase them down, the agent on their tail had stopped by the Dumpster behind Mal's house and pulled out his walkie-talkie.

The younger agent caught up to the older agent as he was calling for backup. The two men argued. Nash mouthed the word *ninja* to the boy, who stared back at him with big eyes. A shot rang out and Nash covered Ben's near yelp with his palm.

Thankfully, the boy hadn't seen the incident so much as heard it.

Nash, however, had a perfect view. He kept the boy's face turned away from the old guy slumped on the ground.

The young guy would have shot the older man again, but a dark sedan, not the same model as the one parked out front, came screeching around the corner. Instead of looking guilty, the young agent—if that's what he was—started shouting orders to the driver. Something *not* right was going on here, and all Nash needed now was for Mal to step out her back door right into the middle of it.

Maybe he should be more worried that she hadn't exited the house by now.

Nash kept one hand curled over Ben's mouth.

The other on his Glock.

Finger on the trigger, he held his breath until the young agent bolted down the short end of the alley while the car drove up the other end and disappeared—but not before Nash had caught a glimpse of the sedan's rental plate.

Removing his palm from the boy's mouth Nash

brought his finger to his lips, warning the boy to remain quiet.

Picking up a flat, chalky-white stone—a native form of limestone—he scratched the license plate number into the wood siding of the garage.

Ben crouched beside him, his panicked breaths coming in hard and shallow. The boy started to turn his head toward the downed agent again.

Nash pointed two fingers at his eyes. *Eyes on me, not on him.*

The boy turned his head back to focus wide-eyed on him.

Nash didn't know if the kid understood SEAL sign language, but he'd always kept his signs simple enough that any BUD/S on his first mission would get their meaning.

The next thing Nash knew Ben was burying his face in Nash's shoulder.

He wanted to put his arms around his son, offer him the comfort and reassurance he needed. But he didn't allow himself the indulgence to pull Ben closer for that first hug.

He needed both hands free. Especially his shooting hand.

Nash shoved Ben behind him, making sure to put himself between the boy and whatever was coming. The boy kept his face plastered to Nash's back—which was exactly where he wanted him to be. As they crouched in the weeds Nash felt himself growing queasier by the minute and it wasn't from the blood loss. The boy was probably worried sick about his aunt—and so was he.

There'd only been the one shot, but that didn't mean she hadn't been incapacitated. By the shooter or the driver. Or someone else. A silencer—even a pillow—could have muffled the sound of a gunshot.

Or a knife.

There was only one way to find out.

He was getting ready to pick up Ben again when Mal came barreling out the back gate. He didn't immediately reveal their hiding place. But he did reach around to tap the boy so Ben could see his aunt was okay.

Now that they knew Mal was okay, he could get Ben to the SUV and let Mal catch up to them.

MALLORY FOUND STAN slumped against the Dumpster in the alley and hunkered down beside him. The agent was bleeding and barely breathing, but he wasn't dead.

"Son of a bitch shot me." Stan gasped for air.

"Shh…quiet, now. Keep pressure on it." Mal pressed his hand to the wound at his gut as she looked up and down the alley.

No sign of Nash or Tyler. Or Ben.

She didn't know how long she'd been out cold. A few minutes, maybe?

Her head still felt woozy. She must have hit her head on the countertop harder than she thought.

When she'd tried to push to her feet to follow Tyler, she'd blacked out. The next thing she knew she'd heard the shot ring out. She managed to stumble to the back door and down the steps before tossing her cookies.

A concussion was the least of her worries right now.

Thanks to the static of Stan's radio, she found it within easy reach under the Dumpster. "Did you call for backup?"

He offered a weak nod.

A curious neighbor stepped out his back door with a bag of trash and glanced their way.

"You," she called to the elderly gentleman who looked as though he was about to head in the opposite direction toward another garbage bin. "Stay with this man until the ambulance arrives. Keep pressure on it." She demonstrated before shoving the radio at her neighbor and reaching for Stan's firearm.

Without hesitation, she wiped her bloody hands on the pants of her Ann Taylor designer suit for a better grip on the weapon. She hated to leave Stan like this, but Ben had to be her priority.

Stan latched on to her wrist. "Tyler—"

"Save your strength, Stan. Which way did they go?"

He pointed her in the right direction. Digging the Mustang keys from her jacket pocket, she raced the few feet to the garage. She stripped the drop cloth from the Skylight Blue exterior of the 1964 ½ classic, opened the door and sank into the blue and white pony leather. Blood from her hands stained the white leather steering wheel and gearshift as she backed out of the garage.

Assuming Special Agent Christopher Tyler was chasing Nash on foot, and that the ex-marine was in better shape than Stan right now, there was still a chance she'd find Nash hiding out in her neighborhood. Loaded down with a small boy and their two bags, he couldn't have gone far. He wouldn't try to outrun the agent—he'd try to outfox him. Maybe even lead him on a merry chase before circling back to wherever he'd parked his getaway car.

Which had to be around here somewhere.

Close. But not too close.

Not a car, an SUV. He'd want to blend in with the neighborhood.

She was wishing for the radio now or some way to communicate with the agent, but Stan had needed it more than she did. Why hadn't she stopped to grab her cell phone? "Come on, Tyler. Flush him out."

The average criminal wasn't too hard to figure

out. When he ran, you ran after him while your partner cut him off.

But Nash wasn't your average criminal. He was better trained and he'd be familiar with their training.

But what he didn't know was that she spent six days a week in the gym and had spent six long years studying everything she could about Navy SEALs in anticipation of this moment.

So if she was part of his plan A...

You and the boy are coming with me.

Somewhere in his contingency plan B, C or D, either he planned to leave her or, if she stayed visible and vigilant, he'd find her. Except she intended to find him first.

Mal never realized how many dark SUVs there were on her block until now. She rolled down the windows and opened the top of the old Mustang.

Listening. Praying there'd be no more gunfire.

Block after block she made her way in a crisscross pattern toward the highway. There were several on-ramps near her neighborhood, which bordered the park. Nash would have parked facing one of them. Somewhere he wouldn't draw a lot of attention.

Somewhere familiar.

She backtracked toward the house where he'd grown up only to be disappointed.

Nash had the advantage over Tyler of knowing

the old neighborhood. But maybe, *maybe* she had the advantage of knowing Nash. If she just put her mind to it, she should be able to figure this out. Unless of course he anticipated her trying to second-guess him.

"Where the hell are you, Nash?" She had to find him before he took off down the highway. Otherwise she might never see Ben again.

That bloodcurdling thought made her want to scream.

"Think, Ward. Think." She prowled his old block tapping the steering wheel.

The street where Nash had grown up was catty-corner from their street.

One block up, one block over.

She was facing the direction of her house now.

Wait—what if he'd never left the alley? It was basically made up of a combination of wooden privacy fences and low chain-link ones. How hard would it be to jump a fence or break into a detached garage? There were two dozen backyards facing that alley. He could have ducked into any one of them. She glanced up the next block toward Jackie's house.

Her persistence paid off; an engine roared to life down the otherwise sleepy street. Streetlights out. Headlights off. Directly across the alley from her house.

Exactly what she was looking for.

The driver pulled out just as Mallory entered the intersection.

She pulled a hard U-turn into its path. The driver slammed on his brakes, coming to a screeching stop inches from her driver's-side door.

Mallory scrambled over the side of the convertible with her weapon drawn. She had Nash in her sights across the hood of his SUV.

Point-blank range. Finger on the trigger.

They stared at each other for a full second.

Nash revved the engine. All he'd have to do was roll forward and she'd be pinned between the two vehicles. All *she* had to do was pull the trigger to stop him. "Let him go!" She could hear sirens in the distance from the fire and paramedic station located right on the edge of the park. The police would follow. All she had to do was hold him off.

He leaned across the front seat and threw open the passenger door. "Get in!"

Ben's dark head bobbed behind his father's.

Nash motioned for her to get in.

"Mal, now!" There was no mistaking the urgency in his voice as the sirens grew louder.

"Ben, honey," she pleaded. "Get out of the car."

Nash put the SUV in Reverse and then floored it.

"No!" Mallory raced after them.

He slammed the brakes long enough for her to catch up. "Last chance."

Up the street a dark figure ran toward them—
she could only guess that it was Tyler. Upon seeing the unfolding scene down the street from him,
the FBI agent hopped into the passenger side of
another vehicle.

That couldn't be Stan behind the wheel. And
why was that ambulance growing distant now?

She looked into Nash's eyes across the open
door and hesitated. Tyler would be on them
any second. But when the SUV edged forward,
she knew she didn't have even that long to decide. Nash would leave her before the agent ever
reached them, and she wasn't about to lose Ben.
Before the SUV could pick up speed, she threw
herself into the rolling vehicle just as the back
window shattered. "What the—"

"Down," Nash ordered, forcing her head into
his lap.

CHAPTER FIVE

"BEN?" MALLORY STRUGGLED to sit up.

"Stay down. Both of you." Nash pinned her to his denim-covered thigh.

"I am," Ben argued from the backseat.

Relieved to hear his voice, as well as the defiance in it, Mal tried to make sense of the past few seconds. Tyler had to have known Ben was in the SUV. At the very least, he must have seen her undignified dive into the moving vehicle. It didn't make sense that the FBI agent would risk their lives to take down Nash.

Mallory held on to Stan's gun and could, in theory at least, force Nash to stop the Explorer. But she wouldn't—not without knowing who was in that other vehicle and why they were shooting at them.

Nash ran up and over the curb on the right. Presumably to go around the Mustang she'd left in the intersection. The SUV's passenger door knocked into the street sign and then swung shut with enough force to catch the lock. As they dropped off the curb and banked a hard left, she felt the jarring impact, heard the sickening crunch and realized they hadn't cleared her father's vintage Mustang.

Engines raced. Tires squealed.

The passenger door rocked on its precarious catch.

She felt the tension in Nash's thigh as his foot worked the brake and gas petals in tandem through each hairpin turn as the other car chased them. Only the single shot had been fired. Maybe Tyler hadn't meant to shoot *at* them but over them, as a warning, or he could have been aiming to take out a tire.

That's what she would have done in his position.

He'd have to be a really bad shot in order to hit the back windshield instead....

Still trying to justify the agent's actions, Mal shifted so she wasn't nose to zipper with Nash's bulging crotch. The center console dug painfully into her ribs and her ass end was up in the air. She needed to formulate a plan, and the undignified position made it difficult to think. But he pushed down every attempt she made to sit up. Or maybe it was just his hands on the steering wheel keeping her in place. Either way, she did not appreciate his elbows jabbing her in the back.

She could hear cars in the distance. But did the lack of a screeching echo mean Nash had lost the other vehicle? Why weren't there police cars on the scene already?

He continued driving at a frenzied pace.

Her stomach dipped as the SUV sped down an incline—the on-ramp—to I-25, northbound. They wove through traffic and then back up an off-ramp minutes later.

Nash white-knuckled the steering wheel until traffic noise faded to the background. After a couple more turns he pulled over. Mallory had lived in this city all her life and had only a vague idea of where they were once she raised her head. The entire chase had taken less than fifteen minutes. But her accelerated heart rate continued to pump adrenaline through her veins.

They were parked on a side street in front of a warehouse. The run-down neighborhood appeared to be equal parts commercial and residential. The kind of neighborhood a person did not wander into after dark.

Her grip tightened on the gun in her hand.

"Did you lose them?" she dared to ask.

"For now."

She shoved her weapon into his side.

He winced and challenged her in the same breath. "We both know you're not going to pull the trigger."

"You don't know me as well as you think you do."

"I know you well enough, Mal. I also know

when the safety is on." He disarmed her with a quick, painful twist that had her letting go of the grip, otherwise she'd have risked losing her trigger finger. "You're not a cold-blooded killer." He presented it to her butt first. "Holster your weapon and I might let you keep it."

"Ben," she said over her shoulder. "Get out of the car—now." Ben scrambled for the door, but apparently the child safety locks were engaged.

"Ben, *son*." Nash put a halt to the boy's escape with that single word.

How dare he use Ben like that? How dare he call himself Ben's father! She hauled back and hit him right where it hurt—in his side—and was rewarded with a grunt. Even though she hadn't seen his injury, she knew his T-shirt had to be seeped in blood. She'd felt it, smelled it while lying in his lap. From what Stan and Tyler had said, it was most likely a bullet wound.

"What the hell were you thinking?" She reached across him for the child safety switch. He snagged both her wrists and she head butted him in the nose.

"Damn it, Mal," he said in a nasal drone that told her she'd hit her mark. "Stop!" He grabbed her by the hair and held her at arm's length. There was nothing warm or familiar in his eyes. "I will leave you and you'll never see him again. Do you understand?" He gave her roots a yank for emphasis. "I got what I came for. You're expendable."

"Please don't hurt my mom."

NASH LET GO as that single word singed his brain.

"Get out," he ordered.

"Not without Ben—" she started to protest.

"Both of you. Now. We're switching cars." He nodded toward a newer-model white Chevy Tahoe parked across the street as he got out of the Explorer on his side and opened the back door for Ben. The boy scrambled out with his backpack, and Nash reached inside for Mal's gym bag. He hadn't meant what he'd said about her being expendable. But he needed her to believe it for now.

He could only imagine the terrifying uncertainty the kid must be feeling at finding that the man claiming to be his father was in reality a brute. But there wasn't much he could do to reassure him right now.

He put a restraining hand on the boy's shoulder while Mal got out of the car. A dog barked in the distance. They needed to get going before they attracted the wrong kind of attention. He ushered the boy across the street.

Mal stormed after them while he unlocked the vehicle with the key fob in his hand. The interior remained dark because he'd had the foresight to turn off the map light earlier. He let the boy in, and the kid scrambled over the seat. "Are we steal-ing this car?"

He dangled the keys for Ben's benefit. "Does it look like we're stealing?"

Nash had cars and cash stashed from one end of the continent to the other.

He didn't like owning newer vehicles, but he'd made an exception for this one, though he'd still gotten it used. He'd paid cash four years ago and then disabled the tracking system before he'd even driven it off the lot.

Then he'd driven it to Colorado to replace an older vehicle he already had in storage.

Even before his escape from Gitmo he'd kept a getaway car in Colorado packed to the hilt with essential supplies, including a police scanner, hop-ing he'd never have the need for it. Not that he wouldn't have stolen one if he needed to. Grand theft auto was a simple game and the least of his worries right now. Getting Ben and Mal to safety was his priority.

Of course the plates were stolen. And he didn't have insurance. So he wasn't truly street legal.

Nash tossed Mal's bag to the floorboard on the passenger side and stepped aside to let her in ahead of him. She stood in the open door-frame and lowered her voice, he assumed so Ben wouldn't overhear. "Isn't this where you're sup-posed to say come with me if you want to live?"

"I thought that was obvious."

"I have questions. Lots of questions, Nash."

"I don't have time for answers right now. Just know that they want me dead more than they want you and the boy alive."

"Which is why you should let us go."

"Which is why I can't let you go, Mal." He'd asked her to trust him, but he and Mallory had a complicated history and were a long way from trusting each other. Trust had to be earned. And as he'd found out the hard way, it could be easily destroyed.

"At least tell me where we're going."

"Where do all SEALs go when they're in trouble?"

The correct answer was water. But she'd get the gist of it. "Coronado?"

There was no need for either of them to elaborate. Coronado was synonymous with the Teams. He was taking them to the Spec War Base in Coronado, California. Once he acknowledged her with a nod, she backed off and climbed over the driver's side seat to the passenger side of the car.

Nash considered it a victory just getting her in the vehicle.

She drew the seat belt across her body and reminded Ben to secure his before she turned her attention back to Nash. "I still have a gun."

"Yeah, I'm the one who let you keep it. And

who also taught you how to use it in the first place," he reminded her. That blast from the past earned him a fiery glare before she glanced away. He clamped down on the memory and allowed himself to slip back in time to that firing range where he'd taught Mal to shoot, and where he'd purchased her graduation present.

"YOU KNOW MY sister has a crush on you." Cara materialized beside him as he pointed downrange and pulled the trigger. He missed center mass—the heart, of the paper target—by a good two inches because of the distraction. But a beautiful distraction she was.

Nash set down his weapon and removed his range muffs in order to give his wife his full attention. "What?"

"You heard me." She teased him with her beautiful smile.

Nash glanced over at Mal. Two stalls down.

"You buy her this gun and she'll be yours forever."

"It's just a graduation present."

"She hasn't even left for the academy yet."

"Okay, so we'll call it incentive. She wants this, and I want her to do well."

"Just be careful with my sister's heart. You know you're going to have to break it someday."

Nash did what he always did when Cara teased

him with the subject of her sister's crush. He distracted her with kisses. "I wish you'd let me teach you how to shoot," he said against her lips.

"I'm not touching that thing."

"I seem to remember you saying something similar at sixteen. And yet—"

She swatted him for being cheeky. Okay, so her sister had a crush on him—it didn't matter. Cara was the only woman for him and had been since they were in their teens. He and Mal had long ago settled into an easy friendship.

"Just for protection," he said, getting back on topic.

"You're all the protection we need." Cara drew his attention to the slight swell of her belly. At sixteen weeks, she was just beginning to show. He gave her baby bump a rub. He'd promised to let Cara and Mal drag him along for maternity clothes shopping later that day—if Cara came with him and Mal to the range first.

Probably her least favorite place.

"Get a room, you two." Mal joined them with her target in hand. "Check this out. 'Shot through the heart, and you're to blame....'" Mal sang a little '80s Bon Jovi, "You Give Love a Bad Name" from the *Slippery When Wet* album.

"Yes, you do," Cara agreed. "'Give love a bad name,' that is." She pointed at him.

"What did I do?" he asked, all innocence, as the sisters ganged up on him.

After packing up their equipment, the three of them exited the shooting range through the gun shop.

"I want you to set Mal up with Kip," Cara was saying.

"Ensign Nouri? What? No."

"Yes," she insisted. "He's single."

"I'm only here for the weekend," Mal interrupted. "I want to spend it with you guys."

"See?" Nash argued.

Cara raised a perfectly sculpted eyebrow as if she'd made her point.

"She doesn't want to go on a blind date," he argued.

"I didn't say that exactly," Mal chimed in. "Maybe we could double?"

Cara looked at him as if she was about to burst out laughing. Okay, so maybe Mal was a little too attached to him. They'd been pals since she was, like, twelve.

Obviously, his wife intended to put an end to her little sister's hero worship by finding Mal a more appropriate hero to worship. But Nouri?

"Is he a SEAL? Is he hot?" Mal fired off a barrage of questions at him as they made their way to the counter to fill out the forms for her gun purchase.

"Define *hot*," Nash said.

"He's gorgeous." Cara went on to describe Ensign Kip Nouri for her sister. "Blond hair. The bluest eyes I've ever seen. Surfer-god hot."

Nash turned to his wife. "You think Kip Nouri is hot?"

Cara patted him on the chest. "He can't compete with your swarthy good looks. But yeah, he's hot." She fanned herself and he playfully swatted her on the bottom for being cheeky with him.

"Are you sure they won't just issue me one at the academy, Nash?"

"They do not issue hot guys at the academy," he said over his shoulder to Mal.

The guy behind the glass display case chuckled.

"I was talking about a firearm." Mal nudged him with her shoulder. "Pay attention, Nash."

"You'll like this one better." He went on to explain to her in detail all the advantages this model had over the one she'd be issued. For one thing, SEALs preferred a SIG without a safety—they didn't have time for that extra step, which could be a matter of life and death.

"I'll like it better. But because you bought it for me," she said. "Thank you for my graduation gift." She planted a kiss on his cheek.

"Don't thank me yet. There's a waiting period."

DUCKING UNDER THE yellow tape, NCIS Special Agent Tess Galena flashed her badge at the local law as she crossed the police line. Cruisers with their red and blue flashing lights blocked both ends of the alley. Neighbors appeared outside their homes in full force. Officers with the K-9 units were shaking down bushes while others were interviewing homeowners. Meanwhile, the FBI clustered around the open back of an ambulance as the paramedics hauled off one of their own.

Tess walked up to the man in the navy blue military-issued trench coat standing off by himself.

"When did you get here?" she asked without preamble.

"Not that long ago," McCaffrey said. "Boarded a military hop from North Island to Buckley as soon as I heard."

She nodded. "So, what do we know?"

"He was here," McCaffrey confirmed. "The animated G-man over there…" He nodded across the alley toward a man in black arguing with another agent as paramedics rushed to close the back of the ambulance. "Says Nash shot his partner."

Two quick blasts of the siren to clear the barricade and the ambulance drove off in silence under police escort. Tess frowned after the departing vehicles. That couldn't be a good sign. "Is the partner dead?"

"No, and if he survives surgery I intend to keep it that way. I called in a few favors. Spread some rumors. No one is getting near him without my knowing."

"So you think Nash shot him."

"I know for a fact he did not."

"So who did?"

"The partner's story is full of holes. Start there."

Galena had a lot of respect for Mike McCaffrey. He had good instincts and liked to challenge her to dig deeper for the less obvious truth—as he had in the case of Cara Nash. The evidence stacked against Kenneth Nash had been overwhelming and had led to his conviction. But over the years she'd come to know Nash as something other than a murderer, so she was willing to take the commander's beliefs on faith. And dig deeper.

"You think the agent shot his own partner," she said.

He flipped open a small notebook to read from his notes.

"You never take notes," she said. He wasn't an investigator. Aside from being the C.O. of SEAL Team Eleven, he was more or less Nash's handler. And was always there when it came to anything that involved Kenneth Nash.

"I want to get this right," he said. "Still, I'm

just paraphrasing his exact words. So, following a distress signal from Ms. Ward, Agent Tyler broke through the front door while Agent Morgan ran around back. The suspect then shot Agent Morgan at the Dumpster. No witnesses." He flipped a couple of pages.

"Agent Tyler pursued the suspect on foot. One block over, the suspect orders Ms. Ward into a late-model black Ford Explorer at gunpoint. Agent Tyler aimed for a tire and shot out the back window."

Tess cringed. "Bad shot."

"Unable to pursue on foot, he returned to his downed partner."

"Maybe it's your note-taking that's full of Swiss cheese. Where is Benji, the son he's accused of kidnapping?"

"Let's assume Nash is carrying him," he said.

"Okay."

"Agent Morgan is sixty-five years old. And a good thirty pounds overweight. For the sake of argument, let's say Nash is carrying an extra fifty, sixty pounds of little boy—which is probably not a problem for him—but let's pretend for a minute that slows him down and that Morgan manages to stay ahead of Nash this whole time. Why run out the back gate at all? Why not cut Nash off at the back door? So I would suggest that the open gate proves that Nash was the one out ahead."

"That makes sense," Tess agreed.

"Okay, now look at this—from back door to back gate to the spot where you and I are standing is a straight shot."

Tess glanced at the open back gate of the six-foot, rough-hewn privacy fence, through the open back door of the Ward residence and into its well-lit kitchen. "Yes, I see it."

"Good." McCaffrey reached over the waist-high chain-link fence on their side of the alley and parted the brush. "Because I'm pretty sure Nash and the boy were right here when things went down."

Tess looked down at the trampled grass—someone had been crouched down in it very recently. Then she noticed the crumbled limestone at the base of the garage and the number etched into the siding. "License plate?"

"That's my guess."

"Hmm, Nash even left us a clue. Did you let the police know? They need to get the K-9 unit over here—"

"The dogs scented all over this place, both inside and out." McCaffrey gestured to the house directly behind them and the garage. "This is where the babysitter lives. They followed the trail, which leads to a pile of broken glass and a crumpled Mustang the police have probably already hauled off to the impound."

"In other words, *parts* of the FBI agent's story are true. What about forcing Mallory at gunpoint?"

"I could see that, but chances are she chose to go with him rather than get separated from Ben. But the babysitter said something interesting when she was interviewed. Apparently Mallory wrote the girl a check for four times the normal amount. Does that sound like someone who's planning on sticking around?"

"You think she was getting ready to run. With him? Or from him?" Tess asked.

"She has no reason to run from him—not that she believes it. I think it's safe to assume that upon seeing the two agents waiting for her on her doorstep, she began hatching an escape plan—a plan that involved taking the boy and running before Nash showed up at her door, too."

McCaffrey shrugged before continuing. "We know she didn't shoot Stan. The neighbor saw her come out the back gate. Morgan was already down on the ground and she apparently stayed by his side for several minutes. During which time she called the neighbor over to stay with the agent until the ambulance arrived. Before she took off down the alley the neighbor says Mallory grabbed Morgan's firearm—so we can assume she was armed when she met up with Nash. Who's more likely to kill whom in that scenario?"

Tess crossed her arms against the evening chill. "You're not always right, you know."

"I've been right about Lieutenant Commander Nash all along. And I'm right when I say the man's not going on a killing rampage two weeks before testifying against the leader of one of the most notorious terrorist cells to ever infiltrate this country. Nash is not some rogue superspy turned terrorist. And the origins of that rumor rest squarely with the FBI."

"And the U.S. Marshal Service—"

"Just lost a protected witness. Yeah, I know, and they're a little anxious to get him back."

"Two of their own are dead. Marshal Reid Thompson's dying words were 'Kahn, came to rescue him.' 'Him' meaning Nash. What would you make of that?"

"Unfortunate choice of last words."

"That's pretty callous even for you, Mac. How does your wife put up with you?"

"Just lucky, I guess. Look, I was recently out to that safe house in the Catskills. I met those men—decent guys both of them. But they died in the line of duty. I've lost men in the line of duty, too. You grow calluses, that's what you do. As for the meaning behind Thompson's words, they've gone to the grave with Thompson. Until they review the surveillance, the only thing of significance is that he mentioned Kahn. And we know that there's only one crooked Kahn *not* in jail awaiting trial at the moment."

"Bari Kahn." She sighed heavily. "I take it Sari's been moved for her protection."

"She's all they've got if Nash is unable to testify."

"But what motive would an FBI agent have for shooting his own partner? And what's the connection to Bari Kahn, if any?"

"I'm not sure there is one. Nash has a lot of enemies, and not all of them on foreign soil. What was the name of that marine guard at Gitmo? The one Nash helped put away? The kid who got his rocks off torturing prisoners?"

"You're talking about Corporal Joseph Tyler." The man had blamed Nash in his suicide note.

"With a little digging I think you'll discover that Special Agent Christopher Tyler was also a marine—and older brother to the late Corporal Joseph Tyler. I'd kill for my brother."

"And I'd like to kill your brother." She was talking about Itch, even though they weren't actual brothers. And they both knew she didn't mean it.

"Still mad at him, huh?"

"I've gotten over him is more like it."

"He wasn't a good fit for you, Tess. A nice guy is not what you need, Ms. Galena. And I hate to say this, but you weren't a good fit for him, either. But anytime you want me to set you up with a SEAL, you just let me know."

"Where are you going?" Tess asked as McCaffrey started to walk away.

"I'm leaving you to your investigation or whatever it is you do. While I reassure the U.S. Marshal Service and the federal prosecutor for the state of New York that Nash will be in court in two weeks. And then I'm going to sit tight and wait for his call."

"And you're so sure he'll call."

He pointed out all the reporters on the perimeter. "Actually I'm hoping he takes Mal and Ben and just disappears."

CHAPTER SIX

MALLORY SETTLED BACK against the passenger seat. A few blocks later, they reached a well-lit intersection with fast food on three of the four corners.

"I'm hungry," Ben said.

"Not now, Ben." Despite the fact that neither of them had eaten dinner, and she was just as hungry, she knew Nash wasn't about to pull up to a drive-through window. "We'll get something to eat later, okay?" she promised with a glance toward Nash, letting him know he'd better keep it.

"There should be a box of protein bars back there," he said. "And here." He handed back a bottle of water he'd already tapped. Mal grabbed it before Ben could. Retrieving her gym bag from the floorboard, she began to dig around, hoping her sport bottle was still in there.

"What are you doing?" Nash reached out to stop her and she slapped a pack of breath mints she found at the bottom of her bag into his hand.

"Getting my water bottle. He doesn't need your germs."

He glanced at the pack of tiny pink mints before

tossing them to the center console. "What kind of germs do you think I have?"

"Cooties," she said, sounding more like thirteen than thirty. It was the same thing she'd said countless times upon finding him with his tongue down her sister's throat. And who knew where the hell his tongue had been for the past seven years?

It appeared someone—not her—had shoved clothes in on top of her workout gear. She pulled out a handful of lace panties and stuffed them back with disgust. Leave it to her kidnapper to grab the slutty underwear instead of something more practical. She found her toothbrush, toothpaste and deodorant floating around loose at the bottom despite the fact that she already carried small makeup and toiletry bags within the gym bag.

Obviously, he hadn't searched the gym bag, because she also came across the clear window wallet with her membership ID and a credit card she rotated for use at the juice bar after a deserving workout. That was sloppy of him. Tucking the flat ID wallet up the sleeve of her suit jacket, she pulled out her pink sport bottle.

"Here it is." She sat back in the seat and poured water into it, then handed the sport bottle to Ben. She passed the near-empty water bottle back to Nash before picking up the breath mints from the console and shaking out a couple to chew on. Then she discreetly slipped the wallet into her jacket pocket along with the mints.

He might not be paying attention, but *she* certainly was.

They took the on-ramp for U.S. 6—Sixth Avenue—at Federal Boulevard.

The sound walls of residential neighborhoods soon gave way to open space as they approached the foothills of Golden, Colorado. Ben was being awfully quiet back there. She really had no cause to be snapping at the kid about being hungry—he was almost certainly more scared than she was.

"How you doing back there?" She twisted in her seat.

"Okay," he said, staring down at the half-eaten protein bar in his hand.

"Hey." She reached out to smooth his hair and then lift his chin. "Are you sure you're okay? Ben, can you look at me when I'm talking to you?"

He narrowed his eyes and did the two-finger point. Mal slanted a glance toward Nash. "Did you teach him that?"

He glanced in the rearview mirror and shrugged.

"We have to keep quiet," Ben said. "Or the bad man will shoot us."

His words squeezed at her heart. "We're safe now." Mal was trying her best to reassure him while envisioning years of therapy. This was not something any child should go through. "I won't let anyone hurt you." She squeezed Nash's shoulder, hoping he'd get exactly how painful it was for her to hear the fear in Ben's voice. "And Nash won't let anyone hurt you, either. Okay, baby?"

"He's not a baby," Nash said at the same time Ben said, "I'm not a baby."

"You'll always be my baby," she said, unwilling to let it go. Though fearing tonight had changed him forever.

"I'm not a baby. I'm a ninja," Ben insisted.

Secure in his seat belt, he reached into his backpack for his Nintendo DS game system to practice his ninja moves. He put his earbuds in and Mal turned back to the front with a heavy sigh. Maybe now was not the time to talk about this.

Within the dark interior of the SUV, Nash shifted. She glanced his way, sensing his discomfort as the sweat dripped from his face, which she sensed had little to do with the heater blasting at their feet. The warm air was making Mallory drowsy, though, and she would have put her head back against the headrest and gone to sleep if it wasn't for the bump on her head.

Best not to drift off right now.

The fact that they were being kidnapped should be enough to keep her wide-awake and alert. She touched the tender spot at the back of her head as she tried to piece together the last hour or so. "Why were you in custody?"

He kept his voice low. "I'm a witness for the prosecution in the al-Ayman trial."

He didn't need to go into detail about the trial for her benefit. The upcoming trial for terrorist Mullah Kahn had been hotly debated and in the news for months. "You're a protected witness?"

The truth was she would have guessed prisoner— the safe transport of federal prisoners was the responsibility of the Marshal Service. "Why are you running? And don't give me a line of bull about not being able to tell me anything."

"Who am I supposed to trust, Mal?"

"Your best bet is to pull in to the nearest police station and give yourself up. I can negotiate your safe return to federal custody. If you're afraid—"

"Afraid—"

He started to snap and then glanced back at Ben and stopped himself.

"He's got his ears on." She referred to the earbuds for the game system. "He's not interested in the adult conversation. In fact, he's probably trying to escape the reality of the danger you've put us in. So why don't you find a nice public place to drop us off?"

"Forget it. I'm not dropping you off anywhere. And I'm not turning myself in." He white-knuckled the steering wheel. His scowl deepened—she had no idea what was going on in that brain of his. The sooner they got away from him, the better.

To that end, she toed her gun from the side pocket of her gym bag, inch by inch, beneath the seat. She'd lost count of how many firearms they had between them. She could only hope he'd forget about this one and then she'd have a backup if and when she needed it. Nash definitely wasn't at the top of his game today.

He cracked his window and turned his face to the blast of cold air.

Mal crossed her arms against the cold but didn't say anything because she, too, needed to stay awake. Why didn't he just turn off the heater?

Every once in a while he touched his side and winced.

He needed medical attention, but she was too busy plotting her and Ben's escape to care. Nash might have saved them from some unknown danger, but she was pretty sure that he was the one who'd put them in jeopardy in the first place.

Why doesn't he just turn the heater off?

Because he was cold. Too much blood loss could cause a person to go into shock. Weakness, fatigue, confusion were all signs, followed by a rapid heartbeat, low blood pressure and finally death.

Even in the dim light he looked ashen. He was probably cold because of decreased cardiac output.

Dead man driving.

"Nash, you need to pull over and let me drive. Right now."

"I'm not pulling over."

"Find a gas station, now," she ordered. Her concern had more to do with Ben's safety. But Nash driving with impaired cognition put them all at risk.

"Yeah. I need to go pee," Ben piped up. So much for the earbuds. Ben seized the opportunity at the mention of a gas station to make his needs known, and he was no doubt still hungry.

"Ben needs to use the bathroom and so do I. And *you* need to get the hell out from behind the wheel." She spotted the blue gas, food and lodging sign just before the exit. "Take the next exit."

Nash must have been even worse off than she suspected, because he didn't put up much of a fuss about pulling off the highway. Ben's mouth watered as they passed several familiar fast-food chains. He set his game aside and sat forward in eager anticipation. But he didn't make a peep as Nash passed one neon sign after another and the busy and brightly lit Kum and Go in favor of a four-pump mom-and-pop stop.

Gas prices were higher in the mountains than in the city. The fact that he was willing to pay even more meant he was cognizant of security cameras and of keeping them away from the big rigs and any burly truckers who might be willing to help aid her and Ben in an escape.

He pulled up to the overpriced pump and they all scrambled out of the SUV to stretch their cramped muscles. The cold mountain air frosted her breath. Mal hadn't been this far west of her favorite ski resort in a decade.

Nash kept Ben close by, letting him push the pay inside button and help with pumping. He shot her a warning look over Ben's head that said she'd better not even think about going inside without him.

Leaning against the hood of the SUV, Mal crossed her arms against the chill and waited until the gas tank was once again full and the gas cap replaced. Then she hurried in ahead of Nash and Ben. She wanted the chance to use her credit card and leave a trail. She'd thought long and hard about their odds.

There'd be people looking for her and Ben, people who could help.

Her boss at the Bureau for one, and possibly Tess.

The more she thought about it, the less likely it seemed that Special Agent Tyler had been shooting at them. He simply fired a single warning shot, missed and hit the window by accident.

And she supposed it made some sense that he'd taken aim at the vehicle—stray bullets in a residential neighborhood did more harm than good. It's just not what she would have done had the situation been reversed. Special Agent Tyler might have used poor judgment, but he did not open fire on them. There was only one bad guy in this scenario, and that was Nash.

It took a criminal to know one.

And just because he was testifying didn't mean he was innocent. More than likely he'd gotten involved with the terrorists group's criminal activities.

Two federal marshals were dead and Nash was near death himself.

And he wasn't talking. Or at least not to her satisfaction.

Only one thing bothered her about her rationalization of the whole Tyler situation.

Nash had let her keep her firearm—or rather Stan's gun. Why would he do that unless he thought she'd need it to protect herself or Ben? Or was he just trying to use it to gain her trust? She'd also proved once again she couldn't shoot him—so why not let her keep it.

Plus, he knew she wasn't going anywhere without Ben.

If it was just her, she'd have gotten away by now. But she had Ben to think about and she wouldn't do anything to risk his welfare. She did not believe Nash would hurt Ben, but she wasn't quite so confident he wouldn't hurt her. He was certainly capable of it.

The only way they could get away from Nash was with a head start.

She simply had to bide her time as he grew weaker and weaker.

But Mal had no intention of involving civilians. She wasn't the only one armed and she didn't know how Nash would react if he felt threatened.

Plus, it wasn't as if she could cry for help and people would come running. It was a sad fact that people tended to ignore a woman's screams. Especially if they thought it was a domestic situation. Screaming "fire" was far more effective than either "rape" or "help."

But instead of running into the quickie mart shouting "fire," Mal finger-combed her hair and buttoned her black suit jacket to cover up the traces of blood on her white button-down shirt—Stan's or Nash's blood she couldn't be sure.

An electronic bell went off as she entered. The man behind the counter sat on a stool watching the ten o'clock news. She glanced up at the screen. But there was no top-of-the-hour news flash or announcement of a manhunt with Nash's picture.

She forced a smile for the clerk and then headed straight to the coolers in back.

The bell went off again as Nash and Ben entered. "Can I have a bag of chips?" Ben asked.

"You can have whatever you want," Nash responded. Mal glanced over her shoulder at him as he said it. Typical of a guilt-ridden absentee father, he'd just essentially promised Ben all those bad-for-him things she never let her son have—her son! Ben was her son. Nash had given up his right to parent Ben all so he could run around playing his little spy games. It was no wonder Cara had begun the process of divorcing him.

"I can't do this anymore, Mal. I'm terrified of losing him. Of having to raise our son alone.... I can't be married to a Navy SEAL."

Spoken like a desperate woman. But one desperately in love.

"You, too," he said. It took Mal a minute to realize she'd been staring at Nash this whole time and that he'd been talking about her grabbing anything she wanted. She made eye contact before looking away from his penetrating brown eyes. Yes, her sister had been desperately in love with the man. But every time Mallory looked at him, she only saw Cara lying on the kitchen floor, in a pool of her own blood, and wished him to hell and gone.

It's all my fault. She hadn't really been listening to what her sister was saying.

"I can't be married to a Navy SEAL."

The prosecutor's closing argument put Cara's fear into context. *"Lieutenant Commander Kenneth Nash, in a PTSD episode, attacked his preg-*

nant wife. When he snapped out of it—saw what he had done—the Navy SEAL turned his attentions to desperately trying to save their unborn child....

"Ladies and gentlemen of the jury, I'm asking you to look beyond the hero to the evidence in this case. Ms. Ward was there and she was not applauding her brother-in-law's actions. You heard her testimony. She was appalled by what he was doing. She drew her service pistol and read the man his rights....

"Kenneth Nash is no hero. He's a sad statistic, yes. Post-traumatic stress is a real issue for our service members returning from war. Nonetheless, he's a statistic who murdered his wife. Just because he can't recall or refuses to recount what happened before he dialed 911 does not let him off the hook."

"What are you mumbling about over there?" Nash asked from the next aisle over. He stood head and shoulders above the convenience store shelves.

"Buying junk food for your kid doesn't let you off the hook. It just makes you a bad father." Mal left the aisle in a huff.

The store was a decent size with several rows. Yet there were no other customers around—it seemed they were the only ones subjecting themselves to high-priced gas and trans fats.

Mal noticed that Nash had returned to Ben's side to help guide his choices. She was comfortable enough with the situation as long as she was between Nash and the door. She grabbed three bottles of water and waited until Nash and Ben worked their way toward the back of the store before heading to the cashier. Once at the counter, she added a map of California to her purchases.

Hopefully this would help her boss piece things together.

"Evening," the clerk said. "White Chevy Tahoe, pump four?" His fingers hovered over the register keys ready to ring up the gas.

"No, my husband will pay for that," she lied smoothly.

The man's smile changed to a scowl as she pulled out her credit card.

"There's a minimum purchase."

The overpriced water and map easily added up to over ten dollars. "Fine, add the gas." She forced her credit card on the reluctant business owner.

The man sighed heavily.

Nash appeared at her side and leaned into the counter with a wad of cash. "I got this, sweetheart." He added a prepaid phone and peeled off two hundred dollars in twenties from a wad that she'd bet was five hundred dollars thick…and stolen from her emergency stash. "May as well wait until the boy's done."

The owner was more than happy not to swipe the card.

"Honey." Mal played along. "Is that our vacation fund?"

Nash pushed his ball cap back on his head and went from America's Most Wanted to Good Ol' Boy in a heartbeat. "These independently owned gas stations don't make any money off credit. You should know that, hon."

The man behind the counter looked as if he wanted to crawl over it and kiss Nash on the lips. "Kum and Go undercuts us by six cents a gallon. Then the damn credit card companies put the screws to every transaction by taking their percentage. It's so a man can hardly make a living anymore."

The clerk extended the credit card toward her. Nash looked at her with amusement in his brown eyes.

Glad he found this so funny. Mal stuck her nose up in the air and didn't bother reaching for the plastic.

"Mind handing me those scissors?" Nash asked the clerk as he pointed to the flowerpot/pen holder behind the counter. The man handed over the scissors and shot Mal a smug look as Nash cut up her credit card.

She turned her back on both of them and went to supervise Ben who was still perusing the aisles.

He carried a red handled basket filled to capacity with junk.

So much for fatherly guidance.

Ben looked at her, all wide-eyed guilt and innocence. No doubt expecting her to make him put it all back.

Under normal circumstances, she preferred he eat healthy snacks.

But she wasn't going to be the bad guy here and make him put back chips and mini doughnuts after Nash said Ben could have whatever he wanted.

"Make sure you add some good choices, too." She brushed back his hair and hugged him to her side. He hugged her back. Despite his brave front, he had to be scared. She rubbed his back and gave him another squeeze before letting him go.

No matter what he said, he was still her baby.

She just made sure not to call him that.

Even though she wanted to.

He added apples and cheese to his basket, then Nash helped him make a rainbow slushy from a variety of choices. Mal grabbed a diet soda and some chocolate for herself.

Everyone was allowed a few bad choices once in a while.

Besides chocolate was a cure-all.

She looked over the nonfood items for anything else that might come in handy.

If she grabbed a box of tampons, would that

be the same as giving in to the idea of a long ordeal? But what if she didn't grab them and got caught without? What then? Nash had said they were headed to Coronado—California wasn't exactly the middle of nowhere.

Oh, what the hell? Tampons were good for plugging up bullet holes.

She grabbed two boxes and a first aid kit.

She might hate him and wish him dead, but she could be humane about it. She also grabbed a sewing kit, tool kit, mini flashlight and batteries—enough for Ben's game system and the flashlight.

She grabbed anything and everything that looked useful.

"Almost done, sweetheart?" Nash called to her in a syrupy sweet voice.

"Be there in just a sec, honey buns," she answered without the sticky sweetness. On her way to the counter, she grabbed three Colorado-tourist-type T-shirts—one child, one medium and one large adult-size stamp of tourism.

Eventually she wanted to change out of her blood-stained clothes, and though she'd rather not wear the lace panties that Nash had packed, she didn't see any underwear displayed—practical or otherwise.

Once she was done shopping, she did a quick calculation of the items in her basket—Nash would have to cough up another hundred dollars, easy. Served him right for stealing her money.

"Look, Mom. It's our house on TV!"

Ben pointed to the small screen. Nash and the store owner turned toward the set at the same time she did.

Moving closer for a better look, she caught the tail end mention of a gang-related drive-by shooting. There were no gangs in her neighborhood.

The alley behind her house had been cordoned off. In the distance an ambulance and police cars surrounded the Dumpster where she'd left Stan in the care of her neighbor. And the victim they spoke of was described as an elderly man who lived alone.

Were they referring to Stan? Or her neighbor, Mr. Covey?

Both had been very much alive when she'd left them.

No mention of a wounded FBI agent.

No mention of a fugitive Navy SEAL.

What the heck?

Mal felt a chill run down her spine.

"Good thing we're moving out of that neighborhood," Nash said for the clerk's benefit. He loaded down Ben with shopping bags and then steered him toward the door, away from the kid's morbid fascination with the television account of events they'd just lived through.

"May I have the key to the restroom out back?" Mal asked.

The owner reached underneath the counter for a key attached to a cable—attached to a hubcap—and set it on the counter.

"Seriously?"

There was that smirk again. "People drive off with the key all the time," the man said.

Really? She doubted that a key attached to a hubcap would deter someone from raiding the place for TP.

Overloaded with enough tampons and whatnot to patch up an entire bullet-ridden marine battalion, Mal snatched the key from smirky guy. "Come on, Ben."

Nash could hardly put up a fuss in front of his buddy about his kid having to use the restroom. They'd already drawn enough attention to themselves that the gas station owner wasn't likely to forget them as just another family of tourists passing through.

That was a good thing, right?

The goose bumps spreading across her skin right now had nothing to do with the frigid air outside. Nash carried his own purchases and used the key fob to unlock the SUV from a distance. The lights flickered and the car gulped twice. The liftgate opened and Ben ran over to dump his bags inside before racing back toward the restroom with her and Nash right behind him.

The place really was not that well lit when compared to the Kum and Go.

"Guess it's boys first." Nash took the key from her just as she was about to follow Ben into the unisex bathroom. From the glimpse she'd gotten, it was small. One stall. One sink. And no windows, only a small air vent from the look of it.

Nash took his bag that held the prepaid phone with him. She off-loaded her bags to the back of the SUV while waiting for them to finish. As if the shovel, rope, duct tape and full five-gallon gas cans weren't enough to freak her out, she uncovered a bulk supply of dry goods underneath an old wool blanket and camping gear.

The amount of food gave her pause—there was enough here to feed the three of them for about a month. Mal closed the liftgate and backtracked toward the restroom. She heard the echo of their movements inside the small bathroom through the vent. The toilet flushed, and then flushed again.

"Is Mr. Covey dead?" Ben asked on the other side of the door, his voice coming through loud and clear without a hint of that earlier fear.

"Is that your neighbor?" Nash asked.

She couldn't hear what was said next over the sound of running water.

Mallory cringed. No seven-year-old boy should be having a casual conversation about death with his fugitive father. She needed to get Ben someplace safe where they could talk about these things. Preferably as far away from Nash as possible. She wanted no part of whatever trouble followed him.

The running water stopped.

The door opened and Nash held it for Ben to exit.

Ben came out wiping his hands on his pants. His face and hands were clean. "The dryer's broken and there're no paper towels. There is toilet paper, though."

"Thanks for the report."

Nash came out, bag in hand, looking as if he'd splashed water on his face, and from the dripping curls underneath his cap it appeared as if he'd slicked back his hair, as well. She grabbed the hubcap from him and without any resistance on his part. Propping the door open with her hip, she hesitated and held out her hand. "Car keys."

"We'll be right here when you're done."

He smiled that sardonic smile of his. He knew exactly what she was thinking—that there was the very real fear he'd leave her here and take Ben with him.

"Ben." She motioned him back toward her.

"I just went."

"Oh, for crying out loud, Mal. Who's the one being the baby here?" Nash handed over the car keys.

Mallory took her time in the bathroom. A glimpse of her disheveled appearance in the mirror had her wondering why the owner hadn't called the authorities on sight. All three of them were a mess. She took her time tidying up as best she could.

Nash knocked on the door. "Hurry it up in there."

Mal continued to take her time. She had a gun, she had the keys to the Tahoe—this was really the best shot they were going to have of getting away from him.

He continued to pound the door with impatience.

"Just a minute."

Could she do it? Could she shoot Nash this time, without any hesitation?

With Ben standing right there? It was still Nash after all, and if she wavered even for a second, he'd take advantage of that weakness. And then there was Ben.... No, she couldn't shoot his father in front of him.

"Mal." This time when he rattled the door, he tested the knob.

She ignored him as a new idea began to form. She didn't actually have to kill him or even shoot him for this plan to work. She'd almost forgotten she still had her handcuffs attached to the back of her belt. She picked up the hubcap and tested its weight. Not heavy, but solid. Unlocking the door as quickly and quietly as possible, she stepped back and waited for Nash to grow impatient again.

This time when he rattled the door, he found it unlocked and burst in. Mal was ready for him. She clocked him hard on the back of the head with the hubcap. His head hit the mirror and the glass shattered. She winced but took advantage of the situation and pounded him again. He went down hard, hitting the sink on his way down.

Maybe it would have been kinder to shoot him.

She slapped one cuff to his wrist and the other to the pipe beneath the sink.

Ben stood in the doorway looking horrified.

"Ben." She held up her hand to keep him outside. Nash was Ben's father after all—the boy didn't need to see him like this. Of course, he didn't need to see any of what he'd already been witness to today. Crouching down, she checked Nash's pulse. Rapid, thready and far too strong for her liking.

Okay, so she hadn't killed him. That was good. But, God, he was burning up.

His dark T-shirt was caked in blood and she inched it up to find an angry red wound. The sutures looked professional enough, but a couple of them had ripped open. She felt a moment of guilt for punching him there *and* for what she was about to do. She rolled him to his side and grabbed both guns tucked to his back. One was her SIG and the other a Glock.

"Should I call 911?" Ben asked from the doorway.

"No, go!" She directed him back to the SUV and grabbed the prepaid phone package that had gone flying across the floor. She hurried outside and tossed the hubcap into the ditch. Snatching Ben by the hand, she hurried him toward the truck.

She couldn't blame him for not wanting to leave Nash. He didn't know his father the way she did— hadn't even met the man until today. Ben slowed her down long enough to grab his backpack from the backseat.

He stood stubbornly outside the open passenger door.

All she could think about was getting him buckled in and backtracking to safety. She needed to call Galena—someone she could trust to give her information. Other than that she did not have a plan.

Home was not an option.

Ben shook off her hand as she urged him to climb into the SUV. "But he's hurt bad—" The boy appeared to be under the assumption that they had to save Nash.

"Get in the car," she ordered.

"You hurt him."

"He'll be fine. In the car now, Ben." He climbed in and slammed his door. She ran to the driver's side and climbed in behind the wheel. Instead of putting the key in the ignition, she attempted to saw into the tamper-proof packaging of the pre-paid cell phone with the key. "We'll call for help and they'll send someone."

To apprehend him.

Ben crossed his arms stubbornly.

She saw the skepticism in his brown eyes as he glared at her from the passenger seat. "He's tough," she reminded him. "You have no idea how tough, Ben."

Mal grew increasingly frustrated with the phone's packaging.

"Navy SEAL tough? Or ninja tough?"

She responded with a sad smile. "Navy SEAL tough."

Tough enough he'd chew off his own hand at the wrist to escape those cuffs. She didn't say that out loud, but she knew Nash would escape—or die trying. She checked the locked bathroom door in the rearview mirror as if expecting him to burst through the door at any moment. Just in case, she put the key in the ignition and locked all the doors before trying to open the burn phone package again.

He would die alone in that bathroom.

Mal pushed the thought from her head…or at least she tried to.

Nash was a Navy SEAL—or an ex–Navy SEAL, whatever—but he wasn't superhuman. He'd been shot up, cut up, sewn up and then beat up—that last one by her. Like a Timex watch, he'd take a lickin' and keep on tickin'. Normally. But he'd been cycling through chills, fever and sweats. Infection threatened to take him down.

That's one of the reasons she'd had him pull over into the gas station—because it wasn't safe for him to be behind the wheel of a vehicle in his condition. And despite being able to pull off his good ol' boy act inside the store, he hadn't even had the strength to fend her off when she'd mugged him in the bathroom—and it wasn't only because she'd taken him by surprise.

By cuffing him to the sink, she wasn't even giving him a fighting chance if someone other than the Feds were after him.

"We can't just leave him?" Ben echoed her concerns.

"Yes, we can." She grew increasingly frustrated with the burn phone packaging. She stopped taking her frustrations out on the plastic and instead looked into Ben's pleading eyes. He sat quietly beside her with the first aid kit in his lap.

"He didn't leave us." He extended his cell phone, the one she'd given him to carry in his backpack for emergencies.

She had no idea he'd had it on him the whole time. Silently sending out a signal from every cell tower they'd passed. Anyone with the right equipment could track them through GPS. Anyone with her cell phone—the one she'd left on the kitchen counter back home—could track him instantly. Because of the child safety app she'd downloaded to both their smartphones.

Her heart threatened to hammer right out of her chest.

The very real threat of childhood abduction was why she'd gotten him a cell phone in the first place. Someone or some entity was probably tracking them right now. In order to rescue them.

So why was every muscle in her body gearing up to run?

Mal forced a smile for Ben so he wouldn't sense her fear. "We'll get him help. I promise."

She had a few numbers programmed into his phone. Her cell. Her work. His school. Jackie, a neighbor and a couple of Ben's friends.

Mal autodialed her own cell phone.

"Where the hell are you?" her boss—Special Agent in Charge David Glaze—roared into her ear.

Not, *How the hell are you?* Or, *Are you all right, Mal?* Or even, *Is Ben with you?*

But, where the hell are you?

He must have some idea—he'd answered her phone.

Maybe not their exact location. But dot-on-a-map close—highway exit close.

"We're fine. How's Stan? Is Tyler there with you?" She tried hard not to let his response rattle her. "I have something I want to say to say to—"

"Morgan's in surgery. Where's the son of a bitch who shot him? Is he with you?"

Mal chose her words carefully. "I have Nash in custody, yes. Are you saying he shot Stan?" Of course it's what she believed herself. She simply wanted to confirm it with her boss. Because then maybe she could convince herself she was doing the right thing leaving Nash behind.

So why did it all feel so wrong?

Ben shook his head frantically.

"Yes, I am. Who the hell else would have?" Glaze asked. "Where can we pick him up?"

She kept an eye on the dashboard clock counting down the seconds. No doubt the call was being traced. "I'd really like to speak with someone from the Marshal Service to arrange transport. He's hurt—"

"I'll take care of it," Glaze cut her off.

Mal hesitated. She glanced at Ben. Glanced

across the highway at the brightly lit truck stop. "We're at the Kum and Go."

She broke the connection before he could tell her to stay on the phone.

What the hell was wrong with her?

She'd just lied to the FBI special agent in charge of the Denver field office.

Mal ripped the battery and the SIM card from Ben's phone. Cracking the car door, she tossed them both to the trash barrel at the pump.

"You broke my phone."

"Yes, yes, I did." She tossed the shell to the floorboard at his feet. "It's okay," she reassured him. "We'll get you a new one."

In reality, she had no idea what the hell she was doing. She was acting on pure gut instinct right now. She closed her door, put the key in the ignition and slammed the Tahoe in Reverse until she was even with the bathroom door.

Then she scrambled for the ditch where she'd thrown the restroom key.

It was a wonder Smirky Guy hadn't popped his head out to see what she was doing with his precious hubcap.

CHAPTER SEVEN

NASH DRIFTED IN and out of consciousness, trying to find a reason to care that Mal had left him chained to the sink. He'd come to the realization that she and Ben were better off without him. Mal was smart. She wouldn't head home.

But she would pick up a phone and call someone.

He saw the empty plastic bag across the floor.

Damn it. She had his prepaid phone.

He pulled against the chain—a weak test of what little strength he had left—and winced against the pain in his side. Wouldn't his SEAL BUD/S get a kick out of this? Sidelined by a one-inch-diameter pipe.

Holding his side with his free hand, Nash took a deep breath, grabbed the pipe with his restrained hand and yanked. The water pipe gave enough to squirt him in the face.

Yeah, should have closed that valve first.

He reached over to shut it off now.

The cold soak and the sound of someone fiddling with the door gave him the strength he needed and with one more jerk he freed himself. He was on his feet, ready for a fight with the length of pipe in his hand, as the bathroom door swung open.

"Nash?" Mal saw the pipe and flinched.

He stayed his hand and tossed the piece of plumbing aside in disgust. As if he'd ever hit her. A well-deserved spanking, maybe.

As much as he wanted to put her over his knee right now, he restrained himself from doing just that. "You're back."

"We need to leave now."

Hearing the urgency in her voice, he straightened immediately. "What's up?"

"Ben had his cell phone."

"What little boy has his own cell phone?" What idiot didn't check the kid's backpack? Or pockets? Nash put a hand on Mal's back and steered her outside. Ben was waiting in the car. "Where is it now?"

"I pulled the battery and ditched it. It gets worse," she reassured him. "I dialed my cell phone and my boss answered. I'm pretty sure all that fuss at the Kum and Go is for us." As they spoke, the flashing lights of no less than six squad cars and a helicopter with its searchlight on were converging on the well-lit gas station across the highway.

"Let's get the hell out of here." Nash opened the passenger door for her and motioned for Ben to crawl into the backseat. "Take this cuff off me. I'll drive."

"No," she said. "I'm a federal agent and as far as I know you're a fugitive. I just put my career on the line for you, Nash. And though I'm not going to hand you over until I figure out what's going on and can ensure your safety, you are in my custody now. Put the other cuff on."

"You can't be serious—"

She drew her firearm. "Do it now. Or so help me I will get the cavalry's attention."

He hesitated as he weighed his odds of successfully disarming her.

Then she lowered her weapon. "You can trust me, Nash. You have to trust me."

Ben pressed his nose up against the glass.

Nash slapped the other cuff on his free wrist and held up his hand. "Satisfied? I'm only doing this because we don't have time to argue." Nash promised an argument later.

Satisfied with his compromise, Mal rounded the car to the driver's side. While he settled in to the passenger seat, she climbed behind the wheel. Stubborn woman.

"Where to?" she asked. They sat at the back of the lot with the headlights off.

"You're asking me?" Nash said.

"Yes, you. Coronado?"

"Not a good idea right now." The scene at the

Kum and Go seemed to be driving business to the little mom-and-pop stop as the parking lot was much busier than when they'd first arrived. "Wait until the next car leaves and then turn on your lights and follow the driver out to the highway."

Mal waited for the next car to leave and did as she'd been told. At the intersection the car ahead of them got in the turn lane to head west. "East," he said. "We need to lie low for a while. Head back toward Denver."

"You've got to be kidding?"

"They will track us to the gas station. We need to throw them off our tail. We can only hope they assume we continued west thanks to your attempted map purchase."

More cars converged on the intersection as she merged onto the highway headed east. Nash decided it was just as well she was driving—it kept his shooting hand free. He kept his eyes peeled as they blended into traffic without incident.

Ben tapped him on the shoulder. "We got this for you."

Nash took the white box with the red cross.

He didn't know what to say to the kid. Clearing his throat, he went for the obvious. "Thank you."

He caught Mal's glance at the rearview mirror toward Ben. He could guess whose idea it was to come back for him. Not hers. But if she hadn't come back, he might never have seen her or Ben again.

"Ben, buckle up," she said. "You, too." She raised an eyebrow in his direction. "And just as soon as we get wherever it is we're headed, you're going to tell me everything."

She even sounded like a mom.

THEY DROVE IN silence for what seemed like hours, once again passing the junction for northbound I-70 and then taking a series of smaller state and U.S. highways into the backcountry this time. Even Mallory, who'd lived in Colorado all her life, started to lose track of the signage along the unlit roads and simply followed Nash's directions.

They'd left Denver around seven o'clock that evening, and it was now well after midnight. "I'm starting to feel lost," she admitted. "Where exactly are we going?"

"Near Leadville. I know a cabin where we can hole up for a bit."

"We passed Leadville a while ago."

"Are we lost?" Ben leaned forward in his seat.

"Take the next exit," Nash said from beneath his ball cap. Mallory would have thought he was sleeping—or dead—if it weren't for the fact that he continued to bark out orders. More than likely he was still sulking because she'd refused to remove his handcuffs. Nash sat up, looking more haggard than rested and plopped his hat on Ben's head. "If you see a sign for Rock Springs," he said to her, "follow it."

She felt a twinge of guilt. The man was probably in more pain than she'd know how to deal with. Maybe she *should* set him free of the cuffs. *Hello, since when do we have sympathy for your sister's killer?* that little voice inside her head started to squawk. If the man went and got himself shot, it would only be because he deserved it.

Mallory hardened her heart.

"I thought you knew where we were going." She merged onto the off-ramp without signaling, just to make sure they weren't being followed. Even though Nash assured her more than once that they weren't.

And since they were no longer on a major artery and a tail *would* have been easy to spot.

In fact, the blackness was so thick up here she had to switch on the high beams.

"I know where we're going, Mal. Just never been there before."

"Who owns this cabin?"

"No one I know." Even in the soft glow of the dashboard lights, he could tell she'd cast a sideways glance at him. "Let's put it this way, no one who'd likely be traced back to either of us. But maybe someone who won't mind us staying there."

"Yeah, that's real helpful."

"Rock Springs." Ben pointed to the reflective road sign.

"Good eye," Nash complimented Ben, and the boy glowed brighter than the retroreflective sheeting making up the sign. This was what he'd been missing all these years without a mother and a father.

No. Ben had a mother. He had her.

And in every way that mattered, she was as good a substitute mom as Cara would have wanted for her son. Maybe it was time she got serious about finding a man that would fit into their lives so that Ben would have a role model and so she'd have—have a…what? If she knew what she wanted, maybe finding the right man wouldn't be so difficult. Who was she kidding?

Right now, as a mother on the run, she figured her future prospects would be limited to criminals. She'd gone from being a victim to being a fugitive with one lie to her boss. No, that wasn't quite true. She wasn't breaking any laws. She was a federal agent and had every right to ensure a fugitive's safety—as well as her own and that of her son—before handing Nash back over to the U.S. Marshal Service.

Still the outcome of Stan's surgery weighed heavily on her mind. She was taking quite a risk. This could turn out very bad for all of them if Stan died. She had so many questions. None of which she felt she could ask Nash with Ben in the back-seat wide-awake.

Nash pulled a map out of the glove box and then broke into her thoughts with a few more left-turn, right-turn directions. And then he was quiet for a long time.

Too long.

"Nash," she said loudly. "Are you awake?"

"Yeah, yeah, I'm awake," he responded groggily.

She hadn't seen another vehicle in at least twenty or thirty minutes. Clearly they were in a rural area where few ventured. The snow already on the ground snuggled up against the shady north side of the trees and more was expected to fall later this week. At least they weren't above the tree line.

A dense forest of evergreen made up of pines, spruces and firs surrounded them, broken only by the occasional grove of aspen or cottonwood.

"Turn right, here." Nash pointed her down a dirt track. It couldn't even be called a road.

"Are we there yet?" Ben asked.

"Almost," Nash said.

"I don't think that bad man will find us way out here," Ben said.

He sounded in good spirits considering the day they'd just had.

But the last thing Mal needed was for Ben to be afraid of federal agents.

"It was bad of Agent Tyler to shoot out the back window—"

"Is that his name, Tyler?" Nash asked. "Makes sense, then."

"What makes sense?"

"He shot that other man," Ben said.

"What other man?" She glanced at Ben in the rearview mirror. She felt as if she was missing part of the conversation.

"He's referring to the other agent. The older one."

"Stan?" Mal slammed the brakes in the middle of the deserted dirt road and shot a glance toward Nash. "You sh—"

She stopped herself just in time. But Ben still caught on.

"No, he didn't." Ben had unbuckled and was leaning over the seat now. "The bad man shot him. He was going to shoot us, too. But we were very quiet and he didn't even see us."

Mal looked from Ben and then to Nash for confirmation. The fact that he didn't say anything was enough. "But Stan—" What had Stan said, exactly?

"That son of a bitch shot me."

She just assumed that son of a bitch was Nash.

"Oh, God." The son of a bitch was Tyler. And

Stan had grabbed her arm and tried to warn her. No wonder Ben had been shaking his head while she was on the phone with Glaze. She just thought, well, she didn't know what she'd thought other than the boy did not want her to hurt Nash.

"Next right," Nash repeated.

"What? Oh." Mal set the car in motion again, turning right onto another dirt road that opened into a small clearing. She refused to let panic set in as they slowed to a crawl along an unmarked road. Snow and gravel crunched beneath the tires of the SUV.

The high beams lit on a rough-hewn log cabin. The carport to the left was big enough for four vehicles and was lined on three sides with firewood and it also housed equipment most people would not leave out in the open.

At least not in the city.

Mallory could make out two covered snowmobiles. And another couple of ATVs. This was obviously someone's recreational getaway.

The firewood fence and large tarps weighted down with small boulders were designed to keep the natural elements out, not the criminal ones. But then she noticed that there was also a shed the size of a barn with a secured padlock.

"We're here." Ben stated the obvious.

Reaching beneath the seat between his legs, Nash pulled out the gun that Mal had hidden there, letting her know he'd been wise to her hiding place all along. Checking the safety, he tucked it away as he got out of the SUV. Now he was one up on her and she was losing track of all the firearms. Her SIG didn't have a safety, which is why she'd switched to carrying her assigned gun.

But he still wore her cuffs and she was still in charge.

Stiff and sore from the drive, however, Mal could barely move. She got out of the car and opened the passenger door for Ben, who was still wearing Nash's ball cap.

They waited for Nash on the porch while he grabbed her bag and took his time getting out of the Tahoe. He stopped to pick up the key beneath a painted rock at the foot of the stairs. The handcuffs limited his movement only to the extent that he needed both hands for what most people could do with one.

"You've been here before." She spoke without thinking. He'd said he hadn't.

"Never," he repeated.

"Are we breaking and entering?" Ben asked with far too much seriousness. Mal squeezed his hand. She was beyond thinking what she should and shouldn't be saying in front of him. The boy had hidden from a gunman and witnessed an attempted murder—having a father who stole cars and broke into houses was probably not such a big deal in retrospect.

Especially when that man could keep them safe. It was one of the reasons she'd gone back for him.

And here she'd been patting herself on the back for being a great mother.

"More like uninvited guests," Nash said, opening the door. "It's okay. They're not going to mind that we're staying here."

Whether that was true or not was debatable.

Mal could tell by Nash's slow and deliberate movements he was having trouble holding his own. But once inside, he got a fire started while she wrestled to keep a wide-awake Ben in check.

There didn't seem to be any electricity, but they found a small water closet of a bathroom in a dark corner next to the stairs without having to venture upstairs.

And there was running water, which was a relief. Some folks winterized by shutting off the water in the winter, especially if they didn't plan on spending time in their vacation home. Others, like the residents of this cottage, which was far from the ski resorts, did so by insulating the pipes and leaving a drip.

There just wasn't any hot water.

After washing up, she showed Ben how to leave a drip so the pipes wouldn't freeze and burst, making them not only uninvited houseguests but also expensive ones.

Then she made Ben lie down on the couch and started removing his shoes despite his protests. "But I'm not tired."

"You will be once you close your eyes." She removed the ball cap Nash had given him, but he insisted on holding on to it as she covered him with a knitted afghan and pulled it up to his chin. "It's been a long day. We all need to rest."

After settling Ben, Mal moved closer to the fire. She missed the car heater already.

She stood in the middle of the room with her hands tucked beneath her arms.

"That goes for you, too, Mal. Get some rest." Nash tossed her a protein bar. She caught it by sheer surprise.

He sat down across from her with his weapon flat on its side, balanced on his knee and pointed away from her and Ben. She took that to mean he wasn't going anywhere and planned to stand watch.

It was too dark to explore their surroundings, though she would have liked to check out the upstairs. There were probably a couple of nice cozy beds up there, but with no heat except for the fireplace, this was the coziest room in the house.

Mal curled up on the opposite end of the couch and shared the covers with Ben. The fire gave the cabin a warm, cozy glow. There was a small kitchen area to her left, and behind her stairs. A low divide between the kitchen and the living areas was lined with bookshelves. There were a few paperback novels on the shelves, but they were mostly filled with kids' books and games. That was a nice surprise. She didn't know how long they'd be here, but at least she'd be able to keep Ben entertained.

She'd been waiting for Ben to fall asleep before demanding answers from Nash, but Ben had been asleep for several minutes now and neither of them had said a word. The boy's restless murmurs reminded her of all they'd been through today.

Nash's half-hooded eyes held hers while she sat with her feet tucked under her legs in the semi-dark, holding a silent staring contest with an ex–Navy SEAL. His long lashes made him look dreamy, though she knew he was wide-awake. His color looked better now than it had all day— night—but she knew that could just be a trick of the firelight.

Beads of sweat still formed across his upper lip.

"You didn't shoot Stan."

"No, I did not," he said.

She expelled a big breath with something close to relief before reminding herself the man was still quite capable of killing. "Why would Tyler—?" She shook her head because it just made no sense.

"*That* I don't know," he said. "But I do know Christopher Tyler has every reason to hate me."

"Why?"

"Classified."

"Is that going to be your default answer for everything?"

"I've only used it once. But pretty much."

His teasing sounded like the old Nash and she involuntarily snorted.

"I ratted his brother out for torturing prisoners." He held up his cuffed wrists. "How about we start this bit of catch-up with you letting me out of these?"

"I would think those bracelets would feel quite natural on you by now."

"You don't know the half of it." He raised his hand to scratch his nose. "I've been busted on so many charges I've lost count. But it's always to catch the bad guys."

As if he could set himself apart from those bad guys now. Body Language 101. An itchy nose was a telltale sign of lies and deceit.

But she didn't need to catch him scratching his nose to know he was trying to charm her. His last seven, almost eight years were one big lie.

He lowered his hands when she did not walk over and immediately release him.

"I haven't decided what I should do about you yet," she admitted.

"I can protect us better without these getting in the way." There was some truth to that argument. He was armed and dangerous. And the handcuffs weren't going to stop an ex–Navy SEAL from causing harm and doing damage. Truth was, if he'd wanted to hurt her or Ben he could have done so by now.

"Protect us from who? Tyler?" She still felt a sense of disbelief.

"Not just Tyler. I'm not running from the law."

"These people who are after you—"

"Al-Ayman," he said before she finished her sentence.

"Al-Ayman, are they going to find you here?"

"I hope to hell not." His mouth held a grim line. "We're pretty much off the radar here. No one can associate me with the town of Rock Springs or this cabin."

She tossed back the afghan and dug the key out of her pocket. He held up his hands and she yanked him by the chain. "This doesn't let you off the hook, Nash." She hovered over him. "You're still in my custody."

His only response was to tilt his chin and look at her strangely.

"What?"

"Nothing." He seemed irritated by her question. "You've just changed, that's all."

She inserted the key into the lock. His skin still

felt cold and clammy, reminding her why she'd insisted he pull over at the gas station in the first place. And then she'd gone and mugged him in the bathroom. "You should maybe get some rest. Hydrate. Take a pain reliever or something."

She turned the key and released him from his bonds.

"Careful, Mal." He rubbed his wrists. "It's starting to sound like you might care."

"Nothing happens to Ben," she said. "Or so help me, Nash, I will shoot you. As for guns, keep yours locked up or under your control at all times. Ben is far too curious for his own good."

She settled back on the couch and pulled the afghan high over her shoulders and closed her eyes.

Mal was surprisingly able to relax fairly quickly, but whenever she felt herself drifting off, she'd force her eyes open, only to find Nash staring at her unwaveringly.

Eventually one of them would have to trust the other enough to fall asleep.

"WHAT'S THAT NOISE?" Tess spoke into her cell phone.

"A C-130 Hercules," McCaffrey said. "I'm at Buckley getting ready to board a flight back to North Island. What's up?"

She covered her opposite ear and pressed her cell phone closer to her face. "Sorry, I know it's late and you're probably anxious to get back home." She glanced at her watch. It was well after midnight. "I'm at a small mom-and-pop gas station here in Eagle, Colorado. The FBI is in the head dusting for prints." She glanced over her shoulder and stepped farther out of their listening range. "I thought you'd like to know that Glaze heard from Mallory. The FBI was using her smartphone to track them with an app called Mama Bear." Once the FBI had realized Ben's cell phone was on the move, they were able to catch up quickly. "They were maybe ten minutes behind when Mal called her cell phone."

"Is Nash in custody?"

"No, they haven't caught up to them yet." Tess paused briefly before going on. "There've been a couple of curious developments I'd like to go over with someone who is *not* on a rampage." She glanced toward the store where agents Tyler and Glaze were inside interviewing the owner while the evidence recovery and processing team scoured the restroom for traces of forensic evidence. A cell phone battery had been discovered in a trash barrel next to the pumps. "Glaze is in an uproar because Mallory lied about her location and then cut the call short. She said they were at the Kum and Go across the highway instead of at this mom-and-pop store."

Tess stood outside the light, pacing along a frozen ditch where the restroom key had been found. "Since they'd pinpointed her to the exit, he believed her. You know the type of place— corporate, clean, security cameras all over. No sign that Nash and company were ever there. However, a review of security footage shows Bari Kahn gassed up his motorcycle at the Kum and Go about four hours earlier. We're sure it was him. We got a good shot without the helmet and ran it through facial recognition software."

She took a deep breath because this was going to be hard for Mac to hear.

"Tyler has convinced Glaze that Nash coerced Mal into lying. That and the marshal's last words combined with the terrorist's presence, are pretty good pieces of proof that Nash and Kahn are in cahoots." She reminded him that Bari had been the manager of the Little Eagle Lodge in Eagle, Colorado—the motel where Jenny Albright, now Jenny Erickson, had worked. Jenny had discovered hidden cameras in a trailer home she'd rented from Bari. With Itch's help, Jenny and her young son escaped from becoming Bari's next victims.

Tess had had the pleasure of arresting Bari the first time.

But despite her best efforts at trying to make the kidnapping and sex trafficking charges against him stick, being a foreign national with ties to terrorism had made Bari a better candidate for detention at Gitmo.

How was any intel worth that man being free for these past six years?

Tess sighed heavily. "You're not going to try to convince me this is all just a coincidence that I'm standing at the Little Eagle Gas and Go, are you?"

"Never said it was," McCaffrey chuckled. "But don't be so certain Nash is there to meet up with Kahn because they're working together. Kahn could be trying to flush him out. Nash could be distracting you. *Or* leading you straight to Kahn."

"If that's his intention it's working. The FBI is following up on leads to Kahn as we speak. I suspect we'll be here all night. Tomorrow we're broadening the search to the town of Eagle. According to the store owner, Mallory attempted to purchase three bottles of water and a map of California on a credit card in her name. And he distinctly remembers Nash mentioning California several times. He also had a lot to say about people who don't return restroom keys, but that's beside the point."

"Sounds like you have your work cut out for you. Do you need me there?"

"No." Tess ran a hand through her dirty-blond

hair, which was probably more dirty than blond right now. "I'm sticking to David Glaze like glue. If this goes south, it's going there in a hurry. Just keep your team on standby. And, Mac." She hesitated. "Tell Itch to give Jenny and Josh an extra hug tonight. He might need to be extra vigilant if Bari is headed to San Diego."

"Will do."

Tess disconnected and crossed the lot toward the store. Glaze came out with two coffees in hand. "Here." He handed her a paper cup. "You look like you could use this."

"Thanks. How's it going in there?"

"I think we're done here for the night. I've booked rooms for everyone at the Little Eagle Lodge. We can continue our search from there in the morning. And set up a command post if we need to. Don't worry—I got you a single." He produced a packaged toothbrush from his pocket and handed it to her.

"Thanks again, Dave." She saluted him with the toothbrush.

"It's David," he said. The agent was actually quite charming when he wasn't red-faced and shouting into cell phones. "I know you have your own agenda for this op, Tess. But he's already shot *one* of my men. If he hurts Mallory I'm not going to be able to guarantee your man's safety."

"He's not *my man,*" she emphasized. "Mallory and Ben are my main concern here."

"Good." He nodded. "Then we're on the same page. As for this operation, we're calling it Mama Bear."

CHAPTER EIGHT

NASH STUDIED MALLORY as she slept. Cara's kid sister, all grown up.

Curled up on the couch like that, she didn't look so grown up. She looked vulnerable. Scared.

And totally unprepared for the events of the evening, yet she'd risen to the occasion. Hell, she'd even challenged him. That was why he'd chosen her as his son's guardian. Protector.

"He calls you mom."

"Yes," she said.

He hadn't meant to say that out loud. Didn't think she was aware enough to answer. Her eyes drifted open again, a sleepy half-mast kind of open. Firelight picked up the red highlights in her hair, but there was something different about it. There was something not quite right to his way of thinking. All those once unruly curls tamed into submission. What a shame.

Nash leaned forward in his seat. Held back a wince as pain radiated from his side. "Does he know you're his aunt and not his mother?"

"Of course."

Which wasn't really an answer, or at least not the one he was looking for.

What did the boy know about his mother? Her death?

Him?

"He's not afraid of me."

She shifted to a sitting position and hugged her knees. "A mistake on my part obviously." Her gaze drifted to the still-sleeping boy, and his followed.

"Just curious," he admitted. "I saw an old photo of me on his dresser."

"He found it in Cara's things. I told him you were killed in action. I thought it best for him to think of his father as a hero." She said this in a way that let him know she thought he was anything but a hero. And she was right.

"And Cara?"

"He knows she died when he was a baby. Ben has grown up healthy and happy. He hasn't needed the details regarding his parents."

"That's good." It was the way it should be.

Except it wasn't.

A boy shouldn't have to grow up without either of his parents. So many times over the years he'd thought about packing it all in. Returning home.

But home to what? A son who was better off without him?

And it would have meant breaking the promise of no contact he'd made to Mal. A promise he *had* kept and would have continued to keep, except under the most dire of circumstances—which these were.

He'd wanted Mal and Ben to live a life without having to look over their shoulders. That kind of life was no longer possible now. He wondered if she fully understood that there would be no career to go back to—and not because she'd done anything wrong.

"You must really hate me right now," he acknowledged.

She sucked in her breath and let it out slowly. "I have every reason to hate you, Nash."

"I'm sorry I couldn't save her for you. For the both of us."

He caught the sheen in her eyes as she turned her head away from him.

Because really, wasn't that why she hated him? Not because she thought he shouldn't have made every possible effort to save Ben's life. And *not* because she truly believed he'd flipped a switch and strangled Cara. But because he was a Navy SEAL and hadn't been home to save his own wife when she needed him.

All because of some petty argument over circumcision. An argument that at the time, when wrapped up in religious convictions, hadn't seemed so petty.

He should have been there to protect Cara. To

fight for her. It was worse knowing she'd been targeted simply because she was his wife. The al-Ayman leader had bragged to his face about knowing the names of every SEAL Team member who'd been involved in a raid that had killed the man's oldest son.

The terrorist group's plan had been to take out the oldest son of every team member. "We started with the Jew's wife because she was carrying his unborn son," Mullah Kahn had bragged one night to Nash, or Sayyid, as he knew him to be. "But it turned out much better than planned. Her murder was pinned on the husband and he was sent to prison where the infidel killed himself."

Nash even found out that the assassin had entered his home posing as a rabbi.

He now knew Cara had stopped by a synagogue, where he'd sometimes attended, several days before her murder and had talked with a rabbi there, asking questions about the Jewish faith and traditions. That was why Nash was so certain they were on their way toward reaching a compromise and working things out. They were both open-minded adults who'd chosen to love each other for better for worse, until death do us part.

Beyond death.

At the time, when Mullah Kahn had first relayed these events to him, Nash had wondered if it was a setup or a test. He'd had a hard time not killing the al-Ayman leader right then and there. But he knew he had to get his hands on that list of SEALs. Discover how invasive it really was and then get word to Mac.

The list turned out to be less a manifest and more of a compilation of random names from various teams—which was bad enough, but less pervasive than a leak or a breach. And from the inside Nash had been able to make sure the list disappeared and that no other assassinations were attempted, let alone carried out.

But he'd also discovered something else about himself. That he needed to clear his name more than he wanted vengeance. And he needed to do it for Ben.

Both he and Mal seemed to be lost in their thoughts in the firelit cabin. There was so much he wanted to tell her, without also dumping all the shit he'd been through on her.

"He's so much more than I expected or deserved," he said suddenly, watching Ben with an unfamiliar lump forming in the back of his throat. "Thank you."

He had her full attention once again.

He wasn't the type of man who felt the need to apologize or explain. Or even offer his gratitude.

But he owed her more than an explanation. Nash searched for the right words but had a hard time putting them together in a way that would make sense to anyone.

"I chose not to testify in my own defense, not because I was guilty, but because I knew I could turn it to my advantage. And that decision has allowed me to go after Cara's killer." He held her gaze as he said, "Her real killer, Mal."

She shifted in her seat.

"I know you and I will never see eye to eye on certain aspects of the truth," Nash continued. "The how and why I chose to deliver Benjamin into this world, for one. But you have to believe me when I tell you that Cara was my world."

How would Mal react if she knew that the man who'd sanctioned Cara's killing had done so for no other reason than that she was his wife? A payback for a mission that he and his team had carried out.

By the time Mal arrived on the scene that fateful day, Cara was already dead—whether or not she wanted to believe it. He'd sent Mal outside under the pretense of retrieving his phone even though he'd already called 911.

He'd sent her out because he'd known then what he was about to do.

They could argue the fact that he wasn't a doctor—or a coroner—and that he had no authority to pronounce anyone dead. Let alone perform a C-section on his own wife.

As a SEAL he'd been EMT trained. And he'd seen enough death and dying to know that the only woman he'd ever love had died in his arms.

Cara's last words to him were "I'm sorry, the baby."

With her dying breath, his wife had been thinking of their child, so how could *he* not? He could have continued CPR until his lungs exploded. He could have given in to his grief and broken down right there.

Neither of those things would have brought her back.

And neither of those things would have saved Ben.

He'd chosen a course of action that very few would have dared taken. But he didn't care about what anyone would or would not have done in his situation.

He actually thought he was years beyond caring about anything. But he'd thought wrong.

If today had taught him anything, it was that he still cared. He cared about Ben. He cared about Mal. Practically speaking, he needed her for one reason, and one reason only—and that's why she was here. But now that she was here, he knew the real reason he needed her was to keep alive the memory of the family that might have been. She was Ben's anchor.

Only she wasn't just Ben's anchor.

She was his anchor, too.

He'd been telling himself he felt a sense of obligation to her because of Ben. But she was that place he dreamed of coming home to long after he'd forgotten how to dream. She wasn't Cara, but aside from Ben, she was all he had left of Cara. Nor was she Ben's biological mother, but she was the only mother he could give his son.

"You don't trust me, I get it. But can you at least believe that I would never intentionally do anything to hurt Ben? Or you?"

"I want to believe you, Nash. And maybe I do. I don't know. But that doesn't mean you haven't already hurt us. Or that we won't get hurt. And please don't pretend you haven't dragged us into something deep here."

"You haven't asked me if I killed those two marshals at the safe house."

Maybe she had just assumed he did.

The way she had assumed he'd shoot an agent for no good reason?

She leaned back against the arm of the couch, staring up at the low-beamed ceiling. "Why'd you come for us? You don't need us. We'll only slow you down."

"Right on both counts."

What if he just told the truth and said that he'd never left? That he'd always been right there in the background of their lives watching from a distance. Apart and separate, but somehow whole, too. Because they were safe. But now they weren't.

"Why, then? Do you really think you're going to raise Ben on the run? Always looking over your shoulder? And what about me? Do you think I'm just going to go along for the ride? We had a good life, Ben and I."

"*Had* being the operative word, Mal."

That life was over. Whether she knew it or not, chose to believe it or not.

He wasn't here to give her false hope. He was here to save their lives.

Uncertainty filled her eyes. If she hadn't been afraid before, she was now. "What are you not telling me, Nash?"

"What do you think?" He pushed to his feet. He needed to have a look around. Secure the perimeter. Find the generator so they could have a hot shower and a hot meal in the morning. He stopped alongside the couch. "I'm sorry if you can't trust me, Mal, but you've got no one else you *can* trust. My cover's been blown. And because of that— because of me—you and Ben are in danger. So I guess you could look at the situation and say that I did bring danger to your door, but I'm trying my damnedest to keep you one step ahead of it. And for the record, I didn't kill those two marshals. No matter what anyone else says."

MALLORY DRIFTED IN and out to the sound of running water and a few short hours later was jerked awake as daylight streamed through the front window. Nash had given her a lot to absorb before she'd dozed off, and she'd had an uneasy night despite the exhaustion. How long had she been out? She looked around to find Ben eating a protein bar at the kitchen table. The contents of his backpack were strewn across the surface and he appeared to be busy humming as he drew pictures.

"Where's Nash?" she asked.

Ben pointed overhead and the sound of running water registered as a shower on her consciousness. Did that mean there was hot water? Because there also appeared to be electricity in the cabin now. She switched off the table lamp beside the couch and tossed off the afghan. A wave of nausea hit her as she sat up. The tender spot at the back of her head reminded her that she no longer knew the good guys from the bad guys.

She certainly did not know which category her former brother-in-law fell into. On the one hand, it appeared as if he'd risked his life to save theirs. On the other? Well, he'd brought a world of hurt down on them that had nothing to do with her or Ben.

Nash had left her gym bag by the chair next to the fireplace. The ash gave off a temperate glow. There was a chill in the air, so she added more kindling and another log to get the fire going again.

Then she rummaged through the gym bag looking for the car keys and came up empty-handed. "How long has he been up there?"

She straightened and glanced around the small space to see if she could figure out where he might have hidden the weapons. Last count they had four handguns—her graduation present, her service pistol, Stan's service pistol and the Glock he'd gotten from somewhere, plus a box of bullets.

Her plan was still to put as much distance between them and Nash as possible. Ben could hardly object to leaving their kidnapper behind in a nice cozy cabin. Even if the thought pricked her conscience.

She needed to contact Tess, someone she trusted. And to get in touch with the Marshal Service directly. She could check out Nash's story and then arrange to hand him over. The burn phone was somewhere, but where?

Still in the car, maybe?

The first order of business was finding a pain reliever for her pounding headache. In the kitchen, she found a bottle of Tylenol and filled a glass with tap water to down the pill. They wouldn't have much time to make their escape.

How long was Nash going to be in that shower?

Mallory switched the tap from cold to hot, only to find it ran tepid.

The hair at the back of her neck prickled and

she forgot all about her headache and plans to take Nash in as she shut off the water. She put a hand on Ben's shoulder. "Stay here."

He continued drawing as she crossed the short distance to the stairs. There was a gun cabinet at the foot of the staircase. She could see a full rack of hunting rifles through the tempered glass. She tried the doors, which were locked. As was the drawer beneath where the ammo was most likely stored, and quite possibly the weapons they'd brought with them.

She grabbed the next best thing, a baseball bat from the umbrella basket beside the front door, and tiptoed up the stairs. With every creak of the floorboards, she stopped to hold her breath and listen. The shower was still running, but her gut told her there was no way in hell the man was taking a twenty-minute shower in tepid water—especially considering their current situation.

There was an empty bedroom and bathroom situated at the top of the stairs. The running water was coming from behind a closed door, which appeared to be the master bedroom, likely with an en suite bathroom.

Mallory brought the bat to her shoulder and pushed on the door.

The door opened inward with a creak, but she was ready to take a swing at the first sign of trouble. The master bedroom was fully furnished but empty of any life-forms. The en suite bathroom door was open and she moved toward it with caution. How embarrassed would she be if she caught him innocently taking a cold shower?

That was not the case, however. He appeared to have passed out on the tile floor before he'd even gotten undressed.

He lay there pale and lifeless.

For all she knew he was already dead.

"Did you hit him?" Ben screamed at her from the doorway.

"No, I did not hit him." She set the bat aside and stepped over Nash's prostrate body. Reaching into the shower, she shut off the running water and crouched down beside him to check his pulse. Same as before. Rapid and far too strong for her liking.

"Is he dead?" Ben asked in hushed tones.

"No, he's not dead." But he was back to burning up with fever and didn't so much as groan when she rolled him over onto his back. At least he appeared to be breathing. She inched up his dark T-shirt and found it plastered to the wound at his side with dried blood. "Hand me a wet washcloth." She nodded toward the sink.

Ben grabbed a washcloth from the top of the stack. After running it under the faucet, he handed it to her dripping wet. Mallory applied it to Nash's T-shirt until she could work the material free from the wound. As careful as she was, he started to bleed again.

The sutures were professional enough, but more than a couple of them were ripped open now. The wound itself looked an angry red and the skin surrounding it felt hot to the touch. She cleaned around the wound as best she could and felt that moment of guilt again for punching him back at the gas station.

Ben handed her a dry washcloth without her having to ask. "I'll get the first aid kit." He scrambled for the stairs.

"Don't you dare die today. Do you hear me, Nash? I'm not letting you cause that little boy any more pain."

After she tended to his wound the best she could, she hooked her arms under his, and half dragged, half carried him toward the bed. He was lean muscled, but heavier than he looked because he weighed a ton. "Nice to know you gained back all that weight you lost in prison."

The mattress dipped from their combined weight as she fell back onto the bed into a semi-reclining position with him in her lap. The mattress dipped again when she slithered out from underneath him. With the lower half of his body still mostly off the bed, she picked up his legs at the knees and turned him perpendicular to the headboard.

She couldn't help noticing the bulge in his pocket and fished out the keys—car, house and a tiny one, which was probably for the gun cabinet. After a thorough search of all his pockets, and finding nothing more useful than the keys, Mal removed his shoes and dropped them one at a time to the foot of the bed. She adjusted the pillow beneath his head.

He was almost as pale as the bedsheets. She brushed his dark curly hair back from his sweaty brow. All the time she'd known him, she'd never seen him with hair long enough to know it curled.

His marine dad probably never let him grow it long and then he'd joined the navy.

"Here." Ben returned with the first aid kit.

Mallory used the butterfly strips to close the jagged tear as best she could. Then she wrapped his entire midsection in sterile gauze. She wasn't a nurse and moved none too gently as she lifted and then rolled his body to accommodate her attempt to bandage him. She'd stopped the bleeding, but they'd owe the homeowner new sheets and possibly a mattress.

Which was the least of her worries.

She kept thinking that Nash should have regained consciousness by now. He lay stark and unmoving against the white sheets.

She brushed the hair from his forehead again. Careful to keep her touch impersonal, she let the silky strands fall through her fingers as she placed the cool cloth on his forehead.

All those times she'd wished him dead and here she was, desperately trying to save his life as Ben looked on. "Is he going to die?"

"I don't know." She gave him the most honest answer she could. "He needs rest. Let's let him get some."

There was nothing more she could do for Nash. Her best bet was to find the burn phone and call for help. But that niggling voice inside her head kept reminding her that Nash had risked his life coming after them and she owed it to him to keep watch over him until she could figure out what was going on here and who all the players really were. Ushering Ben out of the room, she closed the door with a heavy sigh.

The burden of indecision right now was bigger than two hundred pounds of unconscious man. *Give the man the benefit of the doubt, Ward.*

Surprised to find it was almost noon by the time they returned downstairs to the kitchen, Mallory went through the cupboards one by one to take stock of their supplies. She found a stale box of saltines and two cans of Campbell's Chunky soup.

"How about helping me unload the Tahoe." She tossed Ben the car keys.

"Okay." He raced to the door and they were greeted by a cold blast of air when he opened it.

She grabbed one of the kid-size winter coats from the rack even though it had pink stripes and tossed it to Ben. "Mom, that's a girl's."

She assessed the jersey jacket he wore over his T-shirt and jeans. He'd be fine for a few quick trips in and out. "Fine, but it's here to use if you get cold."

The house itself wasn't all that warm, though there was a thermostat by the door that registered fifty-five degrees. The heat was off and probably should remain that way since she didn't know much about the generator.

Mal grabbed the closest thing to a warm coat in her size, which was a wool peacoat, and put it on. Then she grabbed her SIG from the gun cabinet and holstered it before going outside.

Enlisting Ben's help kept him busy and his mind off Nash for the next hour as they made several trips from the Chevy to the kitchen. She tried not to think about the fact that unloading the SUV felt a lot like settling in.

"What do you want for lunch?" She held out the two cans. "Beef stew or clam chowder."

He thought about it for a minute. "Beef stew, I guess."

If Ben wasn't hungry, then more than the Cheetos he'd consumed for breakfast was to blame. She'd hidden the rest of the junk food they'd hauled out of reach.

The truck had been like an icebox, so the refrigerated snacks had held up pretty well. She tossed him one of the cheese sticks and put the rest into the fridge—which was now operating thanks to the mysterious generator that she needed to hunt down.

Nash had both propane and gas in the back of the Tahoe—and it was a very good thing they weren't in the Tahoe when Tyler had shot at them or they would have gone up in flames.

But two bottles of propane and twenty gallons of gas weren't going to get them very far, whichever the generator ran on.

They probably shouldn't be running it 24/7 with their limited fuel supply.

"Okay, I'll rustle up some beef stew. You empty out your backpack so we can see what kind of schoolbooks and supplies we have to work with. And then let's have a look over on those shelves. I bet there're some books you'd enjoy reading and I saw some coloring books, too."

"Mom," he whined. "I'm pretty sure fugitives don't have to do homework."

"Is that so?" If it wasn't so charming coming from the young boy's mouth, she might have stopped to think about how sad that sounded. "That's a big word you're throwing around. Spell *fugitive*."

He propped his elbow on the table and rested

his face against his palm. "*He* wouldn't make me spell it." He was referring to his newfound idol of course.

Big Daddy.

"You want to bet?" She chucked him under the chin. "You have no idea how smart your father is." She wiped at a smudge on Ben's face while he looked at her expectantly. "Go wash up for lunch," she said. He apparently liked that suggestion better than homework and ran off to wash up.

It was inevitable, she supposed, that Ben would have questions about his father now that he'd met him.

"Don't we all?"

And she'd have to figure out how best to answer them.

Before starting lunch, she took the time to wash up and change herself. Swapping out the white bloodstained shirt for the novelty T-shirt with an eagle flying above snowcapped mountaintops and the words Welcome to Eagle, Colorado, spelled out across her chest. And over that she wore her holster and gun.

They were a long way from Eagle.

She just hoped they'd put enough distance between themselves and whatever clues they'd left behind at the Gas and Go.

CHAPTER NINE

MAL CHECKED ON Nash several times throughout the afternoon.

He continued to cycle through chills, fever and sweats without ever breaking his fever. She'd spent the afternoon getting the lay of the land so to speak. She'd taken Ben for a walk up the private road, which in the daylight was less of a dirt track and more grated gravel, to where it intersected with the next gravel road.

"Which way did we come from?" she quizzed him as they took a tour of their surroundings without his realizing the importance of this homework assignment. As well as what good exercise it was for both of them.

"Left." Ben pointed to his left.

"That's right." They'd taken two right turns after the county road. "So it's left turn, left turn to the county road."

She also made him memorize the lot number by drawing his attention to the post and asking him to read the number and then later asking him if he remembered the number and the way out.

They even made a rhyme out of it.

"Seventy-nine," he answered proudly. "Left turn, left turn, county line."

"I'll race you back to the house."

"Hey, that's cheating," he said when she took off.

She let him catch up and then matched her pace to his, letting him win the race in a sprint to the front door.

It took them just over five minutes at a full-out run to cover the roughly half-mile distance to the cabin. As far as Mal was concerned, there was no such thing as being overly prepared.

Whether they wound up using this information or not, it was all good to know.

The burn phone had never materialized, so she could only assume Nash had it well hidden and didn't want her to find it. Fortunately, she knew a thing or two about OnStar and car thieves.

So even though he'd disconnected the battery in the trunk to disable it—and more than likely wasn't a subscriber even if he was the vehicle's owner—she knew how to reconnect the battery. Then all she'd have to do is press that blue button and speak to an adviser about activating the three-month free trial—all without a credit card—at which time she'd state her true emergency.

Thank you, OnStar.

But she'd decided to save that for a true emergency. Since the man had risked his life and taken extreme precautions to keep them safe, the least she could do now was make sure his fever broke before turning him over to the authorities. Though that line of thinking was beginning to sound like an excuse. Especially since she had the car keys in hand even if she didn't have the phone. She and Ben could leave right now. She could connect OnStar and call someone from the road. But she couldn't shake the niggling feeling that she'd be putting all their lives in great danger if she took that course of action.

After she and Ben had unloaded the supplies, she kept the boy occupied the rest of the afternoon by organizing the cupboards. But she could tell his mind was elsewhere—and likely on his father.

She continued to look in on Nash and, unfortunately, his condition seemed to worsen as the day wore on.

She opened another can of soup for dinner and after dishing out some for Ben, she took a bowl of the chicken noodle soup broth upstairs to Nash. But he wasn't conscious enough to do more than choke and cough up what she tried to spoon-feed him. Though she did get him to take another sip of water as she had done on her previous visits. But he was still burning up when she changed out one damp cloth for another.

Her inadequate nursing skills were no match for an infected bullet wound.

Mal sat back in the chair frustrated. She stared at the man, wondering who'd doctored him and who she could call on to take care of him now. But his words about trusting no one kept her in a state of indecision. "Damn it, Nash."

Despite her best efforts, or because of them, he might die.

How would she explain that to Ben? She had a hard enough time keeping him out of the bedroom without giving him false hope that his dad was getting better.

She picked up the soup bowl and headed back downstairs to find Ben sitting at the table. She put the bowl in the sink, and Ben did the same with his. And he had eaten just about as little as Nash.

"Tired?" she asked.

He shook his head. But he looked wrung out.

"How about a bath? And then I'll read you a story before bed?"

The bookshelf was filled with classics and comics. She passed over the *Harry Potter* books, which they'd already read several times at home, and picked up a copy of *The Swiss Family Robinson*.

Then she had Ben get his backpack and ushered him upstairs to the bathroom across the hall from the smaller of the two bedrooms. There were two twin beds already made up. She put her bag on one and his backpack on the other.

"Can I take a bath tomorrow?" he asked.

"I think you'll feel better if you take one to-night." She helped him sort through his few items of clothes—a sweat suit and a couple of changes of underwear and pairs of socks. She pulled out the jersey sweat suit for him to wear to bed after his bath.

Ben yawned and she relented about the bath.

He kicked off his shoes and dropped his jeans into a pile at his feet. "Leave your socks and T-shirt on under the sweats." Since they weren't sleeping in front of the fire tonight, the extra lay-ers of clothing would help keep him warm, even though she'd been running the heat since sundown to warm up the house before bed.

She'd discovered the gas-powered generator in the locked shed during her and Ben's explorations, and had read the instruction booklet cover to cover so she could operate it as needed. She planned to shut it down for the night—she simply didn't know enough about generators, even after read-ing the booklet, to feel comfortable about leaving it running overnight.

After Ben finished dressing for bed, they traipsed back across the hall to the bathroom, where he brushed his teeth and washed his face and hands. He remembered to leave a drip as she'd taught him.

Once Ben was settled, she decided she deserved a hot bath and a complete change of clothes herself.

She had already changed into the novelty T-shirt, but she still wore the slacks to her blood-stained Ann Taylor suit while the jacket hung on the back of a kitchen chair waiting for attention. The stains on her white shirt had long since dried brown, and she had that in a cold-water soak in the kitchen sink.

She had yet to unpack and inventory her own wardrobe.

Aside from her workout gear and the slutty underwear, she'd only seen a T-shirt and a pair of jeans. She hoped to hell it wasn't her skinny jeans.

They'd have to get by on a minimal wardrobe. There was a stackable washer/dryer in the kitchen next to the pantry. So at least she could do a load of laundry later tonight, because she doubted she'd get any sleep.

"Why don't you like him?" Ben asked.

They were talking about Nash. *Of course.*

"I thought you'd fallen asleep," she said. "And who says I don't like him?"

"You're mean to him."

She restrained from defending herself. In Ben's eyes she *was* being mean.

In her eyes she wasn't being mean enough. Okay, so maybe she was.

The mattress dipped as she sat beside him. "It was a lot easier to like your dad when he was with your mother. She was so beautiful that she used to light up the room and everyone in it, including your father."

"Is she really an angel?"

"Of course she's an angel."

"You said he was dead. But he wasn't really."

Mal pulled the covers back so Ben could crawl beneath them. "I did say that. Only because he was going away for a very long time and wasn't expected to return."

"But he's back now."

Mal didn't want to get Ben's hopes up in that department. "You know staying here—with Nash— is only temporary, right? We might be here awhile longer. But it's not forever. Which is why you have to keep up with your schoolwork."

He nodded. "But he can come home to live with us? You'll let him, right? If he wants to, I mean." There was a question in his voice that made it hard to answer with the absolute truth. Even before Nash had said anything, she knew they weren't ever going back home.

"Home might not be such a safe place for us right now."

"Because of the bad man."

He'd narrowed it down to the one bad man he'd seen in action. "There are bad men, but there are good men also. Do you remember who you can ask for help?" She took this moment to reinforce some stranger danger training. She wanted Ben to use caution but not be so paranoid he wouldn't ask for or accept help.

"Teachers, mothers—"

"Mothers of kids you know," she amended for him.

"Policemen, firemen…" He stopped to think for a moment. "Where's his uniform?"

Just like that, they were back to his favorite subject.

"Your dad used to wear one, but he doesn't anymore."

"How come?"

"I guess it's no longer part of his job description."

Ben mulled that over as he settled deeper into his pillow. "I think he should wear his uniform."

She once again removed Nash's ball cap that Ben had been wearing on and off all day. "You already think he wears a cape. With a big red *S* on his chest." She traced the word *Superman* on Ben's chest.

Ben squirmed and giggled until she relented. "I bet the bad man would really be afraid of him then."

"I bet you're right." She got up from the bed

and tucked the covers up to the boy's chin. "Sleep tight. Don't let the bedbugs bite."

"I decided I'm going to be a ninja for Halloween," Ben said. "Or maybe a Navy SEAL." He closed his eyes with a big grin on his face.

Mal had forgotten all about Halloween. She didn't have the heart to break it to Ben just yet that there'd be no trick-or-treating this year. So setting the adventures of the Swiss Family Robinson aside for another night, she turned out the light.

As she closed the door, she heard shuffling coming from the other room.

Mal crossed the hall and found the bed empty. "Nash?" she called out softly.

The bathroom door stood ajar and she half expected to find him passed out on the tile floor again. He stood over the toilet, lid up, braced against the back wall for support. Resting his head against his forearm, he swayed on unsteady feet.

Turning her back, she folded her arms. "Do you need any help?"

He mumbled something that sounded very much like "I think I can manage to shake my own..."

Yeah, you do that.

That's not what she was offering. She only wanted to make sure he got back to bed all right. Because she sure as hell didn't want to have to carry him again.

Mallory gave Nash plenty of time after hearing the toilet flush to pull himself together before even thinking about turning around. When she did turn around, she saw him stumble and reach for the clear plastic shower curtain, ripping it from the first few holes of its hooks.

Mal reached out and grabbed Nash to keep him from falling into the claw-foot tub. He shook her off and turned the squeaky knob for the cold water all the way to the left. The shower rained down on both their heads before he switched it to the faucet.

"Do not even think about taking off your clothes," she threatened as she slicked back her wet hair.

"Ice," he croaked out.

He dropped the plug into the tub and then slid in fully clothed.

"Ice? Is that really such a good idea?" Packing a child in ice for fevers over one hundred and four degrees was an old-school practice. She distinctly remembered Ben's pediatrician telling her that it was a bad idea when her dad had suggested it. Ben's doctor had recommended baby Motrin and then met them at the emergency room.

But Ben had been six months old at the time.

Nash was a full-grown man with a burning fever. A few ice cubes weren't going to kill him. Were they?

But a shock to his system might.

"Just do it, Mal," he ordered.

She raced downstairs and found two trays of ice in the freezer.

Grabbing Motrin from the first aid kit and a Mason jar from the cupboard, she hurried back upstairs. She had him take the pills while she released the ice into the filling bathtub.

He handed back the glass and lay back against the tub, too weak to know or care what he was doing. So why was she listening to him? Luckily, there wasn't enough ice to make that much difference in the already frigid water temperature.

Short on clean washcloths, she grabbed a hand towel and dipped it into the gully beside him. Then she plastered it to his feverish head.

He ripped it off and let the weight of the water drag it to the bottom of the tub.

"You should go," he said, weakly. "Take the boy and go. Don't make any phone calls and don't stop until you reach Coronado. Trust McCaffrey." He turned his head to look at her. "I'm sorry. I'm sorry...."

He closed his eyes and his head lulled back.

"Nash?" He'd passed out but was still breathing.

She patted his face, but he didn't respond. She grabbed him by a fistful of hair and dunked his head. Water sloshed over the side as she raised his head again. He came up with his eyes wide-open and gasping for air. "Are you trying to drown me, Mal?"

"Quit dying already and I won't have to."

Her wet T-shirt was now plastered to her chest.

She reached over and shut off the water, then pulled the plug to let it drain. While he simply passed out again.

She had no hope of getting him out of the tub and back to bed. Despite what he wanted, he needed medical attention. She'd waited all day for his fever to break, hoping he'd sweat it out.

Was it time to try OnStar and give up their location? Or maybe she could backtrack to a gas station and buy another burn phone? With what little money they had left, could they even afford one? "Where'd you hide the phone, Nash?"

But while the cold water had worked some to cool him down, he was now beyond hearing her. And for how long would his fever stay down? And she doubted all that water was good for his stitches.

The bottom line was he needed something that would combat the infection. As part of her brain assessed the situation, the other part—the practical part—urged her to listen to him. Take Ben and get the hell out of there. And go where?

Drive all the way to the SEAL base in California? Call McCaffrey? Or don't call McCaffrey?

The absolute last thing she should do is listen

to the advice of their delirious abductor. But were they safe here or was she just feeling complacent because no bad guys had followed them or come bursting through the doors—yet? No, she felt safe. This place felt safe for now.

If Nash made it through the night, *then* she'd take Ben and call for help.

If Nash made it through the night.

"Damn you, Nash. I told him you were tough. Fight. You've got to fight."

There must be somewhere she could get an antibiotic to help him fight this thing. She still hadn't figured out how he'd gotten stitched up in the first place. A doctor would have had to report the gunshot wound. He must have known somebody or he'd found somebody.... None of that mattered now anyway.

Think, think. She paced a hole in the bath mat.

If she called her doctor about a UTI or sinus infection, he wouldn't even require her to go in for a prescription. But as soon as she placed the order with a pharmacist, it would be traceable.

Too risky.

But there was a doctor right up the road—a horse doctor.

The veterinarian probably had drugs on the premises.

If she left now...

She'd be leaving Ben and Nash alone. Unprotected.

No—they were safe here. But with her luck Ben would wake up scared and alone.

It was, what, a mile up the road? She could run there and then back in twenty minutes. Ben was likely out until morning. But she could leave him a note just in case he woke up. And Nash? They'd probably be better off if he did drown. Then why go after medicine to help him? Why not just shove his head under the water now and be done with it?

Because she could no more drown him than she could shoot him. Like he'd said she wasn't a cold-blooded killer. Plus, there were too many unanswered questions. Not to mention that he was a protected witness and she'd taken him into custody so technically it was her job to protect him.

Guilt made her feet move faster.

She scribbled Ben a note with a crayon and piece of paper from one of his notebooks and left it on the kitchen table. She opened up the mini flashlight, shoved some batteries in it and found an eyeglass repair kit in one of the kitchen drawers. Perfect. The tiny screwdrivers reminded her of lock picks—which she knew how to use—so she took it with her.

It was now ten minutes to ten.

With any luck she'd be back by ten-thirty—eleven at the latest.

She put her suit jacket back on and grabbed the peacoat hanging by the door.

A men's wool peacoat. Navy-issue. The name stenciled inside read Calhoun. Nash said he didn't know who lived here—that he'd never been here before. But how much of a coincidence was that?

She wrapped a scarf around her neck, found a knit beanie and gloves in the pockets and put those on. She left the house wishing she'd changed into dryer clothes. It was cold outside and she was all wet.

She strode past the Tahoe, up to the main dirt road and then kicked it into a run. She couldn't take the Tahoe and risk the headlights being seen or the crunch of tires being heard.

But if she got caught anyway, she'd just flash the badge in her jacket pocket and then take it from there.

As she ran it started to snow.

Big wet flakes of white appeared like glitter in the moonlight.

Mal turned up her collar and upped her pace as she turned left down the gravel road. In the right gear, it could have been a nice run. As it was, she was too aware of the gun in its holster and of Ben and Nash alone in the cabin without her protection to take any enjoyment from the physical activity.

Though it was unlikely they'd been followed, it was still a major concern. Despite all her comforting words to Ben today.

Which was why she had to get Nash back on his feet.

The truth was she was scared. And every little sound in the mostly deserted night made her feel skittish. She could see her breath out in front of her face, and the sound of her own breathing seemed overly loud in her ears.

She ran toward the veterinary clinic as if her life depended on it.

Because three lives did.

At the academy she'd been clocked in at under the five-minute mark for a mile. She could run a competitive 5K in under fifteen minutes. To her best guestimate she'd been running at least that long.

Which meant she'd either passed the clinic in the dark or it was farther up the road than she'd realized. Still no clinic in sight.

It was another fifteen minutes or so before she saw the light in the distance.

The porch light was on. As she neared the building, she saw a Rock Springs Sheriff's car parked out front.

"Great." Mal ducked behind some bushes to wait out the law.

NASH CLAWED HIS way to the surface of his dream.

He was diving with his team. One minute the guys were there and the next they weren't. His tank was running out of oxygen. And he was choking from the lack of air.

It wasn't exactly a real mission. More a compilation of many missions and many dreams. And in all of them he was running out of time.

He'd just returned home from one of those many missions. Cara was there waiting for him with the news he was going to be a father. He'd been both excited and overwhelmed by the news. Worry was etched around his wife's smile as she told him they were going to be parents. How much that had meant to her. And how much it would mean to her if he'd just quit the Teams. So he'd be around to help raise their child.

He should have just quit the Teams. He should have given her that at least.

Why hadn't he just walked away when she'd asked him to? If he had, then Cara would still be alive.

All his fault. All his fault.

Nash sat up gasping for air. Slicking back his hair, he sat there a moment trying to orient himself to his surroundings. The water was so cold—he was so cold—that his teeth chattered. What the hell was he doing in the bathtub with his clothes on? And how long had he been there? The plug was dangling by a chain outside of the tub.

But a sopping-wet towel was blocking the drain. He yanked it free.

His balls were blue and tucked up tight against his body. He sure as hell couldn't feel them anymore. He swiped a hand across his face and pushed himself to his feet. How could he not remember getting in the tub?

Pretty much the last thing he remembered was Mal helping him off the floor of the gas station bathroom. And then sitting across from her in the dark.

These were his first lucid thoughts in…in he didn't know how long.

He stepped into the bedroom. The numbers on the clock by the bed were little more than a blur until the glowing red numbers rolled over from 01:11 to 01:12. A.m., he assumed from the pitch-darkness outside. The house was quiet, too quiet in his opinion. He left the master bedroom and had a peek inside the other bedroom.

Ben was sound asleep. Assuming Mal had fallen asleep on the couch, he headed downstairs to check on her next. She wasn't on the couch— or anywhere downstairs that he could see.

Or even anywhere in the house.

He stepped out on the porch. The Tahoe was still there. He ran a quick check around the outside of the house and then staggered back inside. His gut felt as though the lead slug had never left his body.

The ashes in the fireplace were cold by hours.

He realized then that he didn't have a weapon or even the keys to open the gun cabinet. Worry started to set in, and then he found a note on the kitchen table. "I'll be back. Love, Mom."

Where the hell had she gone?

The door opened just as he lowered the note. He stepped back in the dark and watched as Mal removed the peacoat and unwrapped the scarf from her neck, then hung them both on the rack by the door.

"Where the hell have you been?"

She jumped and put a hand on her chest. "Don't scare me like that."

"Is there a reason you're sneaking in after curfew?"

"I didn't know we had a curfew." She reached into her jacket pocket and tossed him a bottle of prescription pills. Which he fumbled. "You're welcome. Is Ben still asleep?" She joined him at the kitchen table in the small space between the kitchen and the living area.

"He's fine." Nash glanced at the label. "I'm not a horse."

"Then take half. It rhymes with penicillin. It's an antibiotic. I'm going to go check on Ben." She grabbed the ladder-back chair and made no move to head upstairs. "FYI, the veterinarian up the road is more than five miles, each way."

"Where else did you go?"

"Nowhere. Why? I thought you trusted me."

He fisted the bottle of pills in his hand. "The vet is going to miss these."

"Maybe, maybe not. There's fresh snow covering my tracks. By the time he wakes up in the morning, there'll be no sign I was ever there. If he misses them, he'll have a mystery on his hands."

"The thing about mysteries," Nash said, "is that people like to solve them. What if he calls the local sheriff?"

She scrunched her face. He couldn't quite make out the meaning of her expression in the dark. "I don't think he's going to, but if he does, I'm pretty sure the local law has better things to do than going door to door asking if anyone knows anything about a few missing antibiotics anyway?"

"Let's hope so. Otherwise you wasted your time and risked exposing us."

"Yeah, well." She patted the chair rung and then turned to leave. "Thank me later when you don't die from infection."

Her shadowy figure started swimming before his eyes. "Mal," he called out softly. So softly he didn't think she could possibly have heard him.

Except she was there by his side in an instant and caught him before he hit the floor.

"Jesus, Nash. You're still soaking wet."

"What do you expect?" His teeth chattered. "You left me to drown in a tub of cold water."

She slipped his arm around her shoulders. "You're not that easy to kill."

She'd said it with sarcasm. But for all her tough words, he searched her eyes for their deeper meaning. She might hate him. She might even wish him dead. But she was still Mal. They still shared a history that had been full of love and laughter and friendship. And sorrow.

She would not let him down.

Not the way he was letting her down right this minute.

He felt weak as a newborn babe as she helped him to the couch. He was about to throw himself down on it when she made a sound at the back of her throat to stop him.

"Huh-uh." She grabbed his wet T-shirt by the hem up and peeled it over his head. Too numb to argue, he raised heavy limbs and allowed her to strip his shirt in much the same manner she might have undressed Ben. She tossed his wet rag of a T-shirt toward the unlit hearth. It slapped against the cold brick. Without a fire to ward off the chill, the air inside was almost as cold as it was outside.

He huddled there in the cold and moonlit darkness.

His labored breathing took form in the puffs of air. He could feel the heat radiating from Mal's body, and sheer survival instinct moved him toward it before a much stronger instinct, also born of survival, made him take a step back. "I need to build a fire."

"I'll get it," she said. "Get those wet jeans off. And then under the covers."

She built a fire while he stripped out of his jeans and shorts. He left them both in a puddle by the couch while he slipped his shivering body under the afghan and then pulled the blanket up over his shoulders. Instead of closing his eyes, however, he found himself staring at Mal's silhouette.

"I'd feel better if I had a handgun close," he said.

"They're right where you left them."

That's right. He'd locked up all the firearms before going to take a shower because of Ben. He could tell she was correct about the boy being too curious for his own good. "But you took the key."

"I'll get it for you."

She wasn't supposed to be taking care of him. He was the one who was supposed to be taking care of her and Ben. But he allowed her this, allowed himself this because he had to build up his strength or he'd be no good to anyone. They were relatively safe here, but that didn't mean he should let his guard down so completely he couldn't protect them—though it did mean he could relax a bit and let Mal take charge when she needed to. When he needed her to.

Mal was a strong, capable woman.

"I take it I've been out all day? It has only been one day, right?"

She nodded.

"How's Ben handling things?"

"He's seven." She poked at the fire. "He shouldn't have to be handling any of this."

Even as a young girl she'd had a strength, a mental toughness, that her sister hadn't possessed.

The fire picked up the red in her hair and turned it to flame. She'd pulled her straight hair back into a slick ponytail at some point, but a few of those escaped wisps were starting to curl.

She put the poker down, and when she turned she spotted his pile of clothes on the floor.

"Tsk." She stooped to pick them up. "Now I know where Ben gets it from."

She laid his clothes out across the brick and then turned back to face him. "I'll get you your gun. And some water so you can take at least one of the pills I brought back. And you should probably let me have a look at your side. I'm sure your soak in the tub didn't do your stitches much good."

"I'm fine."

She rubbed the back of her neck. "I grabbed something for pain if you need it."

"Enough about me—what about you? How's your head?"

"Probably concussed." She disappeared from his line of vision. Her voice carried from the entry hall. He heard the opening and closing of a drawer. "I woke up with a splitting headache." She handed the Glock over as she circled around to the kitchen.

He pushed it beneath the couch cushion.

This time he heard running water and she returned with the first aid kit tucked beneath her arm and a glass of cold tap water in her hand. He opened the horse pills and didn't bother breaking the huge tablet in two.

"Down the hatch," she said, extending the water glass toward him.

Penicillin was penicillin, after all—he'd scrounged worse.

Then she unceremoniously peeled back the blanket and cut away the bandage that had been wrapped around his midsection. The rest of his stitches had all but dissolved. The skin was white and puckered where his wound wasn't angry red and oozing.

She dabbed at the area with an alcohol wipe.

He clenched down on his back teeth. "Give a guy some warning next time."

She offered a Cheshire-cat-size grin with just as much sincerity. "This looks professional," she said, applying butterfly strips to make up for the missing sutures.

"Professional enough."

She taped a gauze bandage over the whole mess with equal efficiency.

He shifted uncomfortably as she smoothed the tape across the flat of his abdomen and then around his side. Then she gathered the trash and placed it on the coffee table next to the first aid kit.

She braced her hands on the couch.

"Come here." Before she could push herself up, he had a hand tangled in her hair and was pulling her back down. He saw the confusion on her face as he felt for the knot at the back of her head and then found it.

She winced and whimpered as he massaged around the lump. The tightness around her mouth eased. "Don't do that," she protested.

He didn't stop. "Why not?"

"Because it feels good."

But she didn't pull away and he kept on making her feel good.

"It's okay, Mal." He pulled her head down to rest on his chest. "Relax. You doctored me. Let me doctor you." He continued murmuring soothing words as he massaged her scalp. "Rest is the best medicine. We both need to quit fighting and get some."

CHAPTER TEN

MAL WOKE UP the next morning with her face in a puddle of drool and staring at a black ski mask. She jerked her head up from Nash's bare chest. The pint-size intruder stared back at her. "Ben, what are you doing?"

He lifted the mask. "Shhh, I'm not Ben. I'm a ninja." And with that he pulled the mask back down again and tiptoed his way to the kitchen.

Mal wiped the drool from her mouth. Swiped at the puddle on Nash's chest but decided she was better off letting sleeping dogs lie and pushed to her feet from where she'd fallen asleep sitting on the floor.

Her hair had fallen free from its band. She found the colorful band in the carpet at her feet. Despite the chill, heat infused her cheeks. The last thing she remembered was Nash massaging her scalp and then feeling completely relaxed. Even her headache was gone.

Mal rolled her neck, checking for any residual pain. But the only residual anything she felt was the tingle to her scalp as she remembered Nash entangling his hand in her hair. When he'd pulled her down by the hair, she actually thought he was going to kiss her. A rough, demanding kiss full of passion.

And she hadn't done anything to resist.

His lips had been parted and he'd had that unmistakable dreamy-eyed look about him. But while his eyes were glazed with fever and not lust, she'd been anticipating something else—a forbidden kiss. And why was that?

Maybe because she'd been so happy to see him up and about that she didn't even care that he was surly with her. And her outing last night hadn't gone exactly as planned. She'd waited for what seemed like hours for the sheriff's SUV to leave and was beginning to think the sheriff actually lived there by the time the young female sheriff did leave. And then Mal had distinctly heard, "Good night, Grandpa."

Mal had weighed the options of exposing herself.

There was either help right in front of her—or trouble.

In the end she'd had second thoughts about stealing the drugs. But desperate times called for desperate measures. And she'd been very careful to take only what Nash might need, and only took bottles from the back of the cabinet. In retrospect she should have taken only the pills and left the bottles.

Talk about your dumb criminal. Just because she'd known how to pick a lock from the Academy didn't mean she knew what she was doing when it came to breaking and entering.

She glanced at Nash passed out on the couch. That wasn't her drool on his chest. From the look of his glistening muscles, he'd cycled through chills and fever to sweat again. But this time he'd regained his color. That was a good sign.

The fact that she hadn't been sprawled out in her own drool, but in his sweat, should somehow be a lot more disturbing than it was. She gathered the trash from the coffee table.

She felt much more normal as she made her way to the small kitchen. She felt rested, relaxed—despite sleeping while sitting up. It was Sunday. Nash had abducted them on Friday. They'd made it through two nights.

She appeared to have all her faculties about her. And no one was knocking down the door. The excess adrenaline she'd been running on had finally left her body and she no longer felt as if she were wound tight enough to explode.

"Huh-uh." She took the bag of Cheetos from Ben. "Ninjas do not eat junk. We're having a normal breakfast today. Remove your mask at the table please."

He pushed the mask to the top of his head. She whisked it off the rest of the way and set it beside him on the kitchen table. Though she and Ben had unloaded supplies from the Tahoe to the pantry yesterday, she hadn't inventoried them at the time but knew she'd seen cereal and milk.

Mal poured two bowls of Honey Nut Cheerios and then opened a box of milk.

"I don't like milk from a box," Ben said as she poured from the unfamiliar carton into his bowl.

"You haven't even tried it." She added milk to her own bowl, but Ben didn't budge. "Nash must like milk from a box. He bought it."

More than likely he'd bought it for the shelf life and the fact that it didn't need refrigeration until after it was opened. But it was enough motivation to get Ben eating his breakfast.

After breakfast, she went out and checked on the generator, which had shut itself off during the night—which was good since she'd fallen asleep before doing so. It looked as though the home-owner had it running on a timer. The booklet had said they'd get about sixteen hours for every five gallons with all the lights on and everything in the house running. She didn't know how much fuel they'd started out with, only that they had twenty gallons left, which meant they had to conserve.

They barely had enough hot water for a shower, so she used the hall bathroom with its intact shower curtain and cleaned up as quickly as possible. Then she changed into clean underwear and jeans along with her Eagle T-shirt. She found a men's flannel shirt in the master bedroom's closet and put that on over her T-shirt.

She towel-dried her hair, but didn't bother with the blow-dryer that she'd found in one of the bathrooms. Not only would it be a waste of energy, but it would fry her naturally curly hair. And with no straight iron on hand, she had to be satisfied with simply finger-combing product through her hair and hoping that it wouldn't frizz as it dried. Not that grooming was her main priority right now anyway.

She bound downstairs only to slow down about halfway there.

Nash stood in the middle of the living room with the afghan wrapped around his waist. He turned and caught her staring at him.

And in turn stared back at her. "I was wondering where all those curls had gone."

"Well, they're back. And wet."

"Yeah, so are my jeans. And they're the only ones I've got." He picked them up from beside the fireplace.

"I could crank up the generator and toss them in the dryer," she offered.

"I'll live."

Well, he certainly looked better than yesterday. If not a little worse for wear.

"There might be something upstairs in one of the drawers that you could wear." She lighted down the rest of the stairs. Picking up the Gas and Go bag from the bench beneath the stairs, she tossed it to him. "At least you'll have a dry T-shirt."

NASH FOUND A pair of men's jeans in a dresser drawer. He could use a belt, but it was just as well the jeans hung low on his hips and away from his bandaged wound. He tucked the Glock to his back, then downed a couple of over-the-counter pain relievers and another horse pill.

Ben wore a ski mask and peered up at him from the stair rails as Nash headed back downstairs. "A little young for a life of crime, there, Ben."

He lifted the ski mask. "I'm a ninja." Then he pulled it back down and raced past him up the stairs.

Mal came in through the front door, kicking the snow off her sneakers and carrying a load of firewood. "Here, let me help," he offered.

She handed him one log and continued past him to the fireplace, where she stacked the rest. "Where's the burn phone?"

Nash threw his log on the fire. "I tossed it in

your gym bag." He'd carried her gym bag from the car to the house the night they arrived.

"It's not in there." Mal got a strange look on her face and walked over to the foot of the stairs. "Ben, do you have the phone?"

He poked his head around the corner at the top of the stairs. "Maybe."

"Bring it to me please."

Ben disappeared back around the corner. Nash envisioned having to relocate them until Ben appeared with the phone still in the package and handed it to Mal. "You said you'd get me a new phone."

"And I will," she promised. "But this is not the one."

"I'll take that." Nash relieved her of the phone. He was surprised she didn't put up a fuss. Clearly the dynamics had changed since their arrival.

Ben made his way down the rest of the stairs. He'd changed shirt since their first encounter that morning. He was now wearing the same gray Eagle, Colorado, T-shirt they all wore. "Well, isn't this the family photo op?" Nash said.

Mal caught on to his comment and looked a little misty-eyed as she rushed from the room. "Excuse me."

Nash followed her into the kitchen under the pretense of grabbing a protein bar. "Did I say something wrong, Mal?" he asked, half expecting her to call him an insensitive jerk.

"No." She shook her head and turned to face him with arms crossed. "I just need to know your plan."

"The plan is to lie low here until the trial." He peeled back the wrapper on his breakfast. "I assume you're okay with that."

"Have you been undercover in the Middle East this whole time?"

Here came the questions. "For the most part."

"And now the members of this terrorist cell know your real name?"

He nodded.

"And they know about Ben?" she asked.

He held her gaze, and there were no words necessary.

"What about your mom? Does she know you're alive?"

"No, but if all goes well she should be well on her way to visiting family in Israel right now." He hoped. He tore off a bite of the protein bar. It had been a hard choice being so close and not going there to ensure his mom's safety himself—but one he'd thought any parent would understand. His first responsibility was to Ben.

He noticed Mal hadn't asked about herself. She was in just as much danger as Ben or his mom, no matter how tenuous their connection.

"We're safe here for the time being," he said, wanting to reassure her. "Just set aside any plans you have to turn me over early. I'm going in on my own terms."

"What happens after the trial?"

"I think you know. You and Ben will enter the witness protection program." Otherwise known as the Witness Security Program, WitSec. As a protected witness, he was also entitled to protection for his family.

"I'm never going to see my dad again?"

It was a rhetorical question and he didn't bother answering. It would be hard, but not impossible, for her and Ben to leave loved ones behind. That's why their relationship with his own mother only added another wrinkle. It was unlikely she'd be entering the program with Mal and Ben, either. "I was sorry to hear about your mom, Mal."

"She overdosed. For a long time I blamed you. I've blamed you for a lot of things, Nash."

"Then I'll just have to hope you're a lot closer to forgiving me than you were seven years ago."

"You really found Cara's killer?" There was that hint of disbelief in her voice that told him she still had not separated him from her sister's murderer.

"I found the man who ordered the hit and discovered his motive. Conspiracy to commit murder is just one count among his many other crimes. His ties to terrorism will mean he never sees daylight again." Nash had uncovered enough garbage to see that Mullah Kahn never dug himself out of prison.

"And what about you?" she asked.

"You and Ben will be safe. I'll see to it," he said, deliberately ignoring Mal's last question.

IT TOOK MAL three more days to come to terms with the fact that they had no recourse except to enter the Witness Security Program. Though she'd noticed Nash had not included himself in that little scenario.

There'd be no going back to their old life after this.

The three of them had developed a routine of sorts revolving around breakfast, lunch and dinner.

She and Ben would tackle homework between breakfast and lunch while Nash took one of the hunting rifles and went for a walk. But she knew he wasn't hunting, because they had plenty to eat and he never returned with any small game.

In any case, there was also the issue of the different hunting seasons and licenses required for each. And Nash was not going to draw attention to himself by illegally catching game.

After lunch he'd split logs and haul wood while she and Ben got their outdoor exercise. It hadn't snowed since Sunday night and it was still quite nice out during their midday breaks.

She and Ben had just finished their half-mile hike when Ben hauled out the little pedal cart they'd found in the shed. Mal took the opportunity to sit down on the front stoop, while Nash stood off to the side splitting logs. He made it look easy. Place a log end up on the tree stump and then drop the ax, splitting the log in a single swing.

But she winced every time he hauled back and dropped that ax. Even though he brought it down single-handed, that couldn't feel good on his injured side.

"Mind if I give it a try?" She pushed herself up from the stoop.

He removed his work gloves and waited for her to put them on and then extended the ax and even placed the first log for her.

She tested the weight of the ax in her hand. While it wasn't that heavy, there was no way she was going to swing it single-handedly. She brought it overhead two-handed.

"Whoa, whoa, whoa—" Nash stopped her from taking a swing. "You're going to cut yourself in two on the follow-through if you hold it like that."

She repositioned the ax.

"Not so high."

She brought it down and took her first swing. The ax embedded itself in the log. She tried to pull it out but couldn't. Nash used his boot to brace the log against the ground and then removed the ax.

He handed it back and replaced the log on the stump again. "Put your shoulder into it."

She did and wound up with an uneven split. But a split nonetheless.

She split three more logs on the second swing without his help before she got the mechanics of it down and split a log on a single swing. Ben even stopped to watch. By the time she'd split a dozen logs, she was ready to turn the chore back over to Nash and she had a new appreciation for central heating.

In keeping with their daily routine, in the late afternoon, just before sundown, Nash would start up the generator for a couple of hours and the three of them would crowd into the kitchen. One of them would start a load of laundry while the other got to work on dinner. Ben would try and be helpful to the best of his ability. Tonight Nash was making chicken chili from canned ingredients while Ben helped her measure out laundry detergent.

After dinner, she tried to keep Ben busy in an activity with her, but he preferred to shadow Nash in his ninja mask. But always from a distance.

Every morning and every evening, Nash rolled up her yoga mat and tucked it into the wicker basket next to the fireplace. They both used it.

Mallory didn't mind that he used her yoga mat twice a day as much as she minded the prejudice she felt when he pointed that mat northeast for what he called morning and evening meditation.

Whatever he was doing, it wasn't downward-facing dog and it made her uncomfortable. Uncomfortable because he'd never again be the boy who sat at their Easter table and shocked the rest of the Ward family by politely refusing ham, or the man who'd argued with her sister over circumcision and baptism before Ben was even born.

As a result, Ben was both circumcised in the Jewish faith according to Nash's wishes and later, when Mallory was awarded custody, baptized in the Catholic faith in accordance with her sister's wishes. Which was probably exactly how things would have played out had Cara lived. Regardless of whether or not Nash and Cara had gotten back together.

Of course they would have gotten back together.

Since they hadn't even been separated a week before Cara was murdered, it was hard to think of them as anything *but* together.

If Nash was embracing a new religion or culture, she wanted to believe she was more open-minded than to judge him for it—she wanted to believe she was more open-minded period.

She kept hearing Stan's voice. *"It's not unheard of for these guys to turn rogue."*

Nash wasn't rogue.

After dinner Nash sat at the table and read from a stack of old newspapers the homeowner had accumulated and left stacked by the fireplace. She didn't know if he was reading them out of boredom or to catch up on months' or even years' worth of news he'd missed. She'd finished several romance novels herself. Sometimes she'd wake up in the morning and find the newspaper open to a finished or half-finished crossword puzzle. So she knew he stayed awake most nights while she and Ben slept.

When he did sleep, it was in short naps during the day and only while she was up.

They kept their firearms on them at all times and the key on top of the gun cabinet in easy reach of the adults. Most mornings he disappeared for hours on end with a rifle and binoculars.

She glanced over and saw Ben on the chair next to Nash holding up his arm next to his father's. He seemed to be comparing skin tones, which were a similar tan. Then Ben looked at her pale skin and back again to his father's.

"Can I be excused?" Ben asked.

Mal nodded.

"Not so fast." Nash tilted his head toward the sink. "Your plate."

Ben picked up his bowl and walked it over to the sink. He even rinsed it off and put it in the dish drainer. Then he walked back to Nash. "You can play my Nintendo DS if you want."

"No, thanks." Nash barely glanced up from his paper.

"Do you want to play a game of Sorry with me?"

Nash folded his newspaper. "Maybe later."

"Do you, Mom?"

Nash got up from the table.

"Of course." Mal picked up her bowl and walked to the sink. "After we do some schoolwork. Why don't you run upstairs and get your backpack?"

Ben raced upstairs. He was bored and she couldn't blame him.

She noticed Nash putting on one of the heavier coats from the rack. Apparently it was time for another perimeter check.

While Nash was outside, she and Ben spent half an hour together on math and then she put him to work making flash cards with some old index cards she'd found in a junk drawer. He was smart, but she was worried about him falling behind on his lessons.

"I don't think he likes it when I call you Mom,"

Ben said later as they were setting up in front of the fireplace for a game of Sorry.

"Too bad," Mal said, though she should have been more diplomatic.

"Would it be okay if I called you Aunt Mal?"

Mal opened her mouth. But nothing came out.

CHAPTER ELEVEN

MALLORY WENT OUT onto the snow-covered back deck having noticed that Nash had returned. "You're unbelievable."

He glanced over his shoulder at her.

"You kidnap us at gunpoint."

"I've never pointed a gun at you or the boy, Mal."

"You didn't give a damn whether or not we wanted to go with you or not. So here we are for who knows how long. The least you can do is listen to your son when he's talking to you."

"I hear more than you give me credit for."

"You walk away every time Ben opens his mouth. After your missing the first seven, almost eight, years of his life, this is your chance to get to know him and for him to get to know you."

"It's best if the boy doesn't get too attached."

"What the hell is that supposed to mean?"

"You know where this is going, Mal. We go our separate ways after the trial. I wasn't part of the boy's past and I won't be a part of his future. All I care about is that he has a future."

"Yeah, well, as you're walking away, Nash, you might want to think about what kind of memories you're leaving behind. Because he's going to remember you—remember this." She spread her arms to encompass both space and time. "And you can bet that if I knew I only had two weeks to spend with Ben, or my sister, or my mother or my father, I wouldn't spend it putting distance between us. He's already attached, Nash. He's already missing you. The person you're trying to protect is yourself."

She stormed off and left him standing on the deck.

Nash caught a glimpse of Ben in the back bedroom window. The boy ducked out of sight. Mal was right. The only heart he was trying to protect here was his own. He kept his distance from the boy because that was the only way he was going to be able to survive leaving him again. And make no mistake, he'd have to leave his son. For years he'd survived with the single-minded focus of catching Cara's killer.

And Ben was the price he'd paid for these past seven years. Was it worth it? Was it what Cara would have wanted for their son?

He'd wanted justice for Cara, for Ben. For himself. But no maybe about it, he'd let finding her killer and clearing his name take over his life.

Ben and Mal did not need him in their lives.

He could have told her the truth. But maybe it was easier this way. Easier to let them go if they weren't holding on.

THE DAYS WERE growing shorter and the nights longer. And Mal was growing restless. Had they only been here a week? Nash put his arm through the winter coat. "Would you like to come with me today, Ben?"

Ben looked up from the breakfast table and then at Mal.

"Where exactly?" she asked.

He shrugged. "Check some things out."

"Do you think that's such a good idea, Nash?"

"It was your idea, Mal."

"Yeah, well, it's cold. He's not going to be able to keep up with you."

"I'm sure we can find something here that fits. And we'll take one of the snowmobiles." He grabbed the keys from the rack. "What do you say, Ben?"

"Please, can I?" He hurried to set his bowl in the sink.

Mal didn't think it was the smartest idea. When Nash headed out, he went armed. He was keeping an eye on the perimeter and looking for disturbances. All because of the very real danger of being discovered—either accidentally by someone who knew they shouldn't be there or intentionally by someone—the bad guys—looking for them.

So far they'd been lucky. But what if today was the day their luck ran out?

Except was Ben really any safer indoors with her than outdoors with his father? And she was the one who'd insisted Nash spend time with Ben. "I guess it would be okay."

Nash helped Ben find a heavy down vest and gloves that fit. Mal insisted he put another jacket on over it and found him a knit beanie to wear.

MAL ANXIOUSLY WAITED for Nash and Ben to return. She kept herself busy tidying up the cabin. And then herself. It was almost dinnertime, so she decided to experiment with something other than just opening a can of soup tonight.

By the time she was done making dinner, they'd be home. Sure enough, just as she was putting the finishing touches on the meal, she heard the sound of a snowmobile headed toward the shed. She checked outside just to make sure it was Nash and Ben and then ducked back into the kitchen so they wouldn't think she'd spent this whole time worrying about them. Nash and Ben came through the front door stomping snow from their boots and laughing.

"Something smells good," Nash commented as he hung up his coat.

"I've been experimenting."

Ben peeled off his coat and boots and then ran up to her excitedly.

"We saw a couple of deer. And a real mountain lion and everything."

"Mountain lion?"

"He wasn't very big, though," Ben said thoughtfully. "They don't like to eat people. But maybe sometimes if they're really hungry they might try to eat people. Right?" Ben turned to look over his shoulder at his father.

Mal looked over Ben's head to Nash. He looked at her sheepishly and shrugged.

"Sounds exciting," she said.

"I learned how to track a deer and tell if it's running or walking. Oh, and do you know how to cover your tracks?" He kept going before she could even shake her head no. "You walk backward and then you brush a branch over the snow." He demonstrated by waving his hand back and forth. "And then we trapped a bunny. But I did *not* want to eat him, so we couldn't bring him home. 'Cause bunnies don't like to live in cages. But maybe if I was really hungry I would eat him. Maybe, I don't know. Mountain lions eat bunnies because they do not think they're cute. They think they're dinner. And coyotes and foxes eat bunnies, too."

"How about canned pork burritos? Do little boys eat those?"

Ben nodded enthusiastically. "I'm starved. Just not enough to eat a bunny," he added.

"How about grown men?" she asked Nash as he stepped into the small kitchen.

"Sounds like a lot less work than skinning a rabbit. On my part, at least."

Still glowing from the acknowledgment, Mal let the men wait on her as they set up the intimate dinner for three and then ate at the coffee table in front of the fire. When they were almost done, Ben grabbed a board game, which she helped him set up while Nash read the instructions out loud.

Funny how he didn't miss his video games at all.

"I don't like this game," Ben said after being awarded triplets in the game of Life.

Nash reached over and scuffed his head. "But maybe you'll play it as you get older. Everyone does."

"It's your bedtime anyway." Mal pushed up from the floor and grabbed the bowl of popcorn from the square coffee table. A fire crackled in the fireplace.

"I don't see why I have to have a bedtime."

"It's ten o'clock. Well past your normal bedtime. Which is when…?" she prompted.

"Eight on school nights, nine on Friday and Saturday."

"So what are you complaining about?" Nash asked.

"Nothing."

"Then help me put away this game," Nash said to his son.

"Ben, after you're done helping, go on upstairs and get ready for bed. I'll be up to tuck you in later."

"Can my dad tuck me in?"

Mal glanced at Nash. Her throat tightened around her response. "Sure."

Nash nodded and Ben rushed upstairs. Mal made her way to the kitchen. It was nothing to get upset about. She'd wanted them to bond. Just not at the expense of her bond with Ben. He'd started calling her Aunt Mal and now Nash was no longer "him" or "he," but "Dad."

Nash put the game box back where it belonged and then added another log to the fire. The house got pretty cold at night, and they only ran the generator for a few hours every day. And now that he was feeling better, he was usually up to keep both going.

"By tucking in, he means reading him a story." She wrapped her arms around herself.

"I got it," he said. "I'm just going to take a look

around outside and then I'll see to it that he gets tucked in. That is, if you don't mind."

"Why would I mind?" She did not mean to snap.

"You sound like you mind."

She tilted her chin. Honestly, she didn't mind. She reminded herself again that it had been her idea for Nash and Ben to spend time together in the first place. But maybe since they'd spent the day having fun together, she'd found herself looking forward to a little of that fun spilling over into the evening.

She tried not to feel hurt or threatened by the fact that Ben preferred his father's company to hers. Nash was a shiny new toy. And long after he was gone, Ben would still have her. His Aunt Mal.

He had simply been too exhausted by the day's excursion to have the patience for a board game. And now he wanted his father to read him a bedtime story. No big deal. It was a good thing.

"You know he talked about you nonstop today. You got to hear stories of mountain lions, but I got to hear stories of Aunt Mal. We're all struggling with new dynamics here. Ben most of all."

"Thank you, Nash." Her voice sounded rough and she had to concentrate to clear it.

He nodded. She didn't know which one of them her sincerity surprised the most.

CHAPTER TWELVE

NASH MADE A wide circle around the house and garage. Checked the generator and locked up the shed for the night. And then walked as far as the main dirt road. No fresh tracks in the snow other than his own.

He turned back to the house and after hanging up his coat and putting away the rifle, he made his way up the stairs to tuck in Ben.

He still had his handgun, but then he always carried it—that was just a fact of life.

Ben was sitting up in bed with a book in his lap. "Aunt Mal started this one."

Nash took the copy of *The Swiss Family Robinson* and Ben scooted over to make some room for him to sit. "Where'd you leave off?"

"Chapter six. Aunt Mal read chapter five last. We're reading one chapter a night."

"Okay." Nash opened the book to chapter six.

"Can you do voices? Aunt Mal does voices sometimes."

"Your aunt Mal does, huh?" Nash cleared his throat and held his place in the book. "You know,

Ben, it's okay with me if you go back to calling your aunt Mal Mom. You know what adoption is, right?"

He looked down and plucked imaginary fuzz from the blanket. "It's when your mom goes to heaven, and your dad goes to war, and then your aunt Mal takes care of you."

Close enough. "She takes really good care of you, doesn't she?"

"I guess. Yes," he amended when Nash held his gaze until Ben looked him in the eye. "I just don't want to call her my mom anymore."

"The thing is, I think she wants you to…and I want you to. She's taken very good care of you and she's going to continue to take very good care of you. That sounds like a mother to me."

"I wish I had my real mom."

"That's something we all wish, Ben."

"Maybe my real mom will come back."

"No." Nash shook his head. "That's not going to happen."

"But maybe. Aunt Mal said you were dead and then you came back."

"I did not come back from the dead, though."

"'Cause Aunt Mal lied. That's why I don't like her to be my mom anymore."

"So you're mad at her?"

Ben's lower lip quivered as he sniffed back tears. Nash scooted Ben over on the twin mattress to make room for himself. He sat back against the headboard with his long legs stretched out in front of him. "Come here." He pulled his son to his side. "It's wrong to punish someone you love just because you're mad at them. Your aunt Mal is not the reason your mom is gone. She didn't really lie to you—she was just trying to protect you from the truth."

Ben looked up at him with so much trust behind the tears welling in his eyes.

Nash knew he had to get this right. "How old are you now, seven, almost eight? Seven is not a baby, right?"

A smile broke through the tears. "No, I'm not a baby."

Still too young to hear the whole truth, but this was probably Nash's only chance to have a heart-to-heart with his son. Mal was right about the lasting impressions. How to make him understand? He took a deep breath. "There are people who think I'm a bad man who hurt your mom—"

"But maybe you didn't."

"No, you're right, I did *not*. But I had to go away for a while and I wasn't supposed to come back, ever—that was part of the deal." He lifted Ben's chin. "I went away mad. I wanted to hurt the people who'd hurt your mom. Except not only did that take me away from you, but I realize now that it also meant you'd never know the truth. That when you got older you might even believe what you heard or read about me. And I didn't want that for you. For either of us."

Ben was looking a little confused.

"I changed my mission from hurting people to clearing my name. Because that's what your mom would have wanted. Always remember you were born Benjamin Nash. And that's something to be proud of. So, do you think you could change your mission from hurting your aunt to making me proud? I chose her especially for you. I think it would make your real mom really happy to know the two of you had each other. It's not an either/or, Ben. We have room in our hearts to love as many people as we want."

He could see the cogs turning in Ben's brain. "You'd still be my dad?"

"I will still be your father no matter what."

"Is this going to be our house?"

"No, we're only here for a short time."

"I like it here," Ben said.

"I like it here, too."

"I wish this could be our house."

"THIS IS STUPID." Ben crawled down from the chair he'd been kneeling on in the kitchen. "I don't want to make any more of this stuff."

Mal had found a big bottle of white school glue and had been trying to distract him with an old

Silly Putty recipe she'd found in the junk drawer.
The recipe was simple: two parts glue to one part
laundry detergent. Liquid or powder. It didn't matter.

They'd made several batches of both.

Unfortunately they didn't have any food coloring, so they were left with unappealing white
blobs. And Ben wasn't all that interested in playing with those big white blobs. He kept looking
out the front window waiting for Nash to return.
Finally he settled on the couch with his Nintendo
DS and his current favorite video game.

She noticed that he hadn't put his ninja mask on
even though today was Halloween. He'd been in a
bad mood all morning despite the fact that she'd
let him off the hook for schoolwork.

He was probably just now realizing he was
going to miss out on trick-or-treating.

Nash came in through the back door and into
the kitchen, kicking snow from his boots. Ben
didn't even look up.

"What's with the C-4?" Nash nodded to the
Silly Putty on the counter that Mal had shaped
into small bricks.

"Silly Putty," she said. Though it probably did
look a lot like plastic explosives. She put the bricks
in old margarine tubs for storage and went to put
them in the fridge.

"Can I get a couple of those bricks?" Nash asked.

"Sure." She handed over half a dozen containers of the C-4 look-alike. At least now she knew how she could revive Ben's interest in the Silly Putty.

"It's nice out there," Nash said to both of them. "Anyone want to go for a ride after lunch?"

He'd said it loud enough for Ben to hear from the living room, but he was looking at her and waiting for her answer.

"I'd love to." The truth was, after the boys' excursion yesterday she was starting to feel a bit of cabin fever. "Doesn't that sound nice, Ben?"

He kept his eyes glued to his video game and shrugged.

Nash raised an eyebrow.

Mal lowered her voice. "It's Halloween. He's sulking."

"I'm not sulking," Ben said with a sulk to his voice.

"What do you like best about Halloween?" Nash asked.

"Candy," Ben answered. Again without looking up.

"Candy? Anyone can go to the store and buy candy."

"You don't go to the store," Ben explained patiently. This time he looked up from his game. "You probably don't know that because you've never had a kid before." As if this were Nash's first Halloween. "You put on your costume and you go door-to-door. And then you ring the bell and say trick or treat and they give you candy. Except Mr. Covey. He gives you a toothbrush and dental floss. That's because he used to be a dentist. But he gives me candy *and* a toothbrush and dental floss, *if* I promise to brush my teeth regularly."

Mal and Nash exchanged looks. They still didn't know the fate of Agent Stan Morgan or their neighbor Mr. Covey.

Clearly Halloween was something that still weighed heavily on Ben's mind. Despite the fact that he'd seemed to be taking everything else in stride, he was still just seven.

"Hmm…. I thought All Hallows' Eve was a night for remembering the dead. Maybe I have my Christian holidays wrong," he said, knowing full well he had it right. Nash moved into the living room and sat down on the coffee table. "You know I can't take you into town for trick or treating, Ben. But what if I could take you to a real ghost town?"

"A ghost town?"

"There are a lot of old mining towns in and around Leadville and Rock Springs. One not too far from here. We could make a day of it. Even camp out overnight if your mom is up to it?"

Nash looked across the room to her. Had he just deliberately called her Mom?

Camping? She was a city girl. This *was* camping.

"Oh, please, Mom. Please," Ben begged.

Mal felt his pleas with her heart. He'd called her Mom. Nash had called her Ben's mom.

She *was* going kind of stir-crazy cooped up in here. But at the same time she was almost afraid to leave their sanctuary. But a ghost town? Well, if nothing else, this promised to be a Halloween to remember.

"Sure, why not?"

"Great!" Nash said. "If you want to gather some supplies, Ben can help me with the equipment."

They were ready to leave within the hour. Mal made sandwiches they could eat in the car since they'd wound up skipping lunch in all the excitement. And she'd packed enough food for two days even though they were expecting to be gone just one.

While she prepped the snacks and food, Nash and Ben had loaded up the white Chevy Tahoe. They'd talked about taking the snowmobiles—and there was even a shortcut they could take—but in the end they simply had too much equipment.

The long way around still took less than thirty minutes, and they hit the town well before sunset with a bit of time to explore all the old buildings while there was still daylight.

"You have until sundown to get out of town, Black Bart." Ben stood in the middle of the street and pretended to draw on the bad guys.

He ran up and down the boardwalk exploring the doorless and windowless buildings. Nash showed Ben how to set the pretend C-4 as if they were bank robbers blowing up a bank. And it was only at that moment that she was reminded they were skirting the law. In fact, she hadn't yet devised a plan for turning Nash over. Apparently at some point over the past week she'd become quite content to stay at the cabin until the trial.

Their first building to explore was the jail, which still had cells with bars and bars in the windows, but no cell doors.

Next they hiked the half mile up to the actual mine shaft, which was boarded over. Though a child or a determined adult could have slipped inside, neither she nor Nash would allow Ben to give it a try.

Like in most Western ghost towns, once the mine had been abandoned, everything else was, too.

"What kind of mine do you think this was? Gold, silver—or some other mineral?" Ben asked.

He directed their attention to the rusted chute. "The flue makes me think silver or gold. Most likely silver."

"Gold!" Ben's eyes widened.

"Ever pan for gold?"

Ben shook his head. "How do you pan for gold?"

"I guess I'd better show you," Nash offered.

They hiked back to the SUV first where Nash grabbed a tin pie plate. And then they followed the creek back to the flue. The chute angled down the mountain and ended in a long flat section that emptied into the creek.

"This is where the water would flow down. Men would stand around this section here sifting through the sediment for gold or silver whatever was coming out of the mine." He stopped at the creek's edge to cuff his pants. And Ben did the same. "Don't know if it's true or not. But I remember hearing miners wore their pants cuffed, not to keep them up out of the water, but to steal nuggets coming out of the mine."

Nash had working boots on and stepped right up to the water with them. He stooped down to dip the pan and picked up a little of the creek bottom with him and then showed Ben how to sift through it.

"I got a gold nugget!" Ben said almost immediately.

Nash patiently explained about fool's gold and the patience required for panning while the boy dipped the pan again and again. His hands were turning red from the cold water. Nash took a turn until Ben's hands warmed up.

The creek was freezing, but not frozen over.

"I'd like to give it a go," Mal yelled at Nash once it was his turn again.

He handed over the pan and then stood back with his cold hand tucked to the pit of his under arms.

She dipped the pan in and pulled it out to sift through the sediment. "Holy Moly! I hit the mother lode."

"I don't see any gold. It's black." Ben put his chin right up to her shoulder to look over it.

"Beginners luck." Nash pointed out the shiny flakes to Ben. "This little nugget is made up of lead, zinc and silver—silver tarnishes when exposed to air. Probably have a lead mine here. Considering how close we are to Leadville."

"We're rich! We're rich!" Ben danced around.

"Not quite," Nash said as he fished out the tiny nugget for her.

They spent another half hour and found two more just like it. By that time everyone's hands were red and stiff from the cold.

"It's time we head back to town and set up camp and light a fire."

They went back to where they'd parked the Tahoe. It was in the schoolyard between the school and the white steepled church. "Indoors or outdoors?" Nash asked.

Mal studied their surroundings—it all seemed so open. "Can't I just sleep in the truck?"

"If you want," Nash said.

"Outside, outside, outside." Ben jumped up and down. "I want to sleep in the tent."

She could just let him and Nash sleep outside while she slept in the truck. But he looked so happy and excited and they *had* come here to camp. The sun was starting to set and they really needed to set up the tent if they were going to use it.

"Okay, the tent," she agreed. There was no way she was missing out on the boys' fun this time.

Nash showed them how to search for the perfect spot to set up camp. He had them sweep it with pine branches and clear away any rocks that he promised would only give them a restless night. Within very short order he'd assembled their tent, which upon inspection barely had room for their three sleeping bags spread out side by side.

Then he built a fire pit and they gathered wood for the fire.

He showed Ben how to start a fire using only flint and the steel blade of his knife. Mal felt a sudden pit in her stomach at the knife in his hand and grew quiet.

Once the fire was started, they found a couple of almost rotten wild pumpkins and Nash carved one for Ben and stuck a flashlight in it. Again with the knife. She just kept staring at his hands and the knife in it.

He caught and held her gaze and she felt that

pit lift and even managed to shake off the feeling and smile back at him. Actually, when was the last time she'd seen Nash smile? Yesterday and today.

Once the fire was blazing, they set their open can of baked beans right up to the flame. They roasted hot dogs on sticks and Nash showed Ben how to hold his stick so the hot dog wouldn't catch fire.

They ate until they couldn't possibly eat any more.

Ben entertained them by singing Nash the songs from every school recital he'd ever missed. From kindergarten right up through second grade.

Mal broke out the s'mores and Nash told ghost stories that made Ben giggle.

Mal alternated between feeling totally at peace and being terrified. When they were quiet, with the wind blowing, it did sound like ghosts moving through the buildings. She found herself scooted closer to Nash as the night wore on.

Once it was pitch-black outside, they all knew it was time for bed.

Mal pushed herself to her feet. "I'm going to go mark my territory."

Ben giggled. "Girls can't mark their territory."

"Wanna bet?" she teased.

"Need a lookout?" Nash offered.

"I think I can handle it." She grabbed a flash-light, took her gun out of the holster and went to go look for a bush behind the school while the guys headed off in the opposite direction.

When she returned, Nash was putting out the fire and Ben had already settled down inside the tent. Mal crawled in beside him. She took off her heavy outercoat and shoes.

She was wearing what she always wore around the house—her yoga pants and a tank top with a flannel shirt she'd found tossed over it. She settled in beside Ben. Nash crawled in after her and zipped up the tent. As if that was any kind of protection from anything. Now she remembered why she hated sleeping outdoors. It was scary and made her feel vulnerable.

Ben didn't seem to notice or care.

Nash hung the solar lantern above their heads. "Tell me when you're ready for lights out." He folded his jacket and laid his head down on it as if it were a pillow.

Mal thought that was a good idea and did the same. Apparently Ben thought it was also a good idea, too, and bunched his jacket beneath his head. Lying there between them, he had the biggest smile on his face.

Once Mal settled into her sleeping bag she rolled over onto her side to face Ben and Nash. "You can turn the light out now."

Once her eyes adjusted to the dark, the soft glow of moonlight made it so it wasn't pitch-black.

And it wasn't so bad. She was quite warm and there were no rocks digging into her backside.

Once all was quiet, Ben sat bolt upright. "What was that?"

Nash scuffed his head. "The wind."

They got him settled down again. But he did it two more times before Nash put his shoes on to have a look around outside while Mal clutched her firearm. He came back after what seemed like forever to reassure them everything was all right. Finally Ben settled down and Mal wrapped her arm around him, which put her hand smack-dab in Nash's territory.

She accidentally brushed his stubbled cheek and pulled back.

NASH WOKE UP the next morning with his arm thrown across both Ben and Mal. The three of them huddled toward each other in the center of the tent. He was the first one up and out of the tent. For breakfast he made bacon and eggs and pan-fried biscuits. He smiled as Mal swore she'd never tasted anything so good.

After they washed up and stretched their legs with a quick trip through town, it was time to leave for home—Nash caught himself. The cabin wasn't their home. This wasn't their life. This was borrowed time.

And while he was enjoying every minute of it

once he'd decided to try it Mal's way and simply enjoy this time with his son, he felt the clock ticking down with every beat of his heart.

He caught himself watching not just Ben, but Mal, as the two helped pack up the Tahoe to head back to the cabin. Maybe he shouldn't be getting too comfortable. No, that was fear talking. They had so little time left together he wanted to spend every moment with the two of them.

As he drove them all back to the cabin, he had a hard time imagining what his life would be like after this. Different, that's for sure.

Empty. Lonely. Though try as he might, he couldn't picture that life. For so long now he'd been living a life, not of his choosing, but of his choices, nonetheless. He wondered at the freedom of finally being able to live his own life, knowing full well that the life he really wanted was forever out of his reach.

By the time they reached the cabin, it no longer held the feeling of home. It felt like the first time when they'd pulled up to this strange new place. In that moment he realized that he wanted to be more than just a trespasser in his son's and Mal's life.

THE FOLLOWING EVENING Mal stood staring at the blank corkboard in the kitchen. She'd taken all Ben's art down and had paper and crayons spread out all over the kitchen counter space.

"More of Ben's art?" Nash came into the small space fresh from the shower and picked up a drawing from the counter. He'd shaved his head. With his hair short like now, his face looked hardened, with more angular lines. She actually liked his hair long and wavy, but something about this completely masculine style spoke to her softer, more feminine side.

She shook her head and went back to staring at the blank canvas in front of her. "Afraid those are mine."

He held up the picture with his name on it up to his chest. "I look like Mrs. Potato Head."

She'd given him a brown oval for a head and had colored in brown eyes with thick black lashes. And she added an angular nose and red lips, and lots of wavy black hair around his head and finally dots for whiskers. And she'd spelled out N A S H / S A Y Y I D in big bold blue letters.

"No, you don't. Be serious." She waved off his attempt at humor. "It's before you cut your hair."

He turned it over for a second look. "Huh."

"Help me out here." Mal took the picture of him and tacked it to the center of the corkboard. "Sayyid Naveed, Bari Kahn and Joseph Tyler were all at Gitmo." She took the picture she'd drawn of Bari Kahn and tacked it high and to the left of his. Kahn had a fat round head, shorter hair and a longer beard.

"Actually Bari doesn't have a beard."

"Don't judge me. I'm not a profiler. I may have heard of al-Ayman, but I wouldn't know Bari Kahn if I passed him on the street. Can you do better?" She ripped down the picture. "Please, be my guest. Draw me a more accurate picture of the terrorist." She extended a crayon.

"His face is scarred." Nash picked up a red crayon and drew a circle without a beard. And then he doctored the left eye to make it appear droopy and added a scribble to the whole left side of Kahn's face. And wrote B A R I K A H N under it.

"Okay, so now he's creepy monster guy." She tacked the new and improved Kahn up again and added Tyler to the right.

Nash shook his head. "Tyler doesn't wear a turban."

"It's a hat. Marines wear hats."

"Military wear *covers,* but okay." He angled his head as if he was trying to picture it.

She elbowed him for his silent critique. She had used olive-green, desert sand and a color called banana mania to add some camouflage. Then she'd given the marine a peach head and periwinkle eyes to match his brother's and some short brown spikes under and around his hat for hair.

Nash stared at the board with her. "Okay, so what have we got going on here anyway?"

"I'm trying to figure something out. You were all in Camp Six." She tacked what looked like a wooden sign with blades of brown grass on top of a green island, roughly in the shape of Cuba, above their heads. This was obviously to represent Camp Six. "Tyler was a detention guard. You and Kahn were *detainees*. Tyler tortured *detainees*." She quickly drew a rainbow of smaller circles with sad faces and tacked it up next to Tyler. "Did he ever abuse you?"

"No."

"How about Kahn?"

"No."

"Why not?" She stared at him intently.

Nash leaned back against the counter with his arms folded and seemed to stop and consider that for a moment. "I don't know," he admitted.

"But you witnessed the abuse?"

"On several occasions. Plus, it was general knowledge among the prisoners that you didn't want to get on Tyler's bad side."

"How would you describe your relationship with Kahn while in the prison—were you close?"

He scowled as if she didn't understand his predicament. "It was my job to get close to him."

"I get that." She drew another rainbow of circles with happy faces and tacked it up next to Kahn. "How many of Kahn's cohorts were tortured while you were there?"

Nash took a step toward the board. "Mal, you're brilliant."

"I know, right?" She added drawings to represent Mullah Kahn and Christopher Tyler to the top of the heap and then stood back grinning broadly. "We know Christopher Tyler wants you dead because of his brother." She dug a piece of string out of the junk drawer. She tied one end of the string around Joseph Tyler's tack. "We know Mullah Kahn wants you dead so you can't testify. And we know they're both after you. But there's coincidence and then there's coincidence."

Mal outlined a triangle using the string. From Joseph Tyler to Nash to Bari Kahn and then back to Joseph Tyler. "I think there's a connection between Bari Kahn and Joseph Tyler. Maybe even a money trail. He might have enjoyed torturing prisoners, but I'd bet the whole bank of Monopoly money he was also working for or with Bari Kahn. Just like I'd bet Bari Kahn and Christopher Tyler are connected."

Mal reached into an overhead cupboard and got down a bottle and two canning jars that were obviously used for drinking glasses. "Care for an adult beverage?" She got out the ice tray and poured herself a drink over ice. "Found a bottle of Wild Turkey bourbon tucked away. I've been saving it for a rainy day."

"No, thanks," he said. "Alcohol dulls the senses."

She raised her glass. "I hate to drink alone, but sometimes you need to dull the senses."

He eyed the half-empty bottle. "Okay, sure, why not?"

She poured him a drink and they clinked glasses. "To cabin fever."

She pushed the bottle aside and leaned back against the counter.

"This has been hard on you and Ben, I know," Nash said. "And I am sorry."

"What?" She held her hand up to her ear. "Was that an apology, Mr. Nash?"

"I know how to apologize."

"No, you know how to give orders. Other than that you don't say much."

He shifted uncomfortably. "There's not much to say."

"Used to be you wouldn't shut up. You'd get going on a subject and then Cara would look at me and just roll her eyes. Make this man shut up." The corner of Nash's mouth turned down. "Oh, don't get me wrong, she loved you for it. So did I. It was part of your charm." She smiled into her drink and then took a swallow.

"I think that's what I miss most," he said. "Not being able to talk about her."

They were both quiet for a minute. Mal looked into her drink again and then set it down without taking another swallow. She couldn't if she wanted to. Her throat constricted around her next words. "Yeah, well, for me it's not having anyone to talk to."

"I didn't kill her, but I am the reason she was killed." He reached for the bottle and topped off their glasses.

"I've never heard you say that before."

"What, that I'm guilty? Culpable?" He took a swig of the Wild Turkey.

"That you didn't kill Cara."

He searched her face. "Maybe it's just the first time you believed me."

She shifted away from him to face the countertop. "I wanted to believe you." She traced an old cut mark in the scarred Formica. Some wounds were too old and too deep to mend. "My parents, the prosecutor—they wouldn't let me near you. I didn't know how to navigate JAG."

"Belief takes faith."

"Maybe I needed to hear you say it." She slammed her glass down on the counter. "'I did what I had to do' is not a denial."

"But maybe it was the truth."

"And when the military investigators and lawyers asked me questions, I spoke the truth. And when I took the stand, I spoke the truth. You didn't even testify."

"The right to remain silent is one of those rights you read me."

"Such a rookie move."

"Don't beat yourself up about it." He screwed the cap back on the bottle. "I made the deal before the trial was even over. I had evidence to exonerate me, but it was more important to keep it under wraps so I could go after Cara's real killer."

"You—" His revelation turned her world upside down. His casual shrug seemed out of place. "Why would you do that to Ben, to me? My parents? Your mother?"

"Cara was my life."

"Now Ben's your life."

"Mal, you know that's not going to happen."

"Why not?"

"Do I have to spell it out for you? This doesn't end with my testimony."

"It could. You're a protected witness. You could testify remotely. They'd alter your voice and turn your face into thousands of pixels. Nobody has to recognize you."

"Mal, my cover is blown."

"You can walk away with a new identity. Ben and I could go with you…. We'd have to go with you…. We're not ever getting our lives back, are we?"

"I'm sorry, Mal."

"I think I kind of knew." But maybe it was just now hitting her what that would really mean. A laugh escaped and she looked up at the ceiling to keep from crying. "I had this plan to take Ben and run should you ever come after him. It would have worked, too. I keep four different storage sheds, one in each direction leading out of the state. I have money, lots of money." Nash had signed all his and Cara's assets over to her that day at Miramar. "I have Mom's life insurance policy. And once his condition started to deteriorate, Dad put everything in my name.…

"I used to lie in bed at night and dream of starting over. But I guess I never really understood what that would mean. At least we'll all be together if…"

"I'm not going with you, Mal."

She knew that, too. It was foolish to hope.

Suddenly she felt the need for distraction—to turn the subject away from the personal and back to the board again. "There is one thing I haven't been able to figure out." She tacked her own picture near Christopher Tyler's. "I don't know if this means anything, but Tyler transferred to the Denver field office two years ago. He hit on me pretty hard when he first arrived. I mean I couldn't go anywhere without bumping into him. He asked me out a couple times, but I always said no. It was actually beginning to feel like stalking. I was on the verge of going to H.R. when he just stopped. At the time I thought I'd gotten my point across, but now I'm wondering… He used to ask me all kinds of questions about Cara's murder. About you. Like he was digging for information. But then, like I said, he just abruptly stopped."

Nash took a swig of his drink. "Two years ago Bari started growing suspicious of me. Right after a big bust."

"But you stayed?"

He nodded. "I was able to divert their suspicions from me."

"How?"

"I set someone else up to take the fall." He threw back the last of his bourbon. "And then I married Kahn's sister, Sari."

"Excuse me?" Mal couldn't possibly have heard him correctly. She would have doubled over, the pain was so acute. "You remarried?"

"It's not like that."

"What's it like, Nash? All this time I thought what you'd done, what you were doing was some sort of penance for Cara."

"Mal—"

She held up her hand to stop him from saying anything else. "I can't talk about this right now." She set her glass down when what she really wanted to do was slam it. And then she left the kitchen with as much dignity as possible.

NASH TRUDGED THROUGH knee-deep snow with a hunting rifle slung over his shoulder. No matter how much distance he put between himself and the cabin, he couldn't escape the accusation in Mal's eyes. He could have explained away his second marriage as a sham he'd only entered into in order to maintain his cover.

Mal might even have understood.

Sari was his wife in name only, an assumed name at that. It had never been real for him. The union had been forced on them both by her father and brother.

A test of loyalty for him. A punishment for her.

It was easier to maintain the whole undercover facade when you didn't stray far from the truth. Nash had never presented himself as anything other than a grieving widower—a man who'd lost his wife and son in childbirth. It helped explain his lack of interest in women. And family.

He'd played his part. Worked his way up through the al-Ayman terrorist network through the leader's son, whom he'd helped escape from Gitmo. That wasn't exactly part of the script— he was supposed to feed information higher up through a doctor on staff. But he knew it was only a matter of time before the guards stopped buying his excuses for medical attention.

He'd staged a hunger strike, knowing he'd be taken to the infirmary and checked out by the medical staff, or as a last resort, force-fed. Most of the Camp Six prisoners joined him in his rebellion in one form or another.

He and Mac had gone over escape scenarios. Nash knew the prison camps, the base, the entire island of Cuba like the back of his hand, and he also knew that he'd go for it if he ever got the chance. And then he'd gotten his chance.

The government's mission, while parallel, wasn't exactly the same as his, which was retribution for his wife's murder. The disappointment came in discovering that the lowlife who'd killed her had been so close at hand and was already in custody.

So Nash made sure his wife's killer was included in the escape plan.

The murderer even got a taste of freedom, but no more than that before gators got a taste of him. Nash had left the man's corpse to rot in a mangrove swamp.

While Nash could have disposed of Bari just as easily—and to his way of thinking the world would have been better off—Nash needed Bari alive. The younger son of the Mullah Kahn was a worthless piece of crap with a porn addiction and no real ambition. Nash spent four long years dragging the bastard up the terrorist chain of command just to get the young thug noticed by his own father.

A low-level pervert like Bari Kahn eventually found his footing in sex trafficking. Big Daddy Mullah Kahn had more than just his toes dipped in sex and drug trafficking to keep the family terrorism business afloat.

No operative had ever wormed his way into a terrorist organization as deep as Nash had and then lived to tell about it. He'd been feeding information to the intelligence community for seven years. He'd come close to exposure a couple of times. But he'd always been able to either take care of the rat undetected or pin his misdeeds on some other lowlife. Then two years ago his handler had turned up dead—an experienced CIA operative whose cover had been blown. While Nash had been able to mask his emotions at seeing the man dead, his hands were so dirty by that time they'd never be clean again.

But he'd systematically been able to build a case against the man who'd ordered the hit on his wife from the inside. And he'd been able to play it cool even when faced with the ultimate test of his loyalty. Kahn never expected he'd marry his sister. But what choice did he have?

Now the U.S. wanted to try Kahn in a Manhattan court.

CHAPTER THIRTEEN

WHEN NASH RETURNED TO the cabin, all was quiet downstairs. He unwound the scarf from his neck and hung the borrowed winter coat on the rack, then he locked the rifle back in the cabinet. He'd rather have the weapon within easy reach, but locking it up was a concession to Ben's safety. But of course, he kept his handgun on him.

He heard the shower blasting away upstairs and figured Mal was getting ready for bed, which suited him just fine. The less they saw of each other this evening, the better. He couldn't wipe her unspoken accusation from his mind. If he'd had the choice he never would have remarried, but the fact that he had didn't lessen his first marriage *or* the love he felt for Cara.

You do not have the luxury of stopping to think things over.

He needed a distraction in order to get rid of the unsettled feeling in his stomach. So he set about building a fire in the hearth. But not twenty minutes later a feeling even more unsettling came over him. He could still hear the shower blasting away upstairs. But since they conserved the propane, the sporadic use of the generator meant they never had much hot water. No one in this house took twenty-minute showers.

He reached for the gun tucked to his back.

He kept off to the side of the stairs where his weight was less likely to make the steps creak. He didn't know what to expect as he checked in on Ben first. The boy shifted peacefully in his sleep. The hall bathroom was empty. As expected, the sound of running water came from the bathroom in the larger of the two bedrooms.

He tried the knob to the bedroom. The door was locked.

He tried knocking. "Mal?"

She didn't answer. Not that she would even have heard him if she was in the shower.

He would have left it at that, but heard a muffled sob coming from inside.

"Mal!" He knocked louder.

When she didn't answer this time, he reached into his back pocket for an old motel key card he kept there for these exact situations. The lock on the interior door was there for privacy more than safety, so with a little jiggling of the hand he slid the key into position and disengaged the catch. While all his efforts might just get him a slap to the face, he needed to reassure himself that everything was all right, especially since Mal hadn't been in the best state of mind when he left.

Though he did fully expect a slap to the face for breaking and entering into her private domain.

She wasn't in the bedroom when he entered.

The bathroom door was open and the light on. The shower was still running and the muffled sobs were no longer muffled—they were the heart-wrenching sobs of a woman grieving. He should back out and leave her to it.

There were times when he, too, just wanted to break down and cry for everything he'd lost, but he had never allowed himself that luxury. He was afraid if he did he wouldn't stop.

These past few days had stirred up those old feelings.

And that's what pushed him forward.

Mal was probably simply releasing some of the frustration she'd experienced over the past few days. But Nash needed to know that with certainty before he could leave.

Mal was tough, but the events of the past few days had demanded a lot of her.

"Mal," he addressed the closed shower curtain so as not to startle her as he stepped into the bathroom. Instead of the *get the hell out* that he was expecting, another sob escaped from lower in the tub than he would have expected. The shower spray hit the curtain with no silhouette to break it.

He pulled the curtain aside to find Mal huddled in the tub. Knees drawn up to her chest and her hand covering her mouth to muffle her sobs. He couldn't tell the tears from the water blasting her, which was like ice. He reached in to turn it off.

He grabbed the nearest towel and wrapped it over her as he helped her from the tub. She didn't protest, but she didn't help him, either. She simply allowed him to drag her to her feet and then out of the tub. He rubbed the towel over her in an attempt to warm her up. He tried to dry the tears with a corner, but they just kept coming.

She raised her scraggly red head to look at him. The vulnerability he saw there nearly broke his heart.

"She loved you." The words escaped on a broken sob. "How could you?"

Nash tried to lead her out of the bathroom but she wouldn't go any farther than the bathroom door. Leaning back against it, she looked up at him with accusing eyes. "I was ready to believe in you again."

"Mal—" She'd given him the perfect opening to explain away his second marriage. At least that's what he thought this was all about. What else could it be?

He understood Mal felt betrayed on her sister's behalf. There was no closure with murder. Not even in killing the man who'd carried out the crime, and certainly not when you thought your brother-in-law had committed a crime of passion and then found out that he didn't. Only to discover he'd remarried. "I will always love Cara. She was my first…"

His last. His everything.

Mal shook her head from side to side. She didn't seem to be willing to listen. She just kept repeating, "She loved you."

"Mal, stop." He grabbed her chin and forced her to look at him.

"I loved you," she said on a broken whisper.

There it was. That thing that had always been between them. He hadn't been so dense in his teens and twenties not to notice.

Cara had even pointed it out to him on occasion. *"Be careful with my sister's heart. Someday you're going to have to break it."*

Dropping his hand to his side, he held her gaze with his own. "I know."

"I wanted to believe you." She wasn't even trying to hide the tears now. "You could have made me believe you."

He knew that, too.

He could have played on her feelings for him, but he hadn't wanted the responsibility of those feelings then any more than he wanted them now. Not that he had to worry about that anymore since she'd used the past tense for *love.*

She had loved him. But she was over it. He was glad of it. "I only want what's best for Ben. And you."

He moved to reach for her but Mal shrank from his touch, refusing to budge when he tried to help her toward the bedroom.

"Of all the dangerous things I imagined you doing all these years, walking down the aisle was never one of them. I thought you lived in a barbed-wire world. Now I find out it was all white picket fences. Dare I ask if Ben has any siblings? Because you already have one son who's never known his father."

Her barbs cut at the truth, but they were far from reality.

"Do you think I don't know what I'm sacrificing?"

"Do you? Do you really, Nash? Because you've gone on living your life *your* way, while my sister paid the ultimate price because of it. If everything you've said is true, then she died because she married you—a man who chose to be a Navy SEAL. The same man who chose revenge over raising his own son—"

"You think that was a choice?"

"Yes. Yes, I do. What you call sacrifice I call selfish. I see now why my sister was divorcing you. She was the one making all the sacrifices.

She hated your job. What you were. Who you'd become—"

Nash took a step back as if Mal had slapped him. It was like fighting with Cara all over again. Except it wasn't, because Cara had not fought with words. His wife had never said the things his sister-in-law was saying to him now, but he still knew them to be true.

Cara had used silence to get her point across.

He'd hated those sulky moods. And he'd been too eager to dismiss them as pregnancy hormones even though it had been that way since they were teens.

"I took a desk job. For her," he added, sounding defensive even to his own ears.

"But you didn't stick yourself behind it. She knew enough to know those training ops—" Mal used air quotes "—weren't all training ops. And she just couldn't live with the uncertainty of it."

He'd loved his wife and she'd loved him. Nothing Mal could say would change that, but these were the first negative thoughts he'd associated with Cara since her death.

He had never lied to her, not even when he told her he was going on "training ops." It was just the language used in his line of work where classified information couldn't be shared. Cara knew that. And she'd hated it.

Was it any wonder his wife had grown to hate him, too?

He didn't want to fight with Mal in some pseudorelationship squabble. He didn't even know what they were fighting about anymore. "You're right. I was a lousy husband and a lousy father—"

"Do you have any idea what Ben and I have been through?" She adjusted the slipping towel. "I was twenty-three years old, Nash. My sister had been murdered. My mother had just committed suicide. My father couldn't even remember how to tie his own shoes. And on top of all of that, I'm responsible for a newborn. All on my own."

"I was in prison."

"You figured a way out fast enough when it suited you."

"Mal!" He grabbed her by the shoulders and forced her to look at him. "I get it. I'm a lousy human being."

"I loved you," she said again on a broken whisper.

"I gave you and Ben everything I had left to give when I gave you each other."

Nash didn't know how it had happened. Or who kissed who first. Or what he'd seen in her eyes that brought his mouth down on hers in a crushing kiss. But one minute they were arguing and the next Mal was ripping at his jacket as if she couldn't tear it off him fast enough. He only knew that he demanded more, wanted more from her bruised and swollen lips that tasted of salty tears and longing.

He helped her by shrugging out of his coat and when that was accomplished and she'd unzipped his hoodie, he shrugged out of that, too. He dropped his Glock to the top of the pile as he untucked his flannel shirt while she worked his buttons with a greedy need.

Somewhere in the back of his brain, it registered that this was Mal. Cara's sister. But he pushed those thoughts aside because the truth was there was no denying he wanted this. And with the towel pooled at her feet, there was nothing to stop him from exploring all that softness. He filled one greedy hand with a breast while his mouth moved down to meet the other.

He sucked in rhythm to the low moans in the back of Mal's throat.

She fumbled with his belt and made fast work of his zipper.

His breath caught on the intake as she wrapped her hand around him, straining his arousal by stroking his shaft up and down. When she teased his ball sac in her greedy little hand, he recaptured her mouth with his and drove his tongue deep, mimicking the naughty pleasure he'd like to bring her.

Foreplay would have to wait. His fingers fumbled between her legs like a horny teenager's. She was wet and ready for him, and when she wrapped a leg around his hip he drove in hard and deep. His need to be inside her trumped everything.

He didn't care that his pants were still around his ankles. Or that she'd only managed to unbutton his shirt. He wasn't going to last long enough to get his clothes off anyway. Not when she was fully naked and spread before him with her back against the door.

He held her hands above her head and then she wrapped both legs around him.

The sounds they were making were primitive, primal—just like their mating.

Base. Elemental.

He pumped into her. Felt her tight muscle spasms join his earth-shattering release. He buried the sound of his guttural cries in her shoulder. In her hair. In her neck.

First time fast. Second time slow.

He took his time working his way back to her lips. This time he wanted to take things slow. She unwrapped her legs from around his waist and her feet touched down, though she stood on tiptoes. He didn't move away from her or pull out, but moved closer instead.

He looked deep into her dreamy eyes, unable to let go of this forbidden fantasy.

"I'm just trying to figure out how to get my pants off and then get you to the bed."

Without waking up.

In the end it was accomplished with a lot of kissing and tripping.

Moonlight bathed the bedroom and Nash kept his promise to take it slow.

It had been a long time since he'd made love to a woman without Cara intruding on his thoughts. Tonight was no exception. She was there in every kiss and touch. Reproving, disapproving—but he didn't let her in enough to know which and he worked hard to push her aside. Gazing into Mallory's eyes, he knew which sister he was with. His body knew, even though his mind kept wanting to split into two. To tell him this was wrong. When it felt right. Mallory felt right.

He'd be reminded of some snippet of conversation with Cara. Or he'd hear Cara's whispered words when he knew it was Mal whispering in his ear. Not about love. This wasn't love. This was lust pure and simple.

Mal whispered words that made him hot. Words that made their bodies move as one. Words that had them fighting for dominance as he rolled her beneath him.

Words that would last through the night.

He worshipped every inch of her in silence.

This time when he reached his climax he

reached for something deep inside and called out, "Cara," at the exact wrong time.

NASH ROLLED OFF her and simply lay there in the dark. Mal rolled onto her side and away from him. She pulled up the covers and wanted to pretend that what had just happened hadn't. Not the love-making part, but the part where he called out her sister's name during climax.

They lay there in the aftermath of that awkward silence for a long time. Neither of them saying anything. Neither of them finding sleep.

"Mal," he said after a while.

She didn't answer. Didn't care if he knew she wasn't asleep.

The mattress dipped as Nash sat up. The weight shifted again as he stood. She could hear him moving around in the dark. Gathering his clothes. Dressing.

She rolled over just as he was leaving.

He must have heard her, because he turned to look at her. "I'm going to go sleep on the couch. I don't think Ben should find us together like this."

Together? She wouldn't exactly call this to-gether.

"Don't worry about it, Nash," she said in her best *I sleep with all my dead sister's widowed husbands* voice. "I know I'm a poor substitute for Cara."

"Mal," he said in that reproachful *you're not to blame it's all my fault, big brother-in-law* voice.

She waited for him to deny it. Shouldn't he at least be gentleman enough to deny it?

But he simply left. Closing the door with a quiet click on all her schoolgirl fantasies about him forever. Except as she lay there in the dark, still unable to sleep, she went through a play-by-play of the night's activities in her head.

She'd done a very bad thing. Sleeping with her sister's husband. A man she knew was still in love with her sister.

And the only person she wanted to talk about it with was her sister.

NASH WOKE WITH a start. He wasn't going to get any sleep tonight.

He banked the fire in the fireplace, put on his jacket and grabbed his rifle to head out on his security rounds. He had a couple of traps set. Nothing that would hurt anybody, just something that would let him know if anyone came snooping. He crouched down to check on one of the wires that had been tripped. The cougar tracks made him think the cat had tripped it but he figured it wouldn't hurt to take his time and be extra cautious on his rounds. So he moved slowly, deliberately, taking in every part of the surroundings. The activity not only served to make sure the perimeter was secure, but also gave him little time to think about Mal.

Significantly weary after an hour of traipsing around outdoors, Nash headed back to the cabin. He stopped at the bottom of the stairs to kick the snow off his boots.

"Put your hands where I can see 'em," the voice behind him said. "Slowly, turn around."

Nash turned to find an elderly man with a shotgun pointed straight at him.

"Are you the culprit who broke into my clinic and stole some meds?"

CHAPTER FOURTEEN

Seven years earlier

"HE JUST WANTS to talk to you." Mal stood in her sister's kitchen with her back to the Formica countertop.

"I do not want to talk to him," Cara said, pushing herself belly up first from her seat at the kitchen table. "You can't possibly understand, Mal."

"What, that you're eight months pregnant and hormonal?" Mal folded her arms. She could be just as stubborn as her big sister when she wanted to be. Maybe more so.

"Because you're not married to a Navy SEAL. And if he persists on using you as a go-between, I'm going to file a restraining order against the both of you."

Mal ignored the part about the restraining order. "Yeah, well, I'm not married period, but that's beside the point. You can't hold the man's job against him, Cara."

"It's not just his job."

"You can't hold the man's religion against him, either."

"I'm not having my son circumcised." She put a protective hand on her belly. "We agreed we're not raising this child in any singular religion. So I don't see why he's so insistent."

"A lot of men are circumcised. Dad's probably even circumcised. You should ask him."

"Ew. Mal, put away your phone."

Mal tapped out a text to their father.

Too late Cara tried to take the phone away from her. Mal just held it high above her sister's head. Cara hated that Mal was a good six inches taller than her puny five foot two. And Mal used to hate that Cara was very pretty and petite until she'd grown into her own. Now she kind of liked being able to look most men in the eye.

Although she wouldn't hold a guy's lack of height against him if the right man came along, secretly she liked a man better when she had to look up to him.

Like her dad. Or Nash.

Mal held up the return text from their father.

"Drive safe?" Cara added the question mark as she read.

"Just told him I was leaving here tomorrow and that I'll see him soon." She stuck her tongue out at her sister, who rolled her eyes. "Look, I know what the American Pediatrics Whatever says, but maybe you should let Nash have his say in this. It's a guy thing. They have really strong feelings about their penis. Penises? You know what I mean."

Cara and Nash had known the sex of the baby for a while now and apparently had been arguing ever since. Mal had been away at the FBI Academy and blissfully unaware of the domestic strife between her sister and brother-in-law until a few days ago.

"It's not just the job and the baby. You just don't understand," Cara repeated for the hundredth time that evening. "It's everything."

"How can it be everything?" And how could a seemingly great marriage turn upside down in just twenty weeks? That's what Mal wanted to know.

"We married too young, Mal. I never should have dropped out of college."

"So go back to school."

"It's an expensive waste of time. We have enough student loan debt already. Babies are so expensive, you know," she wailed mournfully.

"What? Cara, you have free health care. And Nash just got that promotion to lieutenant commander. That comes with a raise. Don't make it about money."

"Just forget it, Mal. I can't talk to you about this anymore. You just don't understand because you're the fifth wheel in this relationship and you always take *his* side."

"I do not always take his side." She crossed her arms. "And I'm certainly no fifth wheel. I see the two of you, what, twice a year?"

"You have more in common with my husband than I do. He respects you more than he does me. I know it."

"Do not even go there." Mal threw her hand up in frustration. "Nash treats you like a princess—"

"You idolize him, Mal. But you don't really know him and you do *not* know what it's like being married to him. He's gone all the time—three hundred days a year. I may as well be a single parent, because I'm going to be raising this child alone."

Mal heard real fear behind her sister's rant and suspected they had finally circled back to the heart of the matter. Cara was so afraid of losing Nash that she'd rather push him aside than risk losing him someday in an OJT incident.

"I just want a different life," her sister wailed.

"Come here," Mal said, pulling her sister into a hug—at least as far as her sister's baby bump would allow. "I may not be married to the man, but I do know him. Nash loves you. And you've got to love him enough *not* to make him choose between you and the baby and his job. Because he'd choose to make you happy." Mal wasn't one for emotional displays. Letting go of her sister she tried to lighten the mood. "Then he'd be miserable. You'd be miserable. And you'd really hate each other then. Cara, you do not want a different life. You have a perfect life. With a perfect man. And you're about to have a perfect baby...."

Cara looked a little weepy. Maybe Mal had finally gotten through to her.

"You know if anything did happen I'd be here for you and this little tyke." She rubbed her sister's belly. She decided not to add that Cara could take comfort in the fact that if anything did happen to Nash on the job, he'd die doing what he loved, and few people could say that. She didn't think her sister was ready to hear it. "Maybe you should drop by a synagogue and speak with a rabbi. Find out what the big deal is about circumcision from the Jewish perspective. If you still don't agree, at least you'll be able to argue with Nash from an educated standpoint. That's what I would do anyway."

They spent the rest of the evening eating ice cream and watching romantic comedies. Mal slept on the couch because the guest room had been turned into a nursery since her last visit. A crash outside woke her from a sound sleep around two in the morning. She reached for her firearm.

Funny how that had become second nature in just a few short weeks.

Something, probably the wind, had knocked over the trash cans outside.

Mal went to investigate, but it wasn't the wind

trying to set the trash cans right. She stood at the back door watching her brother-in-law fumble with trying to put the lids back on. "Nash, are you drunk?"

Clearly, he'd been drinking.

"Shh." He pressed his finger to his lips in an exaggerated whisper. "I just came to give you your graduation present."

"At two in the morning?"

The kitchen light flipped on.

"What's going on?" Cara entered the kitchen. "Nash, what are you doing here? Are you drunk?"

"I just stopped by to give Mal her graduation present."

"You came here drunk and armed? I'm calling the police," Cara threatened, picking up the phone.

Mal took the phone from her sister's hand before she could dial 911. "No. You don't have to do that. I'll get dressed and drive him back to the base." The last thing they needed was to get the police involved. "Stay," she ordered Nash. "The SIG is still in the box," she said to her sister as she dragged Cara with her back toward the master bedroom.

Mal made Cara get back in bed before her sister blew this whole thing out of proportion. And then Mal threw on a hoodie over her tank top and pajama pants and grabbed her purse and keys to the rental car out front.

"Seriously, Nash," Mal said as she loaded him into the rental car. "You couldn't have picked a worse time or a worse excuse. Next time try showing up sober and in broad daylight. With a better excuse then dropping off a gun."

"Is she mad at me?" he asked miserably.

"I don't know, but I'm pretty pissed." Mal shoved the car in gear and pulled away from the curb. After a few minutes driving toward the base with Nash snoring beside her, she realized she didn't know where on base he was staying.

So she drove to the only other destination she could think of.

She helped Nash out of the car and up the steps. The porch light was on, and a motion-sensor light at the side of the duplex came on as they approached the house.

There were no lights on inside and she hadn't gotten the chance to fire off a warning text. But she rang the doorbell of the bachelor pad anyway, hoping someone was home who could help her.

"Mal?" Kip Nouri opened the door, looking as sleep tousled and gorgeous as the day she'd met him. Too bad this wasn't a booty call.

"Hey, Kip." Well, at least he didn't glance over his shoulder—which was probably a good sign that he didn't have a woman warming his bed.

"Can we come in?" She nodded toward Nash, who was leaning heavily on her shoulder.

"Sure, come on in." He shook his head, likely to clear it from the shock of seeing her again, and stepped aside. Or perhaps it was the shock of seeing his executive officer drunk. Come to think of it, she'd never seen Nash drunk. He was much too serious for that.

Nouri slipped in under Nash's other arm and helped her get him to the couch. Then he disappeared into the kitchen and returned with a lined wastebasket. "In case he feels like, you know, doing the backward bungee."

"Sorry," she said.

He waved off her apology. "What goes down must come up—right?"

He had the *speaking of what goes down must come up* look in his eye. Any other night she might have taken him up on the offer.

"I'd better get back to check on my sister."

"Yeah, sure." He walked her to the door like the gentleman he wasn't. "I meant to call." He made an awkward attempt at an apology.

"It's okay. I was just in town for the weekend."

"I had a good time at Disneyland. And, you know, afterward."

He meant after they'd ditched Cara and Nash to come back to the bachelor pad. Which was what they'd nicknamed the place because four junior officers—all Navy SEALs—rotated in and out of the apartment.

"Me, too." She dropped her gaze to her feet to surreptitiously get another look at him in his boxer shorts. It's not as if she was in that big of a hurry to leave.

"How long are you in town this time?"

"Just the weekend again."

"You want to meet up tomorrow for lunch?"

"Nouri," Nash bellowed from the couch. "Quit trying to hook up with my sister-in-law. That's an order."

Mal flashed Kip the "call me" sign as she stepped outside. He nodded with a smile on his face. His loss if he didn't take her up on her offer. He was twenty-three. She was twenty-three. She wasn't interested in anything more than a hookup with a hot guy. Besides, she didn't even know for sure she was going to be assigned to the FBI's San Diego field office yet.

If she was, then she'd decide if he was boyfriend material or simply a convenient 2:00 a.m. booty call. Or maybe they'd even become friends—with benefits, of course.

God, he was hot. She could feel his eyes on her ass all the way to the car.

She turned to get in and waved over the top of the car.

Sometimes it was just about the sex.

NASH THOUGHT IT couldn't get much worse than being held at gunpoint by a geriatric vigilante until the local law showed up. The woman climbed out of a Jeep Cherokee with the county sheriff's badge on the door.

"Grandpa, lower your weapon."

"Him first," the old geezer said, still pointing at Nash with his rifle.

"Sir, would you mind?" she asked politely with a hand on the butt of her holstered weapon.

Nash lowered his weapon to the ground. Since he'd been standing there for at least fifteen minutes with both his arms and his rifle over his head, *no,* he did not mind lowering his weapon at all.

"Told you poachers had moved in," the old man said to his daughter. Nash could only assume that she got both her looks and disposition from her mother.

"We're not here to hunt," Nash denied, well aware that hunting season was over. "I'm just here with my family."

Mal couldn't have timed it better or worse when she stepped out onto the porch just then. She came outside looking thoroughly ravished—and as if she'd been crying.

"Evening, ma'am," Lady Law said, though it was closer to dawn. "I'm Sheriff Rainey Law and this here is my grandpa. I was just speaking to your husband."

"He's not my husband."

Lady Law was immediately on alert, her hand

back on the butt of her gun as she positioned herself between them.

Nash wondered for a moment if Mal was about to give him up.

"He's my former brother-in-law."

"I see," she said, packing a whole lot of judgment into those two words. Aimed directly at him. "Your brother-in-law," she corrected, "was just telling me you're vacationing up here. The thing is we don't get many vacationers up around here this time of year. In the spring and summer, maybe. Some hunters in the fall. But we're too far off the grid for skiers. I'm going to have to ask how you know the owners."

"Oh, and the other thing is," the old man said, "we'll know if you're lying. We know all the owners around here. Even the ones that don't live here year-round. All my granddaughter has to do is make a phone call."

"Grandpa, please. Let me handle this."

"We're not friends of the owners," Nash volunteered. "We're friends of the Calhouns," he lied. But it was a credible lie. "Bruce married into the Zahn family. You can call him and check if you'd like, but I believe Bruce and Mitzi are still on their honeymoon. Or maybe it's just that they're newlyweds, because when he handed me the keys he told me not to bother him. We served in the marines together, you know, before Bruce lost his leg.

I'm just back myself. Looking for a little peace and quiet."

There was just enough truth to the story that Lady Law appeared to be buying in to it. Though she seemed to be curious about the relationship triangle that would include his sister-in-law and son.

Pops not so much. "That doesn't give you junkies the right to steal medicine from my animal clinic."

"We didn't steal any medicine," he said. Now, that was just a bald-faced lie. Good thing he was such a good liar. Good thing he had lots of practice telling lies. His life often depended on it.

"Grandpa, please. Folks, I don't want to keep you from your beds. I just need to check some ID so that I can write it up. Plus, any drivers or hunting licenses, gun permits," she said, looking at him. "Then I'll be on my way."

"I took the antibiotics from your clinic," Mal confessed before Nash could come up with another credible lie.

Was she crazy?

MAL STOOD FRAMED by the open door hugging herself. She'd slipped into shoes and had thrown on a sweater over her pajama pants and tank top. She glanced at Nash, who stood outside on the porch being interrogated by the local sheriff.

An elderly gentleman, rifle down by his side, stood with a foot on the bottom step, staring up at her. She didn't even know Ben was up, but how could he sleep with all this commotion? The boy raced past her to stand at his father's side.

The lady lawman looked the three of them over. Her concerned gaze came to rest on Mallory. She must look a mess, judging by the way the woman put herself between her and Nash and then put a hand on the hilt of her weapon.

Of course she didn't know what Nash had already told the woman. But everything coming out of his mouth right now was a lie.

Mal was sick of the lies. And the mistrust.

While she'd never been on the run before, she didn't believe that skirting the law was always the best option. Besides, she had a feeling their luck was about to run out. And maybe having the local law on their side was a better option than lying and continuing to go it alone.

"I broke into your clinic and helped myself to antibiotics," she said to the man. "Would you like to come inside?" she invited.

The sheriff seemed surprised, to say the least— a confession and an invitation to search.

Nash cast Mal a murderous look.

Inviting the law into your home was the same as giving them permission to snoop without probable cause or a warrant. Plus, she'd also just confessed to a crime.

But this wasn't their home no matter how good the lie was that Nash had created, and sooner or later the sheriff was going to figure that out. And she didn't know what Nash would do if and when the woman did see through the lies—and she didn't want to find out. So far he hadn't hurt anyone, that she knew of anyway, while they'd been on the run, and she'd like to keep it that way. She did not fancy being an accessory to murder.

She turned and went inside, followed by Ben, who Nash had a hold of, and then Nash. Next the sheriff and the elderly gentleman came inside, in that order. The old man didn't shut the door until she indicated that he do so.

"Please sit." She gestured toward the chairs around the table. "Anyone care for coffee?" she asked, moving into the kitchen. No one took her up on either offer.

"I'm Special Agent Mallory Ward with the FBI. This man is a protected witness in my temporary custody. He is also my brother-in-law. And Ben is my adopted son and biological nephew." Mal swept their shocked gazes. "My badge is in my pocket. May I?" she asked, not wanting to be shot while reaching for her badge.

The sheriff nodded. "Slowly," she cautioned.

Mal pulled out her badge wallet and handed it to the woman.

Nash looked like a big ball of frustration right now. He stood by with tight lips and his arms folded in front of his body. No doubt thinking she was a poor excuse for a fugitive—which she was. She was the law and she believed in the law.

"I know you have to run my badge number to check out my story, but I'm asking you not to." She hoped that pleading their case would gain them some sympathy and maybe even an ally. And gather some information in return.

"Nash is set to testify in federal court next week. There are people who want to make sure that doesn't happen. Two federal marshals have been…incapacitated." She censored the word *killed* for Ben's benefit.

"What's *incapacitated* mean?" Ben looked up at her.

Mal crossed her arms over his shoulders and hugged him close. "We'll talk about that later, Ben." Then she turned back to the sheriff. "So, what do you say?"

"I don't know, Mallory," the sheriff said. Mallory thought it was a good sign that the woman called her by her first name. "You're asking for my blind faith. I won't enter your badge number into the system, but I am going to be checking out your story." She made a few notes and then wrote down

Mal's badge number. "You won't mind if I put a deputy on watch?" It wasn't really a question.

"Yes, we do mind," Nash said.

The sheriff ignored him. "If your story checks out I could have a U.S. Marshal up from Denver in less than twenty-four hours."

"Great, we'll all be *incapacitated*." Nash seemed barely able to keep his mounting frustration in check. "If you make any inquiries…we're all in a lot of trouble."

"The thing is," Mal said, "we don't know the good guys from the bad guys."

"And they shot out our window," Ben added.

"I'll send that deputy around," the sheriff said.

"Unless he's Special Forces–trained, forget it," Nash said.

The old man chuckled at some inside joke. "Why antibiotics?" he asked.

"What?" The question was so off topic it caught Mal off guard.

"Why'd you need antibiotics?" he asked again. "The boy sick?"

She shook her head. "Nash was shot. He's better now, but he was fighting an infection."

"Mind if I have a look?" the old man asked.

Nash looked as if he did mind.

"Humor an old country doctor. Horses aren't the only thing I'm good at stitching up."

"And that's my cue to leave," the sheriff said.

"Before I add unreported gunshot wound to my list of transgressions. Good night, Grandpa. I take it you'll find your own way home?"

The old man waved her off. "Just get my bag out of the truck before you go."

"And do not bother sending that deputy around," Nash said.

"The deputy is already here," the sheriff said.

The old man chuckled. "I'll take that cup of coffee now. And you," he said, pointing to Nash. "Would you mind taking that shirt off for me?"

Nash removed his shirt with a scowl on his face.

Mal walked the sheriff to the Jeep Cherokee and Ben followed. "Thank you," she said.

The sheriff grabbed a black bag out of the back-seat. "Don't thank me yet."

CHAPTER FIFETEEN

"WHAT THE HELL you been doing, son?" the old man asked as he got a look at Nash's torn sutures.

Nash stole a glance at Mal. "I don't know," he muttered. "Running, I guess."

Mal set coffee mugs down in front of them and pulled up a chair next to the doc. No one was going back to bed tonight. Except Ben, who'd fallen asleep on the couch.

"How bad is it?" she asked.

"The stitches are professional enough. Though I suspect they *aren't*." He looked at Nash as he said, "And they're infected all right. I'll get him started on a course of the right antibiotics, remove the sutures and get him started on some larva therapy before I stitch him back up. Unless you fancy gangrene," he said to Nash.

"Larva?" Mal asked.

"Maggots," Nash answered.

"Maggots!" Ben popped up. Apparently he wasn't asleep.

"Come help me make breakfast," Mal said to Ben. "Since I don't think any of us will feel much like eating later on."

AFTER BREAKFAST, THE doctor—veterinarian—borrowed a snowmobile and left to go get his sterile larvae. And Ben headed upstairs to get dressed.

Mal and Nash were alone for the first time since, well, since he'd called out her sister's name during sex. Mal found she had a hard time looking him in the eye and an equally hard time taking her eyes off him when he wasn't looking.

"I thought you said you didn't know the owners," she said, picking a safe topic and trying to satisfy her curiosity at the same time. "How did you know this cabin belonged to my friend Mitzi Zahn's family when *I* didn't even know that?"

He shrugged. "Something you said once."

She hadn't seen Mitzi since high school. Even then they hadn't gone to the same high school; they just knew each other through JROTC and then various drill team and rifle competitions. After high school Mitzi had joined the navy, and Mal was ashamed to say they hadn't kept in touch.

"How can you remember something I said years ago when I can't even remember conversations I had last week?"

"You were sixteen or seventeen and made a big fuss about not being able to go on a coed camping trip. The details stuck."

"Oh, God. I do remember that. So this is that cabin." She looked around the now familiar cabin with new eyes.

She'd been seventeen and her parents had re-fused to let her go on the unchaperoned camping trip at Mitzi's family cabin. While most of her peers were already eighteen, others—like her—were not quite there yet. But none of the other parents had made a fuss—none. She was the only one not allowed to go, and she'd never gotten to-gether with Brett Daniels, because he'd broken up with her over it.

It was just another demonstration of Nash's pure genius. He'd shifted their plans on the fly and had been able to pull the location of the cabin out of his memory. Familiar, yet not familiar enough that anyone would associate either of them with it—since she no longer kept in touch with Mitzi, and neither of them had ever been here. And yet he was able to come up with a credible story about knowing the owners.

"But how did you know all that recent stuff about Mitzi getting married? What did you say her husband's name was, Bruce Calhoun? And he's a marine?"

"Read their engagement announcement in the paper." He nodded toward the hearth. "The stack is about six months old. Local and Denver. I was totally bullshitting about the wedding. I have no idea when it is or was."

"You don't think I should have told the sheriff about us?"

"I had it under control. But what's done is done."

"I was afraid you might hurt them," she confessed.

"Why would I hurt an old man and a woman? The worst that would have happened is she'd have kicked us out as vagrants and we'd have been looking for a new safe house."

That's what this was, a safe house.

She felt safe here. Wished she could stay safe here forever. It had been kind of nice to shut out the world.

She'd almost be sorry to leave it when the time came. At least now she knew who to thank for her safe haven and it would give her a reason to get in touch with an old friend. Mal realized how friendless and empty her life had become only now that she faced a future without any old friends.

Because as much as she wanted to she knew she'd never be able to get in touch with old friends like Mitzi again.

"COOL!" BEN SAID when the doc returned with the maggots.

Apparently the use of larvae was quite common not only in veterinary medicine, but also in modern biotherapy medicine. The sterile larvae were contained in a cage, like dressing placed over the wound. It would take two days for the debridement and disinfection process.

In other words, it would take two days for the larvae to chomp away the dead tissue.

If he'd been wearing that the other night, they never would have fallen into bed. There were just some things a girl couldn't get past. But Nash didn't seem bothered by it at all—though it had to feel weird. Ben was absolutely fascinated by the whole process, and the old doc was his new best friend. The things he was teaching Ben would certainly put him ahead in science once Ben went back to school.

If Ben went back to school.

Of course, he was going back to school.

Maybe not to his old school. Actually there was no maybe about that.

Since they'd never be going back to their old life.

CHAPTER SIXTEEN

NASH TURNED THE police scanner down as Mallory walked into the kitchen. He knew the device would come in handy eventually. "I'm going into town."

"What's up?"

"Probably nothing." Nash glanced over at the old man as he said it. They exchanged a look that made Mal feel excluded from whatever was going on. She and Doc had been playing board games with Ben.

Mal followed Nash to the door. "Probably nothing?"

He put a jacket on over his hoodie. "Just going into town to check on something. May stop by the sheriff's office to see what she's uncovered. And I need to use the burn phone to arrange for my ride to New York. Can I get you anything?"

She shook her head.

He walked out the door.

"Milk," she called out as he reached the entrance at the foot of the stairs. She had a bad feeling about this. She wanted to say be careful. But it came out as, "Milk and orange juice for Ben." Afraid of what he might see in her eyes, she held his gaze only for a second.

He nodded and then disappeared into the locked garage where the Tahoe was hidden away from the casual observer. Mal watched as Nash backed out of the garage and then had to go through the whole production of getting out of the car and shutting the wide swinging door and locking it again.

Doc came to stand beside her. "He'll be back."

She turned to go back inside. "Maybe."

There was that niggling suspicion that this was all coming to an end too soon.

THE TOWN OF Rock Springs, Colorado, was a mile-long stretch from a bygone era and one of the best-kept secrets in Colorado, having escaped the commercialism of the ski industry. It also had a history as colorful as neighboring Leadville. Rock Springs was located in Lake County, adjacent to two natural mountain lakes at the foot of Colorado's highest fourteener, Mt. Elbert.

Nash made two passes through town before parking in front of the corner drugstore on the slushy snow-covered street and then made his way to the sheriff's office on foot. He wanted to ask Rainey Law about the chatter he'd heard over the radio this morning.

Despite being saddled with the oldest deputy/

doctor of veterinary medicine on record, the town of Rock Springs did have an actual police station, and two squad cars—or rather SUVs—were parked out front.

Nash was debating going inside or waiting for the sheriff to come out when the frosted glass front door to the office opened. A uniformed deputy stood in silhouette, putting on his sunglasses against the white glare and sunshine. "Do you want anything while I'm out?" he yelled back through the door.

There was a muffled response from inside and then Nash ducked into a narrow side alley as the deputy accepted the order and pushed through the door to the street.

While in the alley, Nash noticed several caged entrances to the building, and around back he noticed an entrance that looked as though it might be direct access to the jail. He glanced back down the side alley, sizing up the Dumpster and the fire escape above it. The building was two stories with evenly spaced windows and roof access.

Once the deputy's vehicle pulled out, Nash sauntered back onto the sidewalk. It wasn't that he was trying to hide, but the fewer people who saw him close up, the better.

The interior of the station was more homey than modern. There was a receptionist/dispatcher at the counter when he walked in. "May I speak to Sheriff Law?"

"Rainey, there's a hot guy here to see you."

So much for discretion.

"Thanks for that," he said to the young woman.

"You're welcome."

Sheriff Law stepped out of her office and invited Nash in. She looked surprised to see him. "Didn't expect to see you in town."

"I was picking up some chatter on the police scanner between the deputies over in Leadville—" A nondescript sedan pulled up outside her office window just then. A man and a woman in suits and overcoats got out. He recognized the woman as Tess Galena. "You expecting company?"

"Shit," the sheriff muttered as she glanced out the office window. "Stay here," she said to him, and then she stepped out of her office.

"How can I help the FBI today?" he heard her say on the other side of the closed door.

"Have you seen this woman or this child?"

Nash watched through the closed slats as they flashed pictures of Mal and Ben.

"I told you last week, no."

Damn, she was good. That wasn't even a lie.

"How about this man?" the agent, or pseudoagent he didn't recognize, asked. Nash still hadn't seen the man flash a badge. He expected to see the agent showing Sheriff Law his mug shot, but it was actually a photo of Agent Tyler, the agent who'd fired on his own partner in the alley and then on them as they drove away in the Tahoe.

"No, I've never seen that man before."

"What about this one?" The agent held up side-by-side pictures showing Nash as America's Most Wanted and as a uniformed Navy SEAL. Both pictures were two ends of an extreme—he was somewhere in the middle now. The average person if shown those pictures might not even recognize them as him, or even the same person.

For one thing, his tan had faded to his natural skin tone, and he no longer had the wild unkempt hair along with the full beard and bushy eyebrows. Neither did he have a buzz cut or that hollowed, hard-jawed *I work out sixteen hours a day* look that he'd had right after BUD/S training.

He was lean-muscled and fit, but about twenty pounds lighter, and any hollowing of the cheeks came from skipping regular meals, not spending hours at the gym.

"Nope, haven't seen him, either." She crossed her arms. If either man was trained in body language, he'd be wondering why she was being so defensive. He might just attribute it to normal friction between the local law and Feds tromping all over their jurisdiction.

Nash was more worried about what Suzie Sunshine out at the receptionist's desk might say. So far she'd said nothing and hopefully she followed her boss's lead and kept her mouth shut. But Nash wasn't going to wait around long enough to find out.

Like most well-constructed law enforcement offices, the sheriff's private office had two ways in and out. He stepped out through the side door and into a hall. From there he tiptoed up the staircase and then out onto the roof.

The hollowed-out sound of boots running across a roof would have been heard from inside the building, so he crouched next to the exit tower and waited until the Feds made their next move. Fortunately that was to leave the building and drive off.

He decided against going back inside. He'd heard all he needed to hear. He just wanted to get back to Mal and Ben as soon as possible. He made his way up to the roof.

He'd judged the distance between the two buildings at about twelve feet. The average man could jump a distance of ten feet between buildings. The Olympic record was almost thirty feet. He got a running start and cleared the gap with room to spare.

He'd had a lot of practice running roofs in Third World countries.

The gaps between the rest of the buildings and the corner pharmacy were mere inches.

MAL KEPT WATCHING the clock. Nash had been gone all day. What was keeping him? She tried not to think the worst. That he'd either left them—in order to steer trouble away from them—or run into trouble before he could get back to them.

How long did it take to drop in on the sheriff, make a phone call and pick up some milk?

When she thought how normal that last bit sounded, she couldn't help letting a laugh escape.

"Mom, it's your turn," Ben was saying.

She rolled the dice and moved her game piece. When they saw the flash of headlights and heard the crunch of tires on snow, Ben raced to the picture window.

"He's back." And with that, Ben forgot all about his game.

"Ben—" Mal called after him, but he was already out the door. A quick glance outside told her it was indeed the Tahoe pulling into the garage, but she couldn't make out more than the taillights and license plate, so she hurried after Ben. Neither of them had taken the time to put on a coat, and it was freezing outside.

The car door slammed and Nash emerged from the garage with a bag in one hand and a carton of milk in the other. Mal stopped in her tracks. She put a hand to her mouth, wanting to laugh and cry at the same time.

He handed off the groceries to his son, and then Mal turned to follow Ben inside.

"Can I talk to you for a minute?" Nash said as he reached the porch.

She pulled the door closed behind Ben and waited, hugging herself against the cold while Nash kicked the snow off his boots and took his sweet time about climbing the steps.

"Here." He reached into his pocket and handed her a small pharmacy package that looked suspiciously like birth control pills.

"What's this?"

"Plan B."

"You have a backup plan for everything, don't you?" She couldn't help the sarcasm.

"We had unprotected sex."

Which they hadn't even talked about until now, and then to hear him say it like that—so matter-of-factly. Wow. "I'm aware we had sex."

She used his vernacular.

Don't think of it as making love. Try not to feel anything at all. No emotions. None.

She could choose to be a man about it. Or she could be a girl and demand they talk about their feelings when he so obviously had none for her whatsoever. She was so cold now her nose had started to drip and she sniffed.

Be a man.

"I don't know what form of birth control you

use. But if you're on the pill, you've been off it for a week. And if you're not, well…"

"There's always plan B." She tapped the package against her palm before tucking her arms around herself again.

"You're still within the window."

"Wouldn't want that *window* to close, now, would we?" Her teeth started chattering.

"The last thing I want to do, Mal, is leave you pregnant."

At least he didn't apologize. There was nothing worse than an apology after sex. *Sorry, I've got an early meeting.* Or *Oops, that's never happened before.* And how about, *I know, I should have told you I was married?*

But her favorite? *I'm sorry I called out your sister's name during sex.*

Why couldn't he have just said, *"The last thing I want to do is leave you"?* And then let that be the end of it.

"It's cold. You should get inside, Mal."

"What about you?"

"I've got some things to do." He turned and headed back down the porch.

She couldn't help herself. She *was* a girl. She threw plan B at the back of his head and it bounced right off his thick skull. He probably barely felt it.

He ducked and turned with a hand to the back of his head at the same time. "What the—"

"Birth control is not an afterthought. *I* am not an afterthought."

She turned and stomped back inside.

CHAPTER SEVENTEEN

"YOU'RE NOT AN afterthought, Mal."

He'd followed her into the bedroom and she turned around to face him. She couldn't deny the sincerity in his words or those deep brown eyes she'd come to trust again. "What am I, then?"

"You and me..." He shook his head as if it were a bad idea. "It's complicated."

She knew that, duh. That was the understatement of a lifetime. It wasn't as if she could totally disregard the fact that he'd been married to her sister. But maybe it felt more right than wrong.

More natural than not.

Not like slipping into her big sister's grown-up heels and playing dress-up. But more like finding a favorite pair of old sneakers she thought she'd thrown out and trying them back on to find they were still the perfect fit.

How could she have ever believed him to be Cara's killer when the whole time her gut was telling her that he wasn't? Aside from the fact that she'd wanted, needed someone to blame, her heart had been so fragile that it had been constructing walls to guard against him even then. Walls that had started crumbling down less than twenty-four hours after seeing him again.

Or maybe she'd built those walls wanting him to tear them down. To prove that he loved her, too. Only he didn't. Not in the way she loved him.

"I get it. You came back for Ben. I'm just along for the ride."

He tilted her chin so she had to look at him. "I came back for you both."

"You only need me to look after Ben. Because this isn't over when it's over, is it?" It was time she confronted her fear of losing everything. "Once you testify—Ben and I—we don't get to go back to our regularly scheduled lives, do we?"

He shook his head. "No, I'm sorry."

And there it was, the anticlimactic after-sex apology.

I'm sorry I turned your world upside down.

"My cover's been blown out of the water. And I think you know what that means." Nash might have taken down an entire terrorist cell to get his man, but he'd taken himself down along with it. And besides, for every man captured, another dozen escaped.

There was no end in sight for any of them. Cut off the head of the Cobra and he just grew more heads.

Now the many heads of the Cobra sought retaliation, hunting Nash down, striking where he was weakest—her and Ben.

Mal knew that Nash only had two choices.

Stay ahead of the Cobra. Or stay out of the Cobra's sight.

She and Ben would be tucked out of sight in the witness protection program—Nash would see to it in exchange for his testimony. Funny how his kidnapping them all made sense now. But while she knew what he would do in regards to her and Ben, she didn't know which path he'd choose for himself.

Nash was a mongoose. His quick thinking and reflexes would allow him to stay out of reach of the Cobra and strike back more often than not. At least that's what she chose to believe.

"You and Ben are going to be okay. I'll see to it, I promise."

A lover's promises were almost as bad as apologies.

"I know."

Cara had once called her the fifth wheel in her marriage. Mal hadn't really given it much thought at the time. She'd been the tagalong.

In truth, she'd loved Nash since they were kids. She'd never stopped loving him.

Cara had realized it, tolerated it even. Perhaps Nash had, too. Because they always loved her.

He loved her.

Maybe not in the same way she loved him, but love could be complicated. She'd never stopped loving him, not even when she'd hated him.

Maybe she was trying to hold on to him as a way to hold on to Cara. Maybe she was just trying to hold on to something because of this insane situation they found themselves in. Or maybe she just wasn't that complicated and was simply still in love with him.

He pulled her into a hug. "Are we cool?"

She supposed this was as close as he would come to talking about last night. Resting her head against his shoulder, she allowed herself that moment only to feel what it would be like to be loved by Nash. "We're cool. I'm letting you hug me with maggots taped to your gut, aren't I?"

She reveled in his deep chuckle.

The sound of it. The feel of it.

The heartbreak of it.

IT WAS UNUSUAL for them to sit down to dinner at a table like a family.

"I've arranged for our extraction," Nash said.

"When?"

"Tomorrow. At the old mine."

She hadn't thought to ask where it was going to happen. She'd just assumed it would be here at the cabin.

"Gather all your personal possessions. We pack

only what we need and burn the rest. Doc will sanitize the cabin and get rid of the Tahoe."

"We're walking out on foot?"

"First light. So get a good night's sleep." He held her gaze for longer than was necessary to make his point. There'd be no repeat performance of the night before. The hunger in his eyes held a different story this evening.

After supper, a melancholy settled over the household as she made Ben help her with the dishes while Doc tended to Nash's wound. He declared maggot therapy a success and went about stitching Nash up.

Meanwhile Nash had Ben lay out the contents of his backpack on the table—his Nintendo DS. School supplies and drawings. None of that was going with them. Essentially they were walking out of here with the clothes on their backs, a change of clothes and a day's worth of food and water. Plus borrowed coats and boots.

"What about this one?" Ben asked, holding up that very first doodle he'd made at this breakfast table the morning after their late night arrival.

Nash shook his head. He at least had the decency to look as though he felt bad about it. Ben looked as if he wanted to cry but was a real trouper about it. He put the picture back on the pile.

"Say there, that is a nice picture," Doc said. "Is this you and your dad? And your mom?"

"No, that's me and my dad and my aunt Mallory," Ben said while she tried not to cry. "That's my mom." He pointed to the angel.

"You know, I have the perfect place on my fridge. Do you mind if I keep this one to remind me of your visit?"

Ben beamed at the old man, while Mal shot him a grateful look, knowing full well that the picture would still be burned along with the rest. But at least Ben wouldn't have to know about it.

Suddenly this was all too real.

"Time for bed, Ben," she said with a hand to his back and ushered him toward the stairs. "Ow!" Mal flinched as something cold and wet hit her in the back of the head and then rained down her collar. More shocked than hurt, she turned to face Nash. "Did you just throw a snowball at me in the house? What are you, twelve?"

"Tit for tat." He ducked out the front door as if he expected her to chase after him. Of course, she didn't miss the reference about hitting him upside the head with birth control pills or the challenge in it.

Ben followed in a flash, grabbing a coat off the rack on his way out the front, which he didn't bother to shut.

"Well, what are you waiting for, Mal?" Doc asked. "Go! Blow off some steam."

"And be bombarded by snowballs?" Unless…

she snuck out back and around the side of the house. Gathering snow as she went and packing it into a tight ball, Mal peeked around the corner of the cabin.

Those cheaters already had snowballs in hand and a pile at their feet, ready and waiting for her to step out the door. But before Nash had a chance to spot her in his periphery, Mal took aim and smacked him on the side of the head. He yelped. Ben laughed and hit him from his other side.

They took turns rushing and retreating and then ganging up on one another until they were all laughing and winded. Mal got the worst of it, being without jacket or gloves. "Time-out!" she called after one particular brutal assault of snowballs.

She stopped long enough to go inside and grab a jacket. By the time she returned, a light snow had started to fall. Mal stood on the porch to admire the view. Ben and Nash had called a truce in order to start building a snowman. They were working together rolling a big ball around the yard and came to a halt at the foot of the stairs.

Mal went to work on the head while Nash and Ben rolled the midsection. Nash lifted the middle to the base and Mal put the head on top. Then they all stood back to admire their snowman. Nash volunteered his hat and Ben added his mittens to the arm branches that Nash had snapped off a bush.

The best they could do for eyes were rocks from the garden path after much debate about the size and color of the stones.

Ben decided he'd had enough of Crusty the Snowman—made from hard-packed snow and rough around the edges—and would rather throw snowballs again. But Mal was tired of snowballs. Besides, it was late. At least ten o'clock now and they had a long day ahead of them tomorrow.

As two more balls came straight for her head, Mal decided to put an end to it by rushing Nash. She tackled him to the ground, taking out the whole pile of snowballs in that one swift move. She sat back on her heels, straddling him and gloating. Her mistake was in attempting to make him eat a face full of snow.

He rolled her beneath him. Now he had her pinned.

Scrunching her eyes and mouth shut, Mal turned her head away, totally expecting the same face full of snow in retaliation. She felt his ice-cold glove brush the side of her face and looked up to find him staring down at her. His lips inches from hers and inching closer, he looked as if he was going to kiss her.

Mal rolled over on top, but he rolled her beneath him again.

This time there was no mistaking his intent when Ben chose that moment to dump a pile of snow on both of them. Laughing, they turned toward the boy. And in that instant they both must have seen the laser-red dot between the snowman's eyes.

Ben was standing on the other side of that snowman.

"Ben," Mal screamed.

Nash rolled them into Ben and covered them both as the snowman's head exploded. In the time it took for Mal's heart to slam into her chest, Nash had his handgun out and had fired two return shots in the general direction of the sniper.

The sniper had used a silencer, but Doc came running to the front door at the sound of return fire. He fired off a couple more rounds from behind the open door.

"See anything?" Nash called to him.

"Nothing," Doc acknowledged.

"He's lost the element of surprise," Nash said to her. "We don't want to give him time to regroup. When I say go, we'll cover you while you and Ben keep low and run for the snowmobile. Take it and go. Do not stop until you reach the old mining town."

She wanted to argue with him. "What about you?"

"I'll be right behind you. Now go!"

Nash emptied his clip while she and Ben ran toward the garage. Doc continued to fire off several more rounds. She flung the door wide and swung her leg over the first machine she came across. She tucked Ben in front of her. "Hold on," she said as they slipped from mud to snow.

DOC PROVIDED COVER while Nash ducked back inside the cabin.

"What do you need me to do?" Doc asked. "I've already called Rainey for backup."

Nash tossed the old man the keys to the Tahoe and then scrambled to reload his weapon. "Get to the old mining ghost town over the ridge. Find Mal and Ben. She'll want this…." He handed off Mal's SIG and then tucked his Glock to his back. "I'll meet you there."

"And you?" Doc asked as they divvied up the rest of the weapons.

"I'm going to hunt this guy down. Find out what he knows."

They left the cabin and scrambled to the barn. "Sure there's only one shooter?" Doc asked as he opened the door to the Tahoe.

Nash kick-started the snowmobile. "No, but I am sure we're about to have a hell of a lot more company."

He slammed his night-vision goggles down. Nash waited for Doc to drive out of the barn and then he took off in the direction the shots had been coming from. Unless he missed his guess, the guy had taken off as soon as he lost the element of surprise and they started firing back. There'd been no exchange after that first round had been fired off. He probably had a night scope on his rifle, but he'd fired from close range, so it probably wasn't a long-range sniper weapon.

At best Nash was dealing with an ill-equipped amateur. But this amateur had to work for somebody—somebody definitely on the wrong side of the law.

If the police or military had come in hot, first of all, they wouldn't have sent one ill-equipped amateur, but it would have been an easy takedown. He, Mal and Ben had been out in the open. Exposed, vulnerable…

For a moment he saw Mal's softly parted lips and that look in her eyes as he'd been about to kiss her. There was no denying to himself that he wanted her. He wouldn't let her down, not the way he'd let Cara down. But there was just no future for them.

CHAPTER EIGHTEEN

MAL TORE THROUGH the snow-covered terrain on the Ski-Doo using her natural night vision—at fifty or sixty miles an hour, it was too easy to override the headlights and there'd be no time to stop in the two hundred feet of light anyway.

Plus, by using her natural sight and the moonlight to guide her, she had a better chance of staying out of the sights of any gunman that might be following them. She'd also have a better chance at seeing a drop-off or a fallen tree in her path.

She pulled Ben tighter. His small hand gripped the steering bars in front of hers. He'd given up his mittens to the snowman, so she'd given him hers. Her grip had gone numb, but that was as much from white-knuckling the handlebars as the snow and cold.

She'd snagged both helmets, which in addition to providing safety in case of a collision, also gave them some sense of protection against flying bullets. Except, of course, the high-powered, armor-piercing kind, but she tried not to think about that as they sped along. Though she couldn't help wishing she at least had her handgun.

She trusted Nash wouldn't have sent her and Ben into the night if the danger were greater than what they were fleeing from. He had their backs. She just had to keep going. She knew she was headed in the general direction of the ghost town, but she'd only been there once. Nothing looked familiar, especially in the dark.

Slowing the snowmobile only after they hit the deer trail, she had no choice but to turn on the headlight. The narrow path was filled with sharp turns and trees that appeared out of nowhere. Pine needles daring to get too close. The rumble of the snowmobile engine seemed overloud bouncing back at her from the eerie silence of the aspen grove that surrounded them.

Her imagination ran wild as they went through the snow.

When she came to a fork in the path and would have gone right, Ben pointed left. He'd been this way with Nash more times than she had, so she veered left, hoping he'd inherited his father's sense of direction and not his mother's.

Just as she was beginning to think they'd taken a wrong turn, the trees thinned and opened up to reveal the small mining town, now a ghost town built into the side of the mountain.

NASH FOUND THE amateur sniper in a snowdrift alongside the road with a bullet to his head. Caucasian male. Mid-twenties. Crew cut. Prison tats across his knuckles spelled out FREEDOM. He wore a faded green camo jacket and overalls.

Could be military, ex-military or some pseudo-military faction. Nash had plenty of run-ins with hate groups while undercover. But they weren't likely the ones hunting him down in order to kill him—at least not at the moment.

The dominos in the fifty-city raid of sex and drug traffickers he'd taken down all had connections to the al-Ayman terrorist network and the man he was about to testify against, Mullah Kahn. And *this* guy did not fit the profile.

Definitely not a professional. Fresh tire tracks in the muddy snow indicated a getaway car. So this guy's partner or partners had shot him and then left him. Maybe al-Ayman was hiring out its dirty work to locals—that would be one explanation. But something didn't sit right and it all came back to that FBI agent shooting his partner and then shooting at them…Nash and Ben.

Nash riffled the dead man's pockets, looking for some clue as to his identity, or more important, some clue as to his employer's identity, but came up empty-handed. That's when his ears perked to the sound of three-hundred-horsepower engines.

At least three or four snowmobiles were headed straight for him.

Nash hopped back on his Ski-Doo just as three snowmobiles crested the hill at fifty miles an hour. The drivers were dressed all in black from helmet to boots. Nash circled back toward the cabin and headed into the open terrain of a backcountry bowl.

He would lead his pursuers away from the ghost town. Away from Mal and Ben.

They weren't exactly shooting at him, probably because it was hard to aim at a moving target while driving a speeding snowmobile, but they sure as hell weren't trying to flag him down for some friendly riding competition, either. Could be they wanted to take him alive—or maybe not. That became clear when the lead driver pulled alongside and tried to use his superior high-performance machine to steer Nash into a tree.

Nash barely missed the tree. He came out on the other side, kicking until he unseated the other driver, who went tumbling through the snow. The other two drivers throttled forward to flank him on either side. He throttled back and tried to outmaneuver them rather than outdistance them. But they had him at every turn. He was so engrossed in losing them that he almost didn't see the sheer drop-off ahead.

He didn't have time to think, let alone gauge the

stopping distance needed for the snowmobile. He dove off into the snow as his machine took flight over the cliff. Pursuer number two used his hand-brake to slow his machine down.

But it was too late. Nash watched the man's slow-motion slide off the cliff.

Pursuer number three had plenty of stopping room and a gun pointed at Nash before he'd even regained his feet. Nash slowly stood and raised his hands.

And then with two deft moves Nash knocked the man's gun hand with his left forearm, while at the same time his right forearm connected underneath the helmet at the guy's throat. The man's head snapped back and he dropped the gun, but he immediately came back fighting. They matched each other blow for blow and block for block.

Nash got in a couple of good shots, but then his opponent came back strong with a roundhouse kick to Nash's injured side. He knew instantly that blood soaked his shirt. Several times he thought he was going to pass out, but he protected his injured side and kept fighting.

"Enough," a familiar voice said.

Nash felt the cold barrel at the back of his head. "Thought I already got rid of you once, Bari. Still doing your father's dirty work, I see?"

Somewhere in the back of Nash's brain, it registered that the driver he'd knocked from his snowmobile had caught up with them. And that driver was someone he knew.

Nash raised his hands and driver three got in one last sucker punch. The guy's fist connected with his side and Nash doubled over.

He would have come up fighting, but Bari cold-cocked him with the butt end of his own rifle. And then his world went black.

"HE SHOULD BE here by now." Mal turned to look at Doc.

They'd parked behind the old stable yard but had taken shelter inside the old saloon. Though it was just as cold inside as out. It was the only building in which the second floor was still intact.

The buildings had long ago been stripped to the bare walls, so the only place to sit was on the stairs or on the bar. Mal was too nervous to do anything but pace the hardwood floors.

At least she had her gun now. And they had the rifles that Doc had brought with him. So far they were alone, but that's also what worried her.

"He'll be here." Doc had eased his old bones down on one of the bottom steps. Ben was burning off his own energy by making a game of skipping up and down the stairs.

All they could do was wait for Nash. Because he would get there. Mal had no doubt.

CHAPTER NINETEEN

NASH WOKE UP back in the cabin, duct-taped to a chair. Or rather, his legs were duct-taped to the chair legs while his hands were duct-taped behind his back and possibly to one of the back slats. Either way, he could rip through his restraints in seconds, but it would be loud and he'd have to come up fighting.

He needed to know what he was up against first. Or find something in his back pocket that would allow him to rip through the tape with a little more stealth.

Bari had removed his helmet and stood before Nash with his grotesquely disfigured face. Left lid drooping. Left side of his mouth in a permanent scowl.

A payback from Sari.

"I thought I killed you once already," Nash taunted him.

Bari snarled at him. "Where is she?"

"I have no idea where your sister is," Nash lied.

Well, that explained why he was still alive. Sari was to testify along with him. Although her knowledge of Kahn's terrorism activities was limited, it might be enough to convict her old man and her brother after he was hunted down.

If Nash had to die, at least he'd die knowing justice had been served.

"I could cut you into little pieces." Bari was using his knife to clean underneath his fingernails. He'd probably seen some bad guy do it in a movie and thought it looked intimidating. "But you know how squeamish I am. My friend here—" he nodded over his shoulder to the driver of the third snowmobile "—is not so squeamish."

"I know you're a weasel. So I'm not surprised you'd have someone else do your dirty work." Bari had at least a half dozen armed men in and around the place. Nash had been sizing them up as they came and went.

"An eye for an eye, maybe." Bari used the knife to point to his drooping lid.

"You shouldn't have threatened my wife—your sister—with acid."

"Do not degrade my family by calling my sister your wife! I never would have married her to a Jew." Bari spat in Nash's face.

Nash turned the other cheek. And then turned cold eyes back to Bari.

"Naveed/Nash, you duplicitous infidel. I still love you like a brother." Bari patted Nash's battered face and then made a big production of wiping his own spittle on his black snow pants. "Why must you insist on suffering at the hands of my colleague?" Bari leaned in closer. "My colleague whose brother you sent over a cliff. Besides—" Bari shot snowmobile rider number three a dark look and then spoke loud enough for him to hear "—we both know he was an idiot for not braking sooner. What my colleague doesn't believe but that I know for a fact is that we could inflict unimaginable pain, hack you into a million little pieces and you still would not talk. Am I not right?"

Bari stood there with his arms thrown wide as if he were asking the rhetorical question of the universe.

Nash was beginning to wonder if this speech had a point or if Bari just liked hearing himself talk. He must love the fact that with his father and brother in jail, he was left in charge. A mistake on Nash's part for not ensuring that he'd killed the man.

"So let us put an end to our differences. You are going to tell me where my sister is in exchange for a quick and painless death."

"Bring it on, Bari. You had it right the first time."

Bari turned to his colleague. "What did I tell you?" He turned back to Nash. "See, this I knew. Which is why I'm not going to hurt you, my brother—brother-in-law. But I will hurt what is left of your family."

Nash felt a cold sweat coming on.

"They are over in that old mining town on the hillside, right? The one that looks like an old Western movie set. There are what, seven?" He verified with his henchman. "Seven buildings rigged with explosives. Imagine finding someone had done all the groundwork for me. All I had to do was construct a detonator."

Bari waggled his cell phone in front of Nash's face.

That cold sweat turned into a trickle of fear unlike Nash had ever known. "You son of a bitch."

"Leave my mother out of this and tell me what I want to hear."

"I don't know where your sister is." Nash ground out the words.

"I hope you're feeling lucky." Bari's thumb hovered over the keypad. "Pick a building."

"I'm not going to pick a building."

"Then I will. What about the church? You're Jewish. I'm Muslim. What's one less Christian house of worship to either of us?" His thumb continued to hover. "I can hear those wheels turning inside your head. Odds are seven to one I'm wrong. Maybe you know where they are. Maybe I do not. You think if I blow up the wrong building, then they're safe because they will run out into the street."

Bari studied Nash's face. "That's not how this game works. I have a sniper in place who will ensure that they stay inside wherever they're at."

"Is he as good as the guy you sent earlier?"

"What do you mean earlier?" Bari seemed genuinely confused. "I don't know what you're talking about, Nash, so let's get back to the matter at hand, shall we? Unless you think your FBI agent sister-in-law can find and disarm the bombs you set, tell me what I want to hear," he demanded. "And then I let them live. It's your choice. You can save three lives or one. But you can't save them all. I'm done playing games."

He started to lower his thumb.

"Los Angeles!"

"Even the unbreakable break," he said to his man. "I'm going to need more than that."

"I don't know where she is right now!" Nash stood prepared to lunge with the chair still taped to him. When Bari hesitated, Nash pressed his advantage. "But I know where she'll be a few short hours from now."

"I'm listening."

"She's coming here. To the ghost town."

"You lie."

"I'm not lying. The U.S. Marshal Service is

extracting me this afternoon. Sari will be on the helicopter with them."

"He's lying." The henchman reverted to his native tongue, calling Nash's character into question. Bari argued back in angry, rapid-fire Arabic, knowing full well Nash was fluent, but convinced he'd outsmarted him this time.

"I'm not lying," Nash pressed his advantage. "Think about it, Bari. They've got to get her from Los Angeles and then deliver both of us to New York. Why do you think Mal and Ben are down there? We didn't know you were coming. I was to clean up here at the cabin and then we were all going to spend the night in the ghost town so as not to miss our ride."

"Shut up, the both of you," Bari roared. "Let me think."

Nash knew when not to press and settled back into his chair. Bari looked at him from his superior standing height. "If you're lying..."

He let the threat hang in the air.

"Bring the car around," he ordered the sentry posted at the door.

"I'M GOING TO go look for him," Mal said as dawn crested the sky.

Doc stopped her at the saloon doors. "He'd want you to stay here."

"Perhaps you've never heard the old military

axiom, Never leave a man behind. He wouldn't leave me. I'm not going to leave him—"

They heard the crunch of tires on snow and stopped arguing. A dark SUV drove up and then stopped in the center of town. Mal pulled out her gun and Doc had his rifle at the ready.

A man got out from the passenger side and moved to the front of the vehicle. "Come out, come out, wherever you are," he said with exaggerated nonchalance. "I have something you want."

Two more men exited the back. One dragged Nash out behind him.

Doc squinted against the snow's glare. "What's he wearing?"

"Explosives," Mal said. "Or silly putty."

Ben tried to push his way past her to get a glimpse of his father.

"Ben." She grabbed him by the arm and made him look her in the eye. "I want you behind the bar. Do not come out unless I say so."

He must have recognized her mom voice, because he didn't argue.

"Where the hell is Rainey?" she mumbled under her breath. Mal exchanged her handgun for a rifle and trained it on the man holding Nash. She was a decent shot. She could take him out. "You take the loudmouth."

Until now she'd only seen Bari Mullah Kahn in pictures with the caption FBI's Most Wanted.

"I wouldn't do that if I were you," he shouted. Though he couldn't possibly have heard her. "He held up his cell phone. I know these buildings are rigged with explosives and I have the detonator. If you do not believe me, perhaps a little demonstration is in order?"

"He doesn't know about the silly putty," Doc said.

"What if that's not what he's talking about?"

"There are no good choices," Doc said.

"Nash has even fewer."

"He wouldn't want you to give yourself and the boy up for him. We don't even know why Kahn has him strapped to a bomb. Maybe he wants to throw us all down a mine shaft and then seal it up. I've got to believe Rainey is out there somewhere."

Unless they hurt her.

Mal glanced over her shoulder toward the bar where Ben was hiding. She liked their odds better in here. Even Nash's. She fixed a bead on his captor's head.

"We're not coming out, Kahn. What we have here is a standoff."

"YOUR WOMAN PLACES less value on your life than you do on hers."

"Never said she was my woman."

"I could blow them up now and be done with it."

"And risk turning away the helicopter? Besides which, we have a deal. You hurt them and I have no reason to cooperate," Nash threatened. "She's smart. She has you all figured out." A weaker woman would be cowering in the corner. Or worse, trying to save him.

Nash could see Bari's growing frustration with the situation. "You underestimate me, my brother," Bari said. "While you spent six years living among us, I spent six years learning from you. Observe…"

Mal stumbled out of the saloon with her hands in the air. Another of Bari's henchmen held her at gunpoint. Doc also came out at the end of a barrel. And a third man dragged Ben by the scruff of his collar.

Nash took a halted step forward. "Just let them walk out of here."

"Not until after the fireworks."

His men walked the trio across the street to the jail. Like most of the buildings around town, the jailhouse had paneless windows and no hanging doors. And the single cell had no cell door. Only one guard stayed back to guard them while the rest of the men spread out around town.

"You'd better not be lying about that helicopter," Bari threatened.

"Guess we'll know in a minute," Nash said. "Got a flare?"

"It's broad daylight."

"Look around, Bari. From the air, this is nothing more than a couple of dilapidated rooftops in a dense forest of pine trees on a mountain range full of dense pine. The only clearing big enough is between the old schoolhouse and the church. The pilot needs to know where to put down. That's where you set it off."

"You'll light the flare." Bari gave him a little shove in that direction with the barrel of his gun. "Just try not to light up yourself in the process."

"Whatever floats your boat."

Bari shouted in Arabic for his men to take up positions close to the buildings and out of sight. He grabbed a flare from the SUV and had the driver move the vehicle back behind the buildings. And then Nash and Bari set off down the middle of the street toward the church steeple.

Nash caught glimpses of shadows moving between buildings. He went over the number of Bari's men and their positions. It was possible the sheriff had arrived with reinforcements. And just in time.

They'd reached the clearing.

He could hear the helicopter in the distance.

Bari couldn't help taunting him one final time as he handed Nash the flare and backed off from the landing site. "The redhead and the boy will fetch a good price on the open market."

Nash wrapped his fist around the flare. "You said you'd let them go."

"I said I'd let them live." Nash wanted to wipe the smug smile off the man's smug face.

The helicopter grew louder. "Then it's a good thing I lied about your sister being on that chopper."

"You double-crossed me?" Bari seemed to find the idea incredulous. "You will pay." He pressed the keypad of his cell phone detonator, but nothing happened.

Bari screamed in outrage and lunged for him. Nash snapped the cap off the flare and struck it against the cap to light it. Bari retreated. A spark could easily ignite an explosive vest. Nash used the other man's fear and the high-intensity bright light from the flare to temporarily blind the other man. After that it was easy enough to disarm him.

The sheriff and her reinforcements saw their opportunity and took it to gain the upper hand on the rest of Bari's henchmen. The sniper fired into the battle, but all he accomplished was giving his position away. The helicopter crested the trees and the SEAL sniper on board took Bari's sniper out.

Significantly impaired, Bari struggled to maintain his distance and aim his weapon. He stumbled backward, firing off wild rounds. Nash tossed the flare to the landing zone and then rushed the terrorist before he actually hit something.

Nash had Bari under his control in a matter of seconds.

"You thought this was C-2?" Nash pointed to his duct tape vest bomb that Bari had constructed back at the cabin. "Child's clay."

He might have taught Ben how to construct a bomb, but he would never have used real explosives to do it. None of these buildings were rigged. If Bari wanted the upper hand, then he should have thought to bring his own C-2 or C-4 to the party.

The helicopter circled the town and landed. Nash handed Bari off to one of the SEAL team members. He only recognized a couple of the guys. The face of his old team had changed in ten years. But one very familiar man walked up to him and held out his hand. "Good to see you." Mike McCaffrey drew Nash into a bear hug.

"It's good to see you, too." Out of the corner of his eye, he watched the team's sniper, Kip Nouri, walk straight up to Mal. Nash tried to control his jealousy. It wasn't as if either of them would get the girl in the end.

CHAPTER TWENTY

"YOU LOOK GOOD," Kip Nouri said with a cheeky grin.

She looked a mess. "You mean for a gal who just wrestled an armed man to the ground."

"Might I add that was a real turn-on? Seriously, you okay?"

Mal couldn't help smiling back at him even as she shook her head. Same old Kip. Even though he wasn't. His jaw seemed harder somehow and he looked more mature even if he wasn't. Although maybe he was, because he didn't seem to be having any trouble keeping eye contact. "We are now. You're a sight for sore eyes, Ensign."

"It's Lieutenant now. Lieutenant Commander soon." He looked embarrassed to be correcting her. "And who's this guy?" he asked as Ben came up and glued himself to her side.

"Ben," the boy answered.

"You look just like your dad," Nouri said. "Give me a fist bump, Nash Junior."

Ben and Nouri bumped fists. A total guy thing.

"Well, I have to go set up on a rooftop until Mac gives me the all-clear."

"The saloon still has a second story," she offered, not knowing what else there was to say.

"It was good to see you again, Mallory Ward. Believe me when I say I'm wishing I'd never accepted no as your final answer."

"I know," Mal said. They never met up for that lunch they'd talked about, because her sister had been murdered the morning after she'd dropped Nash off at Kip Nouri's bachelor pad. He'd called around noon and she had still been at the hospital, or maybe the police station by then, but in either case she'd been in no condition to answer.

He'd called again after he'd heard about what had happened. Left a couple of sympathetic messages. She blew him off for a whole week before she finally picked up and told him she didn't want anything to do with Nash's teammates. She'd asked him not to call her again and he'd respected her wishes. Simple as that.

"Nouri," Commander McCaffrey shouted. Or maybe it was Captain McCaffrey now. "Get your ass up on a rooftop."

As Mal watched Kip walk away she looked back on that moment almost eight years ago and realized he was probably the last real boyfriend she'd ever had. Even though she wouldn't have called him that at the time. He at least had potential.

The few relationships she'd had since qualified as dysfunctional. Guys she could dump with no regrets right after the sex had played out. If she happened to come across a decent guy, she'd run as fast and as far as she could.

Or got inside his head and really messed him up.

She glanced over at Nash. He was talking with Mac and the female helicopter pilot.

If it had been anyone but Nash, she would have said that was the reason she'd fallen into bed with him. Because things were going great and she wanted to screw them up. But that wasn't the reason and now she had to live with the guilt.

She'd heard the chatter. They were waiting on the U.S. Marshal Service.

The marshals were transporting the other witness—Nash's wife—to this very location and would be here within the hour. The FBI and the SEALs were working together to ensure that the route and the location were secure before giving the Marshal Service the all-clear.

At the moment, the SEALs were sweeping the buildings with bomb dogs.

Mal didn't want to meet this other woman. Her sister's replacement.

Technically, Mal had slept with the woman's husband, and that made her the other woman. She didn't think she could look his wife in the eye and lie to her. And she sure as hell couldn't tell her the truth. That she was in love with Nash and had been for a very long time.

The special agent in charge of the Denver field office—her boss, Dave Glaze—had arrived on the scene and had made it clear that she was to stick close to his side. That might have been comforting if Christopher Tyler wasn't glued to the man's other side.

So she kept her distance while Dave was busy with the sheriff men.

Doc was busy with the injured, so she didn't even have him for company. There had only been the one fatality during the shoot-out—the sniper that Nouri had taken out. But she heard passing comments from fellow officers regarding other bodies that had turned up in and around the cabin.

She felt more like a captive now than when Nash had first kidnapped them. She and Ben were not allowed to leave—not that they had anywhere to go anyway. Their house was no longer their home, and their home of the past few weeks—the cabin—did not belong to them.

There was a second SEAL team in the process of securing it now.

But it was still the one place she wanted to retreat to when she saw Tyler headed their way. "How you holding up?" Tyler asked with passable concern.

"Fine." She crossed her arms.

Ben moved from her side to stand behind her.

"Look, Mal. I know how it must have looked from your perspective—"

"Like you needed target practice."

"I was aiming for the tire. Like I told Dave, I just wanted to stop a fugitive from getting away with you and the kid."

"He's not a fugitive."

"I'm going to go by my dad." Ben raced up the street toward Nash before Mal could stop him. He didn't feel safe with her. Not as safe as he felt with his father. Nash looked up as Ben came to stand beside him. He put a hand on Ben's shoulder and nodded to her with a rather grim look on his face.

"Excuse me," Mal said to Tyler.

Mal crossed the street to the saloon while Dave and Rainey were arguing over prisoner transport. Dave was playing the FBI jurisdiction card and Rainey was none too happy about it. For now the prisoners were all hooded and zip-tied, sitting in the middle of the street under heavy guard—local, FBI, SEALs and military K-9s. There were in fact more guards than prisoners.

Mal just wanted a moment of peace and quiet and then perhaps she'd seek out her sole friend in all of this confusion—Kip Nouri. She stepped behind the bar and slipped through the panel door to a small office that Bari's henchmen had come through.

They'd grabbed Ben and taken her and then Doc by surprise. That seemed like ages ago.

Thank God Bari Mullah Kahn and his men couldn't tell the difference between C-4 and homemade Silly Putty.

She stepped from the small office and then out the back door.

A couple of deep breaths of mountain-fresh air to quiet her thoughts and she was already feeling better. She knew why Dave couldn't allow her and Ben to leave, but she was having a hard time coming to grips with it.

FBI SPECIAL AGENT Christopher Tyler waited exactly five minutes before following Mal into the saloon. Nash didn't wait five seconds before following Tyler.

Nash left Ben with McCaffrey's wife, Hannah, and Tess Galena.

Commander Hannah Staton McCaffrey had been a combat pilot since before women were even considered combatants. With three kids to worry about, they no longer paired up for routine missions because of the risks involved, but as Mac put it, he knew nothing was going to keep his wife away from this one.

Nash was just glad to have women he trusted watching over Ben.

The CH-46 Sea Knight helicopter would keep the boy occupied long enough for Nash to go check on his aunt. He wished he could think of Mal as Ben's mother—she earned it—but he just couldn't. That was Cara's place in his heart.

He was still trying to figure out Mal's.

But he knew it did not begin or end with her sister.

He pushed his way through the swinging doors of the saloon. A quick look around showed nobody on the first floor. He kept to the side of the stairs as he made his way up to the second floor. There had been doors at one time, but there were none now. The smaller rooms to the back of the building were all dark. But the largest room at the front of the building had light pouring in through the windows and he could see a body on the floor. Nash drew his gun and entered with caution.

The moment he did he had a gun pointed at his head.

"She's upstairs with the new boyfriend," Tyler said from behind him. "I have no wish to hurt her. You're the one I want. She's better off without you. The world is better off without you. Now, hands above your head, nice and easy."

Nash could see the body on the floor belonged to one of Bari's men. He raised his hands above his head. He remembered Tyler exiting the saloon and calling out all-clear to his superiors.

Nash wondered why Tyler didn't step in to take his gun, which he still held in his hand.

"You're Joseph Tyler's brother. Your brother was a guard at Gitmo." Nash did not have to guess—he knew this for a fact.

"My brother was a marine and a patriot. You're not fit to lick his boots, Nash."

"Your brother was an asshole and a sadist. One of the worst I've ever come across."

"Yeah, well, he pretty much said the same thing about you. How you were the camp leader. You started that hunger strike—"

"In protest. To draw attention to the mistreatment. Your brother maimed and tortured prisoners and small animals for the sheer pleasure of it."

"You're no better than animals, the lot of you. You think because you were born here that you're different than them? Than him? You still have that same Middle Eastern mentality they all have." He pointed with his gun to the dead man on the floor. "You're just like him. And you deserve to die just like him. I read your file. You're so dirty not even the government knows what to do with you—one of the unclean. It was only a matter of time before some higher muckety-muck decided to burn you anyway. I'm doing Washington a favor."

"You have no idea what you're talking about."

"I know my brother went to prison because of you. I know he hanged himself in Leavenworth and it wasn't a fake suicide. The whole time you were at Gitmo—sucking up to the enemy, planning and plotting to help them escape—you were spying on marines."

"If your brother and the men arrested with him were acting like marines, they wouldn't have been on my radar. It's men like your brother that give the military a bad rap."

"Shut up. Just shut up. Here's how this is going to go down," Tyler said. "Dead guy shoots you with his gun. I shoot him with mine. Everybody rushes in and I'm the only one left standing to explain the situation."

Nash had tried to talk the guy down. Had given him the benefit of the doubt because of his brother, but now it was time to act.

Nash lunged at Tyler and they fought. The guy had him dead to rights.

He heard the click. And then two shots fired.

And knew he should be dead.

Tyler fell to the floor. And Mal stood right behind him with a gun in her hand. "I shot him."

"He would have killed me."

Nouri swung through the window. He looked at the two bodies on the floor. Looked at Mal still holding the smoking gun. And then exchanged looks with Nash. "We have an insurgent and agent down," he said into the mic.

And then it was left to Nash, not Tyler, to explain the situation.

MAL SAT OUTSIDE on the dilapidated boardwalk as they carried the body of Special Agent Christopher Tyler out in a body bag. Dave looked at her with pity in his eyes. He was a fair man and Nash's story had checked out. One of the bodies, with a bullet to his head, found by the side of the road near the cabin belonged to an ex-marine with ties to both Christopher and Joseph Tyler.

The first sniper—the one who'd blown the head off Crusty the Snowman—had not been working for al-Ayman, but rather for money or vengeance on behalf of the Tyler brothers. The kid had probably freaked after his failed hit and Tyler had shot him, either because he was a liability or because he was a loose end.

"I'm going to be looking into Stan Morgan's shooting, personally. There was an attempt on his life while he was in the hospital that set back his recovery. If it wasn't for Tess, I might not have realized in time to save him and spread the rumor that he'd died. I should have caught on faster. There's no doubt looking back now, that Tyler's demeanor changed after that shooting at your house," Dave told her.

"I'm glad that Stan's going to be all right."

"Officially, Tyler will be ruled as shot in the line of duty. I just wanted you to know that your name will be kept out of all of this. Looks like your ride is here, Mal." He nodded toward the convoy of four white vans entering the town. "Good luck, Mal."

He offered his hand. Mal stood to shake it.

He was a fair man and a good boss. She was going to miss working with him.

Shooting a fellow agent in the back without warning—even a bad one—was not how she had wanted to end her career. Tucking her hands into her back pockets, Mal watched her old life begin to fade as Dave walked up to the driver of the first van and introduced himself as the officer in charge.

Because the Feds had jurisdiction over terrorism, the prisoners were loaded into three of the four secure vans for transport by the U.S. Marshal Service.

The dead bodies were bagged and loaded into the other.

As the four vans drove off, two white SUVs pulled in.

The SEALs had finished their sweep of the town and surrounding area and had given the all-clear. With the immediate threat contained or removed, everyone in the ghost town seemed more relaxed.

Yet Mal paced outside the saloon. Nouri stood nearby without flirting. Nash had given the SEAL strict instructions to guard her. But suddenly he disappeared somewhere with McCaffrey, only to return a short while later with Ben. Nouri stood off to the side as Ben ran straight up to Mal and hugged her.

A woman in jeans, a fitted white blouse and a fringed suede jacket, looking as if she belonged to the old mining town in another era in her cowboy hat and boots, got out of the lead SUV with tinted windows, instead of off a horse. She wore her holstered weapon concealed rather than on her hip. And she had a laptop case strapped across her body instead of a saddlebag. Definitely from this era.

She flashed a badge in their direction.

"Jane Bowman, U.S. Marshal." The woman tipped her hat to Nash. "Lieutenant Commander, good to see you alive and in one piece. Mallory Ward, Benjamin Ward and Mr. Nash. Would you folks come with me please?"

Bowman led them past the vehicles with their tinted windows to the small schoolhouse on the hill. Mal glanced in passing before refocusing her attention on the small hand in hers and where they were going.

"I'm told there's limited seating in this town." Bowman glanced at them over her shoulder. "I wanted some privacy as we go over what to expect as you enter the witness protection program."

Mal felt Nash's hand at the small of her back as they stepped across the threshold of the schoolhouse. The back had been completely stripped, but there were a couple of dusty benches and tables up front still bolted to the floor with rusty hardware.

Bowman removed the strap of her laptop bag from around her neck and placed it on the desk at the front of the room. She turned around and propped up against it. Before they even had a chance to sit down, an older woman entered through the side door to the schoolyard. "This is my colleague, Corin. Corin is a child psychologist and she's going to take Ben out to the swing set. As much as he would like to stay, Nash is going to go with them." She looked pointedly at him and he ushered Ben out the side door behind Corin.

There was no door to close behind them and Mal had a clear view of the rusty old swing set and seesaw in the snow-covered gravel schoolyard.

"We like to have minors evaluated before entering the program," Bowman said, recalling Mal's attention to the front of the room. "Especially those who've been through a traumatic event like your son. He may try to test you or act out some when you first settle into your new life, but trust me when I tell you that kids are usually more resilient than their parents. Corin's going to be with us for the next couple of weeks, and then once we get you settled, we'll arrange for weekly therapy sessions to help Ben transition."

Mal nodded.

"If you'd like to see a therapist I can arrange for that, as well. Other than that, I'm your new best friend. There are no secrets between us, so feel free to spill the beans. Rule number one—I will never lie to you and Lord help you if you lie to me."

"Is Nash coming with us?"

"No. He's not entering into the program."

Mal's gaze wandered outside again. It was more or less what she'd expected to hear. Ben twisted in the swing. Nash leaned against the metal pole and the psychiatrist stood nearby, chatting with both father and son. "What about my dad?"

"I'm sorry," Bowman said. "With his Alzheimer's he's not a candidate for relocation and could be a liability. Don't be nervous. No one in the history of the witness protection program has ever been killed following the rules. I'm good at my job. Right now I need you to empty your pockets and place the items on the desk. Remove any jewelry, including piercings. Any clothing with your name on it? Body art or tattoos?"

"Nothing up my pockets and nothing up my sleeves."

"Did you bring a purse with you?"

"All I have on me are my badge and my SIG."

"I'll need them both."

Mal handed them over. And tried not to cry when giving up her badge.

"I'll try to find you a job on the periphery of law enforcement, but I can't promise you anything. You'll receive a sixty-thousand-dollar-a-year stipend from the program and all your assets will be liquidated and turned over to you again if not found to be from criminal gain. Any accounts in the Cayman Islands? Or hidden money?"

"I keep four storage units." Bowman entered the locations into her computer as Mal explained what the woman would find in each one.

"Aliases and false IDs were my next question. You're a treat for me, Mal," Bowman said. "I'm used to relocating a more criminal element." A voice broke through the static of Bowman's walkie-talkie. "All right," she answered. "Excuse me for a minute," she said to Mal, and then went to go take care of business.

Mal moved toward the door. Corin was sitting on the swing rocking back and forth while Nash was crouched down to talk to Ben. Ben was nodding and trying hard not to cry. Much like Mal.

The helo could be heard starting up outside.

"They told me to wait in here."

Mal turned toward the soft cultured tones. A woman wearing a head scarf, a hijab with an accompanying veil and a niqab for the face was staring back at her with the most exquisite exotic eyes. There was no mistaking that this woman was Nash's undercover wife.

"Do you look much like your sister?"

Mal shook her head. "No. She was a strawberry blonde and petite. Less freckles."

"I meant was she as beautiful as you? I worry, I think, that I cannot compete with his love for her and that he finds me unappealing."

"Oh, I kind of doubt that." Mal folded her arms and started out the door, hoping to discourage further conversation.

But that only brought the woman in closer. "My name is Sari, by the way. Do you know my husband well?"

"Not at all," Mal lied. Was it really a lie?

Was she now looking at a stranger she only thought she knew?

"I think you do." The woman called her on it. "A woman knows these things."

Mal leaned back against the doorframe and

locked eyes with the other woman. "Do you know him as well as you think you do?"

"I know that if he chooses me it will be because he feels obligated."

She dropped her scarf and veil at the same time.

Mal sucked in her breath. The woman's beautiful face had been scarred by acid.

"This was for rejecting the ugly suitor my family had chosen for me. My brothers punished my vanity. I did not have any suitors for a long time. Then Sayyid came to work for my father." She referred to Sayyid Naveed, Nash's undercover identity. "My father and brothers wanted to test his loyalty. They told me they would kill us both if he did not choose to marry me. I think he knew this to be true. I have known his kindness, but I have never known his love."

Sari put her scarf back on. "We are both competing with a ghost for a flesh-and-blood man. I wish you well, sister of my heart."

"REMEMBER WHAT I told you?" A lump formed in Nash's throat as he said it. The boy nodded and Nash scuffed his dark head before pushing himself to his feet. He only remembered seeing his dad crying once, when Nash's grandfather died, and that was not the last impression he wanted to leave with Ben.

Corin nodded to him and took the boy's hand.

Nash looked up as Sari stepped out of the schoolhouse. Mal stood in the doorway right behind her. The team was making its way to the helicopter. He stopped one of his old teammates and asked him to see that Sari got to the helo.

Mal took those few steps out of the schoolhouse and he met her halfway. He knew he should say something, but there just weren't any words.

Mac was calling him. The marshal was calling her.

"I can't do this," she said.

Her tears were his undoing.

"Yes, you can," he said. "Mal, you're the strongest woman I know."

"I'm not that strong without you." She tried to bury her head in his shoulder, but he wouldn't let her.

"Look at me." He held her face so she had to look at him. "Ben needs you to stay strong. I need you to stay strong." His words came out harsh. Much the way he'd talk to one of the guys.

Her tears dried instantly. "I need you not to do this."

"I have to testify—"

"I'm talking about setting us aside."

How did he explain to her that he wouldn't have much of a life after this?

But maybe he could, a little voice inside him insisted.

He'd much rather have them safe, and he wasn't sure he could have both.

Someone called his name.

"I'm coming," he shouted back, though he didn't move right away.

"Do you think this is what Cara would have wanted? For you to be so focused on avenging her death that you've lost sight of everything standing right in front of you? Please promise me you'll come find us when this is all over."

She threw herself into a kiss with so much promise he wanted to savor it, but all he could do was tear himself away. "I have to go."

Nash didn't allow himself to look back until the helicopter was in the air.

Mal stood in the exact spot where he'd left her.

"She loves you, I think," Sari said.

"I know." He settled back against the jump seat and closed his eyes.

"I think you love her, too."

He opened his eyes, looked at his wife in name only and thought maybe he should apologize for that but didn't. He couldn't.

CHAPTER TWENTY-ONE

MALLORY WARD DIED the next day in a fiery crash along with her nephew and adopted son, Ben. She'd lost control of a late-model Chevy Tahoe on an icy back road coming down from the mountains, according to the *Denver Post*.

"Read it. Let it sink in. And then forget about it." Jane Bowman put the dated paper in front of her at breakfast. They'd been holed up in a Seattle hotel for two weeks now. The story was buried deep within the pages of the Denver newspaper and would be of little interest to anyone, but it was a symbol of the end.

Jane—the sadist—had made her write her own obituary. Even though she'd broken down several times during the attempt.

"That's all right get it all out." Jane encouraged tears up to a point.

Mal wondered if her colleagues at the Bureau would believe it.

Had anyone attended their funerals?

Corin was at present keeping Ben busy with crayons. He'd re-created every one of those pictures he'd had to leave behind at the cabin and then some. Most were of Nash. Though he didn't seem to be as pissed with his father as she was.

The one thing Jane did not allow was television.

Especially not terrorist trials on C-Span.

"Enough of that," Jane said when Mal started to pore over the details of her death for a second time. "Happy birthday, Megan Warren." Jane set the Washington State driver's license with the Seattle address in front of her. "I shaved a year off. You're the only thirty-year-old I know who can say she's twenty-nine and mean it."

"I appreciate it."

"I thought you might."

Jane had been working overtime these past two weeks to keep Mal's spirits up.

So far the rules were simple. Mal had gotten to pick her new name. Jane suggested keeping the initials M.W.— a trick that made it easier to cover up if she screwed up signing her own name. Which Jane had made her write over and over again until her hand cramped. Because Meg and not Megan was a pet name for her mother used by her father and known only to the family, Jane had let her keep it.

Ben got to keep his first name. Only because he didn't have much of a paper trail at his age.

New names.

New city.

New job. New school.

New house.

Tomorrow was the first full day of their new lives.

FOUR MONTHS INTO their new life, Mal/Meg was sitting in the doctor's office. "Megan." Dr. Elizabeth Bacca entered the exam room with her nose buried in Megan Warren's medical record. "Something's not right here."

"Is the baby okay?"

"Test results confirmed you are pregnant. Congratulations. And the baby's fine." The doctor put a reassuring hand on Megan's knee. "But you've mentioned you have a son, and your medical record is telling me you've given birth before, but your cervix is telling me you haven't. Mind telling me what's going on?"

"I think we're going to need to call someone." Mal/Meg punched Jane's number.

MEGAN WARREN WAS late to work after her doctor's appointment. Her supervisor tapped his watch as she snuck by his office. Mal/Meg almost burst into tears as she slipped into her chair. She was clerking in the district attorney's office. It was a good fit for her background, just not a good fit for her.

She'd been telling herself for months she'd go

back to law school. But she had no real drive or desire to do so.

She sat at her desk staring off into space.

At first she didn't notice she'd skipped a period. Then two.

She'd blamed the missed periods and weight gain on stress. Until a pee stick provided evidence to the contrary. She'd called for the doctor's appointment after the positive home pregnancy test. Which the doctor had just confirmed. And then on top of everything she'd screwed up when filling out her medical history and had had to call Jane to straighten out her screwup.

What else was she supposed to do except sit here and take it all in?

Only the district attorney knew the truth of her situation. Her coworkers thought her newly widowed—the backstory used to explain the melancholy that seemed to have settled over her—and that her husband had been killed in Afghanistan.

Where he had been for more than a year. Which would make her a slutty widow in the eyes of her coworkers once they found out she was pregnant.

Mal opened up the word processing program on her computer, but instead of finishing up the briefs she'd started yesterday, she typed up her resignation. Five minutes later she walked into the D.A.'s office and then turned it in. Five minutes after that she packed up her desk and waved goodbye to her stunned supervisor on the way out the door.

Fifteen minutes after that, Megan Warren walked through the doors of her sterile life. But instead of throwing herself down on the bed for a good cry, which was what she felt like doing, she threw clothes for both her and Ben into an overnight bag.

She didn't really have a plan at this point. She only knew she wanted to escape her life. Mal signed Ben out of school for the day and just kept driving.

"How was school?" she asked, making conversation.

He shrugged. "Okay, I guess. I just got there."

The new Ben was both quieter and moodier than the old Ben.

But she supposed he could say the same about her. This wasn't their life. This wasn't supposed to be their life. Nothing about it fit either one of them. They were almost to the Washington–Oregon border before she decided their destination should be Disneyland. They'd spend a week, maybe two, in the happiest place on earth—or was that Disney World?—and then they'd be happy.

Mal pulled over to the side of the road and got out of the car. She made it a few yards into the field of wildflowers before bursting into tears. She wasn't headed to Disneyland; she was headed to

San Diego—the last place she should be going. Even though it was unlikely he was anywhere near there.

The trial in New York had been over for months. Nash had done the smart thing and had testified remotely as a pixilated image.

She thought that meant he was trying to protect his identity.

Having his cover blown was not the same as putting it out there in TV land for the whole world to see. Right now the average Joe wouldn't recognize him on the street.

But she'd hoped that everything Nash was doing, he was doing it to be with them.

Then she realized she'd been about to do something extremely stupid.

"Mom, are you okay?"

"I'm fine," she said. "Come here, talk to me." Ben joined her under the tree. She brushed the bangs out of his eyes. "How would you feel about having a little brother or sister?"

"Okay, I guess."

"Good. Because I'm four months pregnant and in a few short months we're going to have a baby."

Ben sat and thought about that for a minute. "I think my dad gave you a baby because he didn't want us to miss him so much."

She pulled him into a hug. "I think you're absolutely right."

"You're what?" Jane Bowman had flown in from Denver and stood in the middle of Megan Warren's kitchen while Meg continued packing.

"Moving to Oregon. Nothing I'm doing is against the rules. It's not like I'm ditching the name."

"But quitting your job? Buying a run-down winery in Willamette Valley? What do you know about running a winery?"

"Nothing. Absolutely nothing."

"Then isn't this a little drastic? My God, you're going to have a baby. A baby!"

"His baby," she emphasized. "This life doesn't fit, Jane. It's not me. It's not Ben. We have to move on for both our sakes and the sake of the baby.

"Ben," Mal called to him. "Rabbi Adler should be here any minute."

"Rabbi Adler?" Jane asked.

Meg shrugged. "He's exploring his options. Anyway, Corin thought it would be okay. And I don't see the harm in it."

"Mrs. Warren, sorry. I did not realize you have company." A rabbi, not Rabbi Adler, knocked on the door and stepped across the threshold. "Is Ben ready?"

"I'm sorry, who are you?"

"Rabbi Sandler. I'm helping the rabbi out today. He asked me to stop by and pick up Ben. We're meeting him back at the synagogue."

"Yeah. No. I'm sorry, Ben's not feeling well today."

"Oh." He looked taken aback.

"I'm sorry. My sister's in town and we're visiting." She gestured toward Jane.

"Are you moving?" the man persisted.

"Just packing up something for charity. Tell Rabbi Adler we look forward to seeing him again next week."

Rabbi Sandler seemed to linger even as he was leaving.

"Was that weird to you?" Mal asked Jane.

"Totally weird." Jane called for backup and Mal brought Ben into the kitchen with her. "Probably nothing, but let's be smart."

CHAPTER TWENTY-TWO

HE KEPT TO the shadows, following the rabbi into a dark alley. There the rabbi approached an old car. He opened the trunk and began to disrobe. He tossed the tunic on top of a body. He did not get the chance to close the lid or draw his weapon. Nash put the silencer to the back of the man's head and pulled the trigger, then shoved the assassin into the trunk alongside his victim.

"You should have let me take him in," Jane said.

"And give him the chance to talk?" Nash turned. Not the least bit surprised to find the marshal one step behind him.

She kept her firearm pointed at the ground as she approached. "How long have you been shadowing her?"

"Long enough."

"Then you know she's moving? You should go to her. She asks about you all the time."

"No, I'm not good for them," he said.

"Really, Nash? Because I've been spending a lot of time with Mal and Ben, and I'm beginning to think that you're the best for them. I'm actually not sure Mal will stop moving around, running away, until she finds you." Jane paused. "And as much as they need you, I'd hazard you need them just as much."

Nash didn't know what to say. Jane suggested a life he dreamed of every second of his days, but he'd given up on it. Could it really work?

"I don't know. I just don't want anyone else to get hurt," he said.

"I know. And I also know that you won't let that happen. So, what do you say, Nash? Are you ready for your next mission?"

MOVING-IN DAY. "Well, what do you think?" Mal ended the tour in the winery beneath the house. "It used to be a bed-and-breakfast. So it's kind of big, but I'm having a panic room built with the extra space."

"It rocks," Jane said. "I hope you don't mind that I brought you a housewarming gift."

Ben led Nash in by the hand then.

"Hi," he said.

"Hi," she said back, because she was at a loss for any other words. She covered her mouth with her hand to keep from crying. "You're here."

"I'm here," he echoed.

He stood there staring at her. At her belly. Then he dropped to his knees with his head resting against her baby bump. "I'm here if you'll have me."

She realized he was crying. "It's okay, my love," she said, smoothing back his hair. "You're home now."

EPILOGUE

IN THE DAYS and weeks and months that followed they had a lot to work out as a family. As a couple. On paper they were already married as Nate and Meg Warren.

"I think we should renew our vows," he was saying as he put Carrie down for her afternoon nap. Carrie reminded them so much of Cara with her strawberry blond hair and sweet cherub mouth. Nash was a good father. Making up for lost time she supposed.

"To what purpose?"

"So that we can get the dress and the cake and invite people…"

"We don't know any people."

"Okay then, let's do it so that you know you're my wife."

"I already know that." She turned her back on him to finish putting Carrie's clothes away in the baby dresser.

He came up behind her and wrapped his arms around her waist. "So that you know I'm your husband." He planted a kiss on her neck that sent tingles up and down her spine.

"I already know that, too. Husband."

"Sometimes I wonder if you believe it," he said, thinking out loud.

She turned in his arms and wrapped her arms around his neck. "I believe it," she said, standing on tippy toes to give him a kiss. A full on the mouth, hearts exploding kind of kiss.

"How about so that you believe that I love you."

She pulled back. Did she believe it? "We should probably let her sleep," she said, leaving the baby's room ahead of him.

"I do love you, Mal." He never made that kind of slip so she knew it was intentional on his part.

She turned to face him. "I love you, too."

The only difference was she meant it soul deep. She believed that he loved her. But not in the way she loved him. And not in the way he'd loved Cara. Or even Ben. Or even Carrie. But she was okay with that. Because she loved him enough for the both of them.

"Come here," he said, tugging her by the hand into their master bedroom. "It's time for the new parents to take a nap, too. Before the big kid gets home from school."

The sex was good. The sex was really good. And he'd never made the mistake of calling her

Cara in or out of bed again. Still there was that one time.

Why'd it have to have been their first time?

Because it was also something she'd likely never forget. And yet she'd probably trade the world to disappear to that little cabin in the woods again.

"We need a vacation." Mal collapsed to the bed exhausted.

"You mean a honeymoon."

"If that's what you want to call it."

"You didn't answer my question about renewing our vows, Mal."

She thought he might try to put the moves on her and then she'd have to further reject him by being too tired. But he didn't, he just snuggled up against her backside and held her. Okay so she was going to have to put the moves on him or feel rejected.

"Why do you want to marry me, Nash? And it can't be because you love me, or because I'm the mother of your children."

"Oh, I don't know then…. Can it be because you're smart and sexy? Not to mention the way you handle a weapon really turns me on? Especially an axe." He rolled her over onto her back. "What do you need me to say? I could think of a whole list of reasons why I love you, Mal. And I know I still wouldn't hit on the right one. What is it you're looking for?" He held her in silence for a few minutes. "I need to go away again for a few days."

She tensed in his arms and tried to pull away, but he wouldn't let her go.

"This is why I love you. Because you never ask even though you want to. I wish the reason you didn't ask is because you trust me."

"I do trust you. That doesn't mean I don't worry."

"I'll only be gone a day or two. And when I get back I want to put a business proposition to you. Retirement is driving me crazy."

"Are you retired, really?"

She worried that these little trips of his were dangerous.

"Yes, really."

"Then what's the proposition? Why not tell me now?"

He stared down at her for a long minute. "I feel dirty, Mal. To go as deep undercover as I have gets in your pores and I don't feel like I've washed myself clean, yet. I've seen things, done things… Mostly just stood by and watched, weighing my actions or inactions against the consequences and hoping that I didn't make matters worse. I'd like to atone for that in my own way."

He had her attention, but she was still trying to figure out exactly what it was he was trying to say.

"I tried not to look the other way when kids

were involved. Helped those I could, but I don't feel like I've helped enough. I think we should go after missing and exploited children. Parental abductions to foreign countries. That kind of thing."

"You said *we*."

"That's right, *we*. My wifey and me. I think this is something we could do together. I'm not talking about putting our own kids in jeopardy. Or even both of us leaving them with a nanny. But we could open up our own agency of sorts. Operate on a sliding scale for those who can't afford us. We both have mad skills and money. What do you think?"

"You're talking about a detective agency. Hmm, I like this idea of yours." She settled more fully into him.

"Then believe that I love you, Mal. Because you are my partner in all things."

She didn't wait for him to lower his head. She brought him down for a kiss.

The kind of kiss that said *I love and I believe you love me*.

"We still have a half hour before Ben comes home from school."

She whipped his shirt off over his head. He took his time with her blouse, taking an excruciatingly long time with each button until he could push it aside. Next came her jeans and then his.

He kissed her again. His hand sliding up her rib cage to cup a breast.

"You know that night that you think I called out Cara?" He lifted his head to undo the front clasp of her bra.

"Must we talk about my sister now?"

"I think we must," he teased. "Because my wife uses her sister as the measure by which I love her."

She pressed back into the pillow to pull away from his words.

"I was reaching into my brain trying to tell you something that Cara said. I just said it at the wrong time and in the wrong way."

"Uh-huh," she agreed as his hands continued to explore where she wanted his mouth to go next.

"Let's for the sake of argument say you had a crush on me and Cara and I both knew it. And sometimes it was even discussed. Cara had always worried that I'd break your heart. I felt like I'd failed her by falling into bed with you for very lustful reasons. Because breaking your heart felt wrong. Cara was my conscience and worked her way into my subconscious. But I knew exactly who I was making love to at that moment."

"Even if that's a lie it's a very sweet lie."

"Believe me, it's the truth. I love you and I'm going to keep telling you I love you until you believe me."

"Then I'm never going to believe you because I don't want you to stop telling me."

"We have to stop now because the school bus is going to pull up any minute to drop off Ben."

"We could play beat the clock…."

"Oh, I'm sure I could. But I'm not going to." He started to get up from the bed. "I've decided to withhold sex until you believe me when I say I love you."

She pulled him back down again.

"Okay, okay. I believe you."

"Say it again like you believe it. Like you can see it in my eyes."

She looked up at her husband. "I can see it in your eyes."

"Mallory Ward, will you do me the honor of becoming not just the mother of my children, but my wife, by renewing our vows?"

"I will," she said on a sigh. "I love you, Nash."

"I love you, too, Mal. I can't promise you an easy life, but I can promise you that we're in this together."

NASH NEEDED TO check up on his mother and Mallory's father.

He knew Mal didn't like him disappearing like he did and still worried that it was somehow connected to the life that he'd once led. The truth is he *was* retired, though he was looking forward to both of them coming out of retirement and putting their skills to good use.

But he did disappear sometimes to check up on family. His marriage to his second wife had been easily annulled. When he thought of Mal it wasn't as a number, his first or second or even his third wife...

It was as his first in his heart. Now and forever.

Cara had been his first love and he would probably always think of her that way. But he believed what he'd told Ben about the heart having room for as many people as you could love. Nash's own heart had proved to be more resilient than he ever would have thought possible. But the reason he didn't tell his wife where he was going on these trips was because parts of both of their hearts had been left in the past.

And every now and then he'd check up on that past for both of them.

He knew he'd find his mother at his father's grave site today on what once was his parents' wedding anniversary.

Her back was to him as he stood in the shadow of a tree trunk.

"Are you a ghost?" she asked without turning around.

He knew she could see his shadow self from her peripheral. "Yes," he answered honestly.

"What kind of life is that for a man?"

"Right now a good one. I'm happy. I married again. You have a new granddaughter. And a grandson who remembers you."

"I always liked Mallory," she said without his having to tell her. "She brought the boy to see me several times a year while you were gone. Did you know that?"

"I do now."

"What's the baby's name?"

"Names aren't important."

"I can almost picture what a pretty little thing she must be."

"I can't stay long. I just came to tell you…"

"Son." The question in her voice stopped him from leaving. "Same time next year?"

"Never the same time, but sometime. Some-time next year," he promised before disappearing.

* * * * *

LARGER-PRINT BOOKS!
GET 2 FREE LARGER-PRINT NOVELS PLUS
2 FREE GIFTS!

HARLEQUIN

super romance

More Story...More Romance

LARGER-PRINT BOOKS!

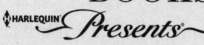 HARLEQUIN *Presents*

PASSION GUARANTEED SEDUCTION

GET 2 FREE LARGER-PRINT NOVELS PLUS 2 FREE GIFTS!

YES! Please send me 2 FREE LARGER-PRINT Harlequin Presents® novels and my 2 FREE gifts (gifts are worth about $10). After receiving them, if I don't wish to receive any more books, I can return the shipping statement marked "cancel." If I don't cancel, I will receive 6 brand-new novels every month and be billed just $5.05 per book in the U.S. or $5.49 per book in Canada. That's a saving of at least 16% off the cover price! It's quite a bargain! Shipping and handling is just 50¢ per book in the U.S. and 75¢ per book in Canada.* I understand that accepting the 2 free books and gifts places me under no obligation to buy anything. I can always return a shipment and cancel at any time. Even if I never buy another book, the two free books and gifts are mine to keep forever.

176/376 HDN F43N

Name _____ (PLEASE PRINT) _____

Address _____ Apt. #

City _____ State/Prov. _____ Zip/Postal Code

Signature (if under 18, a parent or guardian must sign)

Mail to the Harlequin® Reader Service:
IN U.S.A.: P.O. Box 1867, Buffalo, NY 14240-1867
IN CANADA: P.O. Box 609, Fort Erie, Ontario L2A 5X3

**Are you a subscriber to Harlequin Presents books
and want to receive the larger-print edition?
Call 1-800-873-8635 today or visit us at www.ReaderService.com.**

* Terms and prices subject to change without notice. Prices do not include applicable taxes. Sales tax applicable in N.Y. Canadian residents will be charged applicable taxes. Offer not valid in Quebec. This offer is limited to one order per household. Not valid for current subscribers to Harlequin Presents Larger-Print books. All orders subject to credit approval. Credit or debit balances in a customer's account(s) may be offset by any other outstanding balance owed by or to the customer. Please allow 4 to 6 weeks for delivery. Offer available while quantities last.

Your Privacy—The Harlequin® Reader Service is committed to protecting your privacy. Our Privacy Policy is available online at www.ReaderService.com or upon request from the Harlequin Reader Service.

We make a portion of our mailing list available to reputable third parties that offer products we believe may interest you. If you prefer that we not exchange your name with third parties, or if you wish to clarify or modify your communication preferences, please visit us at www.ReaderService.com/consumerschoice or write to us at Harlequin Reader Service Preference Service, P.O. Box 9062, Buffalo, NY 14269. Include your complete name and address.

HPLP13R

ReaderService.com

Manage your account online!

- Review your order history
- Manage your payments
- Update your address

*We've designed
the Harlequin® Reader Service
website just for you.*

Enjoy all the features!

- Reader excerpts from any series
- Respond to mailings and
  special monthly offers
- Discover new series available to you
- Browse the Bonus Bucks catalog
- Share your feedback

Visit us at:
ReaderService.com

RS13